FURY

THE ADAM BLACK THRILLERS #BOOK 4

KARL HILL

BLOODHOUND
— BOOKS —

ALSO BY KARL HILL

TWENTY YEARS AGO

Two men sat at a table in a quiet bar in Glasgow city centre. It was afternoon, in the knuckle of winter, the day cold and dreary.

One was thirty-five, the other twenty. The older man looked tired. Pasty complexion, a furrowed brow, sad bloodhound eyes. Thin wispy hair, prematurely grey. The other – the younger man – was altogether different. Coarse dark hair cropped short, delicate features, eyes the colour of blue agate, his expression candid and clear.

They sat, drinking pints of lager placed on cardboard beer mats. Smoking cigarettes. The ashtray on the table was already half full. Their conversation was low, almost a murmur. The others in the pub hardly noticed them. This was a place where men drank usually in solitude, happy with their own thoughts, content, provided there was a full glass in front of them.

Also on the table was an open penknife.

"Let's do it," the older man said.

"If you want to."

"I do."

The younger man shrugged. "Don't you trust me?"

The other gave a small sad smile. "Easy for you to say. You've had your turn. It's mine now. Three's the charm. I want my charm. We seal the deal. Then there's no going back, right?"

"A blood oath. I get that." The younger man took a gulp of lager, leaving a smear of froth on his upper lip.

"Clean yourself up."

The younger man wiped his mouth with his sleeve.

The older man glanced round. No one gave a damn. They could have been invisible. He pulled out a cream-coloured silken handkerchief from his trouser pocket, and spread it carefully on the Formica tabletop. He placed his hand above it. He picked up the penknife with his other hand, pressed the tip into his palm, bursting open the skin. He drew the tip down four inches. Blood oozed onto the handkerchief. He placed the knife back on the table.

"This really is beyond the call of duty," said the younger man.

"Humour me."

"Very dramatic. You can trust me."

"You should know about dramatic. Blood binds."

"Blood binds," the younger man echoed. "If you say so."

He took another gulp, picked up the blade, cut it deep into his palm, clasped his friend's hand. Blood mingled, dripped onto the open handkerchief.

The older man's face broke into a broad smile. "Easy. Now you keep your end of the bargain. Your turn to do the hard work. My turn to enjoy."

"That's only fair. Any thoughts?"

The wrinkles on the older man's brow deepened. "What do you mean?"

"Thoughts on what you'll do with them?"

"Ah. I don't have your imagination."

"Which means?"

"I might copy you. They were works of art. Do you mind?"

"That would be plagiarism. Or something like that."

"Plagiarism is a copy of literary work," the older man chided. "But what you did was literature, in its way. They were... beautiful."

It was the younger man's turn to smile. "Flattery gets you everywhere. You'll need the right equipment. I'm not giving you mine. That would be too easy."

The older man nodded slowly. "Of course. Any advice?"

"I found a broad blade with a serrated edge was useful. And metal snippers. Heavy duty."

"Metal snippers? Sounds a bit... over the top?"

"For cutting the ribs away from the spine. It's awkward. And the bones are stubborn there."

The older man chuckled. "Makes sense." He lifted the handkerchief from the table, put it in his pocket. He raised his glass. The other did the same.

"To the... how did you describe it?"

"The Blood Eagle."

"To the Blood Eagle." They clinked glasses, took deep draughts.

"Now," the older man licked his lips, "find me three women."

1

Three letters.
Sent to three different people.

Two by first-class post. The third, delivered. Each identical. Each simple, and direct, and written in neat precise handwriting.

I know one of you murdered my wife. I don't know who. But I swear to Christ above I'll find the truth before I die.

I've written it all down, from the start. Every little thing. In a book. A book of my life. A book of our lives. This makes it very special. Intimate, one might say. Everything detailed, except the name of a murderer. The missing piece.

We need to pay for our sins. For me, I'll meet my penance in hell, where I belong. Where we all belong. We are monsters, each of us. I know it. You know it.

The book, I no longer have. It's in the safekeeping of someone who I believe has the power to uncover the truth.

Someone who will find the person who killed my wife.

Someone who kills monsters, like us.

His name is Adam Black.
Now he's coming after you.

2

Learn to stop being surprised. Surprise is failure. And in our line of work, gentlemen, failure is death.

Observation raised by Staff Sergeant to the 22nd Special Air Service Regiment

"**W**ake the fuck up, Captain Black!"

In an act of simple caprice, which was unusual for Black, he had customised the alarm on his mobile phone, using his own voice. The words were echoes of the morning call he and other soldiers of the 22nd Regiment of the Special Air Service would get, usually at 0500.

Black didn't need an alarm. His body was tuned into waking at such an extreme time. Habit, instinct, training. He didn't know what it was. It just happened.

This particular Saturday morning was no different. Black wasn't the type to linger in bed, absorbed in his own thoughts.

He got up instantly, changed, and went for a four-mile run in the park adjacent to his flat.

Thus the morning started. Black could never have imagined what would follow. Two events transpired in the space of the next two days. Events which changed his life. Both surreal. Both remarkable.

The first took place in a coffee shop three hours later, in a town called East Kilbride. Black spent time there most Saturday mornings, sipping a flat white at 8am in a corner of a Starbucks. He went because it was open early, and situated on the periphery of the main shopping centre, which was rarely busy. He sat in a corner, in a particular booth, and read a newspaper, cover to cover.

Black was the only customer. The staff knew him. They fixed him a coffee before he ordered it. The conversation was always polite, but sparse. Black was a man who preferred silence to small-talk. He wasn't trying to be rude. It was just his way.

He sat, a solitary figure. Lightly tanned. Flat, rather harsh cheekbones. Dark hair cropped short. Lean, hard muscularity. Attractive, in a hard-bitten way. Plain grey T-shirt, blue jeans. Black didn't care about fashion. It was July, and it was warm. No need for a jacket.

He sipped the coffee. It was strong and good. Black would openly admit he was a coffee addict, sometimes drinking ten cups a day. Sometimes more. This particular morning, he'd also bought himself a doughnut. He reckoned his body could cope with the calories.

Black looked up. A man was standing at the counter. He was elderly, maybe seventy-five, maybe older. He spoke quietly. He was ordering a pot of tea. Black gave him no more thought. He resumed reading his newspaper. A minute passed. Black sensed a presence. The man was standing over him, carrying a tray.

"May I join you?"

Black stared at him for a full five seconds.

"Excuse me?"

"Thank you," said the man. He placed the tray on the table, and sat opposite. Black remained motionless. The man lifted the pot, mug and a little carton of milk from the tray onto the table, and put the tray on the floor by his feet.

"They do decaffeinated tea here. You can't tell the difference. I've been told by the doctor that I have to watch my heart. So no caffeine."

"That's interesting," Black said. "Have we met?"

The man poured the tea into a large stoneware mug, dropped in the milk, and stirred with a wooden stirring stick.

"I'm not allowed sugar either."

"Sorry to hear that. Can I help you?"

"Though I see your dietary requirements aren't just as restricting." The man nodded at Black's doughnut.

Black had heard enough. The man was deranged.

"Enjoy the tea," he said, and made to leave.

"Please, Mr Black. Indulge me. I won't take too much of your time."

Black sat back, appraised the man sitting opposite. His initial guess was right. He was in his late seventies, and looked it. A face grey and lined, hollow cheeked, dull rheumy eyes, regarding Black behind silver-framed spectacles. Bald, except for wisps of silk-fine white hair straggling over his ears.

He knew Black's name. He didn't seem to pose any instant threat. But in Black's life, death presented itself in many surprising forms.

"And you are?" he asked.

"As you get older, the memory begins to play tricks, don't you think? Sometimes you're convinced something happened, but it didn't happen at all. Sometimes, something actually did happen, but you have no recollection of it. Would you agree, Mr Black?"

"I forget things as much as the next man. Right now, I seem to have forgotten where we've met before. Perhaps you'd like to remind me?"

The man gave his head the merest shake, as if dismissing the statement. He lifted the mug of tea to his lips and took a careful sip, and then placed it back on the table.

"Can't taste the difference." He paused, then continued.

"When we met last, you were different."

Black said nothing.

"You were younger, of course. And less... intense."

Black waited.

"I had forgotten all about you. And then, suddenly, I saw a picture of you in a newspaper. Adam Black. Hero. Saviour. I saw that picture, and a memory flashed into my mind. Perhaps we'd met before. But I wasn't sure. Maybe I was imagining it. Then I checked."

It was Black's turn to sip his coffee. It was cold. It had lost its flavour. It tasted bitter. "You still haven't told me your name."

"My name will mean nothing to you. But your name? Your name means everything. I checked, and there it was, and the memories came back."

Black took a deep breath. He had no idea where this was going, but knew he wanted to leave.

The man was wearing a dark-blue raincoat, buttoned up to his collarbone. He manoeuvred his body to one side, and reached into a pocket. Black had both hands on the table. He waited, senses heightened to a new level.

The man took something out. A book. Roughly the size of a thick paperback. Bound tightly by rough brown string. He placed it on the table in front of him. The cover was plain white. Written in block capitals in heavy black felt pen were four words.

The Book Of Dreams

"I had to check." The man tapped his index finger on the book cover. "I had to know if you were real, or if I'd imagined you."

"And am I real?"

"Yes, Mr Black. As real as it gets."

3

Black was intrigued. He would hear the man out. If anything, his Saturday morning coffee stop had livened up a little.

"I've kept this book for thirty years. Perhaps it would be better described as a journal. Do you keep a journal, Mr Black?"

"It never occurred to me."

The man gave the slightest shrug. "It's not for everybody. But as one gets older, it takes on a new meaning. I can open this book, and reminisce. Relive moments of the past. Some good, some bad. A window into forgotten memories. My memory is dying, Mr Black. Then I saw a picture of you, and a memory came back. I checked my journal, and discovered the memory was true."

Black's lips twitched into the semblance of a smile. "And was it good or bad? Often people I meet are left with bad memories."

"My wife died eight years ago." He hesitated. "Or maybe nine. The years become muddled. Are you married, Mr Black?"

"No."

"Do you remember my wife?"

Black shook his head. *Where the hell is this going?*

"Why would you? It was long ago, and you only met her once. It's all in here." He gestured to the book. "You were younger then. A lawyer in the city. We were shown to a big room, and we sat at a table so polished we could see our reflections. And the place smelled of fresh coffee. And a whole wall was lined with books. Hundreds of books. We knew right away we were in the wrong place."

Black raised an eyebrow.

"Because," continued the man, "with a room like that, we knew you'd be too expensive. And you were."

Black sighed. The conversation was reaching a dead end. He made a mental note to change his coffee venue. "I'm sorry about that. As you say, it was long ago. It was nice talking to you..."

"That's what my wife said. She said she liked talking to you. She thought you were a nice man. You listened. But you couldn't help us, in the end."

"I hope you got things sorted out," said Black, trying to finish the conversation.

The man spoke as if he hadn't heard. "They didn't turn out well. I saw your photograph in the paper. I read about you. And it triggered a memory that we'd met. I delved into my Book of Dreams, and you were there. So I suppose it's fate that we should be having this conversation."

"How so?"

The man stared at Black for several long seconds. Black met his stare, waited.

"We met you in your offices in the afternoon. It was July, and it was hot. Something happened later that day, to my wife."

"What happened?"

"I saw your face. Memories came back. Lots of memories."

"What happened to your wife," repeated Black.

"She died."

The man paused.

"She was murdered. And I need your help."

4

———

Black sat back. The man seemed genuine enough. He knew who Black was. He had gone out of his way to follow him here. There was a grain of truth in his voice.

Black licked his lips, choosing his words carefully. "I can think of three questions. One – why did you and your wife want to speak to me in my office? Two – why do you think your wife was murdered? And three – you still haven't told me your name."

The man gave a weary smile.

"I've been busy, Mr Black. You're not the only person involved. There are others."

Black tried to pin him down.

"I'm sure there are. But let's stick to the basics. You say you visited my offices. Eight years ago? At that time, I was working in a firm called Wilson Fletcher and Company. Why did you want to see me? I'm assuming it was legal advice."

The man took another sip of his tea.

"It's a little jumbled, so long ago. She needed help. There was a man."

"Yes?"

"He was following her. A stalker."

"Your wife was being stalked."

He seemed to hesitate. "Yes."

"That's a police matter. Why would you need legal advice?"

"The police said it was a civil matter. That we should speak to a lawyer to have him stop following her."

"It's called an interdict."

"But you wanted money up front. And we couldn't pay."

Black reflected. More truth. In those days, he was chasing the buck. If the clients couldn't pay, broom them fast. An unfortunate trait of most city lawyers. But then, he had a wife and child to support. Now both dead. Changed days.

"We left your office. Later that day, my wife was dead."

Black thought back. Eight years ago. Probably a fifteen-minute meeting. Taken place in another lifetime. Black had no recollection.

"You said she was murdered."

"She was."

Black raised an eyebrow. "Is that what it says in your Book of Dreams?"

The man kept his stare on Black, sitting motionless.

"The book says nothing. It's blank."

"Then what makes you think she was murdered?"

Now the man's eyes glistened. With tears.

"I just know."

Black nodded.

"You have a feeling."

The man's lips suddenly curled in anger.

"Don't mock me, Mr Black!"

"I'm not. But I don't see how I can help you."

"But you can. I'm giving you this book. Call it a gift. You're not the only person who knows. There are others. They know about you. They know you have the book. They'll come looking. They'll want it very badly. Keep it safe."

"Who are you talking about?"

"Find who murdered my wife. I saw your picture in the newspaper. I read what you did. I believe in you, Mr Black."

The man shuffled out of the booth seat, and stood.

"What's your name?" asked Black.

The man looked down, staring at his shoes, frowning.

"I don't know."

He turned, made to leave. He hesitated again, cocked his head.

"Do you believe in God, Mr Black?"

Black gave a cold smile.

"I gave up on him a long time ago."

"The devil is more reliable. And death. It rides a pale horse. I see that pale horse when I sleep. Sometimes I see it when I'm awake. Why is that?"

Black had no logical answer to give.

The old man left the coffee shop. Black watched him leave.

The whole episode was bizarre beyond words. Black considered the object the man had left behind.

The Book of Dreams.

5

Black didn't stir immediately. The old man had left. The book was on the table before him, but Black's thoughts were on other matters, on events taken place in the recent past. Events the old man had referred to.

Black's exploits had been published in a variety of mainstream newspapers, in glorified detail. Plus photographs. Of Black now, and of him in his younger days, when he served in the 22nd Regiment of the Special Air Service. Where the hell they got them from, he had no idea. Black hadn't asked for the attention, but it was a reality he had to accept, given the dramatic circumstances. He had rescued the Prime Minister's daughter, held captive by a killer in a remote cottage on the Island of Jura. It was front page news. The stuff of high adventure and derring-do. At least that was the media's spin on it. The truth was much darker. During the process, the killer had died, falling to her death on rocks at the foot of a cliff by the sea. Black had survived, by sheer luck. He had landed on a ledge, fifteen feet from the top, virtually invisible. The impact had rendered him unconscious.

He'd awakened to find himself in a soft bed in a health spa

somewhere in the rolling countryside of Perthshire. Compliments of the Government Department he worked for. A secret, mysterious organisation, comprising carefully selected individuals like Black. He had been asked – *ordered* – to stay, convalesce, recharge the batteries. Also, it brought some breathing space for those in power to carefully choreograph Black's return to the land of the living.

Black grudgingly acquiesced. Eight weeks later, and he was front page news. A national hero. His face was splashed on the cover of virtually everything.

But the affair had a tragic side. His friend and mentor, Colonel Mackenzie, had been murdered. Black decided, upon his sensational resurrection, to resign. They didn't try to persuade him to stay. The organisation lived in the shadows, and Black, unwittingly, had allowed in too much sunlight. He left, to return to his law office above a shop on the south side of Glasgow, and after a while, people forgot all about Adam Black.

Until now. He stared at the book. To open it, he would have to cut away the string, and to put it bluntly, he couldn't be bothered. The encounter had been strange, but Black put it down to the wandered mind of an elderly man. Nothing more. He picked it up. The cover was rough and worn. He didn't have a jacket, and it was too big to put it his trouser pocket. He would have to carry the damned thing. He toyed with the idea of tossing it into the nearest bin. But he reckoned the old man might want it back sometime, should they ever meet again, which was something Black hoped to avoid.

He left Starbucks, nodding at the girls behind the counter, carrying the book, and promising to himself that he would stick it in the glove compartment of his car, and do his utmost to forget its existence. And another promise he made himself – he would definitely have to change his Saturday morning coffee venue.

6

If you run out of bullets, use your knife. If you lose your knife, use your bare hands. If you lose your hands, then you just fucking smile, and kill them with your good looks.

Rare moment of humour expressed by Staff Sergeant to new recruits of the 22nd Regiment of the SAS.

T he second incident took place the following evening. An incident as bizarre as the first.

Sunday night. Black and his girlfriend, Rachel Hempworth, were leaving the multi-cinema complex at the Quay, in Glasgow. A space of about forty acres devoted to bland glass-fronted buildings housing restaurants, amusement arcades, a bowling alley, a cinema, a casino, all clustered round a car park catering for three hundred cars.

Black hadn't been to the cinema in years. He didn't own a television. Rather, a radio, and an antiquated CD player. It was all he needed. But Rachel had insisted. She was a cinema buff, preferring film noir. When she mentioned this to Black, he unashamedly admitted he wasn't entirely sure what film noir was.

"Stylish, low-key Hollywood movies," she had explained, smiling, as if instructing a simple matter to a small child. "Crime dramas. Usually in black and white. Fifties stuff. Right up your street, I would imagine."

Black returned the smile. "Right up my street because... they're fifties stuff? Before my time, I think."

"Because they're crime dramas. Hard-boiled detective, usually with a drink problem, gets the bad guys after much angst and pain and self-recrimination. Definite similarities to the life of Adam Black."

"A drink problem?"

"I've seen the Glenfiddich bottle hidden in your filing cabinet."

Black shrugged. "Clients should be able to detect drink on the breath of their lawyer. It gives them that warm, fuzzy feeling of reassurance, knowing that lawyers are human after all."

Rachel laughed. "I've never yet met a lawyer who's human."

Black grinned, and held out his hand. "Pleased to meet you."

Rachel's choice of film mildly surprised Black. It was the opposite end of the spectrum to film noir. It was the latest Hollywood blockbuster starring the world's biggest movie star – Victor Cromwell. Rated by some glossy magazine as the most handsome man on the planet. A thriller costing close to $200,000,000. It had smashed box office records on its opening weekend, and would propel Cromwell from super stardom to mega stardom, or so the tabloid press predicted.

When Black had asked Rachel why she was keen to see the movie, her response was succinct, and to the point.

"He's got a nice arse."

There was little Black could say in response.

They'd bought tickets online, avoiding the queues. The film – *Violation* – was two and a half hours long. Black predicted an ordeal. Rachel bought Coke and popcorn, which they shared. They had seats at the back. The place was full. The lights dimmed. The movie started.

By 11pm, they were leaving the cinema, heading for the adjacent car park. Despite himself, Black enjoyed the movie. The plot was clever, the tension high, the set pieces superb, the acting good. Victor Cromwell had played his part well. A lonely, broken vigilante, with nothing to lose, the world against him, betrayed at every turn.

Black was not oblivious to the similarities.

"I'll bet he gets an Oscar," predicted Rachel.

"For his acting or his shapely arse?"

"Both, I would think."

The air was clammy, the night felt close, the sky clear and bright with a million stars. The car park was illuminated by overhead metal lamps, casting a white shimmering glow on the concrete surface. Even at this hour, it was T-shirt weather, which suited Black fine. He was never one to overdress. Jeans, scuffed trainers, bleached blue T-shirt, black leather bomber jacket.

Rachel walked beside him. In her heels, she came up to his shoulder. Slim, hair red as autumn leaves. Being a journalist most of her adult life, her eyes were curious, searching. Seeing things most couldn't see. Unlike Black, she was dressed elegantly. Pale-green summer dress, green heels, matching green silk scarf.

They were approaching the car when Black's phone buzzed. His first thought was who the hell was trying to phone him at this time, on a Sunday night.

Which meant trouble.

Black answered. "Yes?"

"Is that Adam Black?" The voice was English, lacking inflection. Impossible to detect from which part of the country.

"Who's asking?"

"I need to speak to Adam Black." A whisper of recognition played on Black's mind. Somewhere, he'd heard this man before. A whisper, then it was gone.

"Speaking," said Black.

A silence followed.

"I'm glad I've got you."

"Pleased to hear it. Who are you?"

"I need your help."

An echo from the day before, thought Black.

"Good for you. You need my help. I need your name. If I don't get it in three seconds, then I hang up."

The voice replied.

"Victor Cromwell."

7

B lack stopped. Rachel gave him a bewildered look – *what's up?* she mouthed.

"That's not a common name," said Black.

"No," responded the voice. "Uncommon."

"A strange coincidence. We've just been watching a movie where the lead actor shares the same name."

"I hope you enjoyed it. I tried to put on an American accent. The producers prefer that. More appeal to a wider audience. To me, it always sounds false. A mangled mishmash between Cockney and Australian."

It was Black's turn to meet the comment with silence. His mind geared up to overdrive. A hoax? Black thought not. He didn't know what the hell to think. Accept it. Deal with it.

"It sounded fine. What can I do for you, Mr Cromwell?"

"Can we meet?"

"Regarding what exactly?"

"I would rather we meet. Face to face. Then we can talk. Are you free tomorrow?"

"Where are you?"

"Glasgow. I'm staying at the Radisson Blu. Can you come to me? I would really appreciate it."

Black took a deep breath. The situation was so absurd, it could only be real.

"Fair enough."

"Excellent. Twelve noon. Room 82. Thank you, Adam."

Black disconnected. He regarded Rachel for a long moment.

"I think I must be going insane."

8

Radisson Blu. A two hundred and fifty room, glass-fronted structure of irregular dimensions, squatting opposite Glasgow Central Station, in the city centre. In the late morning sunshine, the frontage sparkled, like a canvass of silver and gold. It was 11.30am. Black hated being late. Plus, being early gave him the opportunity for reconnaissance. Black had seen danger in all its forms. No reason why a meeting with a man claiming to be Victor Cromwell in the Radisson Blu should be any different.

Black sat on a high stool at a bar on the ground level. Large windows of darkened glass looked on to the street outside, bustling with people. A pub opposite had seats and tables on the pavement. Men and women sat on metal chairs in the sunshine, sipping cold drinks. Glasgow was busy in the summer heat. The lounge at the Radisson Blu was not. *No wonder, at the prices.* There were a handful of people, sitting on sofas and leather chairs scattered about the room. Black noted in a corner a woman, fortyish, sitting at a low wicker table, a tall glass in front of her. She was striking. Short auburn hair, olive complexion. Plain white T-shirt, tight blue jeans. A suede handbag on her lap. She was listening to the man who sat opposite her, facing away from Black. Smartly dressed – his white cotton summer jacket couldn't mask wide shoulders and broad back. Dark hair, bound into a ponytail by a yellow band. He was talking. Black couldn't hear the details of the conversation. The man's voice was low. Whatever he was saying, the woman listened with rapt attention. She was not smiling. Her eyes were wide, her face solemn. Black had seen fear before, saw it now. It wasn't Black's concern.

Black had a Coke with ice, and a straw. He sucked up some of the cold sweet liquid. To his left, the main foyer. People entered, exited through electric revolving doors. Bellhops in blue uniforms carried luggage, pushed trolleys. People checked in, checked out. Three receptionists sat behind a counter, staring at computer screens, answering the telephone, polite, smiling. To one side, broad carpeted stairs enclosed by glass casements, leading to a large function suite on level 1. Three lifts.

The bar tender wasn't busy. He was checking the gantry, cleaning the marble surface of the bar with a cloth. Wearing a crisp white shirt, black velvet waistcoat, looking attentive and efficient.

Black resumed his attention back to the corner table. The woman was crying, trying hard to stifle sobs. The man leaned over, casually, slapped her with the palm of his hand. The incident took all of two seconds. So quick, one could have questioned if it had happened at all. No one saw. Except Black. The woman stared back, mouth dropped in shock, blood drained from her face. It must have stung. She bit back more tears.

Black had seen enough.

He eased himself off the stool, took his drink with him, made his way over to the table. The man looked up. Black gave an easy smile. The man was maybe in his early thirties. Round face, thick neck. Eyes like dull black pebbles. Massive arms.

Under his jacket, he wore a white silk shirt, open wide at the collar. One hand resting on the table, one on his lap. Hands like shovels. The woman was lucky her neck hadn't snapped. The man was Eastern. Hair glossy black, scraped back from his forehead. Romanian. Or perhaps Albanian. He spoke in fluent English.

"Can I help you, pal?"

Black sat on an empty chair, placed his drink on the table. He nodded at the woman. Her eyes darted bird-like, from Black, to the man next to him.

"You don't need to be scared," said Black quietly. He gave the man his full attention. "It's a hot day. You should cool off." He picked up his glass, and still smiling, tossed the contents into the man's face.

The man recoiled, face dripping, shirt sodden. Black stared at him, square on. Black didn't possess the same bulky muscle. But he possessed a lifetime of lethal expertise, which emanated from his easy smile, his unwavering gaze, his almost-languid demeanour. Violence oozed from Black, raw, palpable.

"What the fuck are you doing?" shouted the man.

"You like to hit women?"

"What?"

Black slapped him across the face. "Hit me. Like you hit her."

The man stared at Black, frozen.

Black slapped him again, across his right cheek. A hard, stinging blow. The man gasped. Elsewhere life went on. The barman continued cleaning the bar; the few people sitting, carried on their quiet conversations. The revolving doors turned. People came and went. The world kept moving.

Black held the man's stare. "I said hit me."

The man licked his lips.

Black's smile vanished. He leant across, his face only inches from the other man's. "I don't get it," he said, his voice a shade above a whisper. "You can hit her. But you can't hit me. I don't understand. Perhaps you can explain."

The man remained still. Black read his eyes and read all the signs. Shock. Bewilderment. Fear.

Black resumed his smile. A waitress was approaching the next table. He caught her attention.

"You couldn't bring over a pen, and maybe a scrap of paper," he said.

She nodded. "Of course, sir."

Black sat back. The woman was staring openly at him. "What's your name?"

She glanced at the man opposite.

"You don't need to worry about this piece of shit. What's your name?"

She replied in a mumble – "Elena."

"Nice. Where are you from?"

Another frightened glance at the man opposite.

"Forget about him."

The woman lowered her head, not daring to look. "Poland," she whispered.

"Whereabouts?"

"Warsaw."

Black nodded.

"A beautiful city. The Vistula River sparkles like spun silver in the winter."

She looked up, a tremulous smile playing on her lips. "Yes."

The man had a drink on the table. It looked like whisky.

"Do you mind?" Black picked up the glass, put it under his nose. "Single malt. Good choice." He drank it in one, replaced the glass on the table.

The woman returned with a pen and piece of A4-sized hotel notepaper.

"Thank you." Black wrote something on it, pushed it across the table to the woman. "That's my name and number. If he ever hits you again, all you do is phone me. Any time."

He turned to look at the man. "And if you lay one finger on her, I'll kill you."

He stood, and nodded politely. It was 11.55am.

He had a meeting with a Hollywood movie star.

9

Room 82 wasn't a room at all. It comprised a suite of several rooms, on the seventh floor. Black took the stairs up. He got to a wide, carpeted corridor, found the door, and knocked.

A man answered. Medium height, compact, wearing a dark suit, dark tie, blonde hair cropped into a boyish crew cut. Thick neck, broad shoulders. Possibly the same age as Black. Late-forties. Pale blue eyes regarded him with a professional detachment.

"Mr Black?"

"Yes. I have an appointment. With Victor Cromwell."

The man answered with a small courteous nod.

"Of course you do." Black detected the unmistakable lilt of an American accent. West coast, maybe? Impossible to say.

Black was beckoned into the interior. He entered a spacious living room, decked with brown leather sofas, coffee tables, and on a long metal and glass unit, a television the size of a small cinema screen. Framed black-and-white photographs of parts of Glasgow dotted smooth white walls, some dating back a hundred years. At one end, a dining table for eight. Beside it, a Chinese vase half the height of Black. The carpet was thick, luxurious. Nice in the winter, thought Black. A little stifling in the July heat.

The man made his way to the opposite end of the room, to a set of double frosted-glass doors, imbued with Charles Rennie Mackintosh designs. He knocked gently. A pause of several seconds. He opened the doors. Black glimpsed another room, similar to the one he was in – more couches, chairs. The man entered, closed the doors behind him.

A minute passed. Black waited. The room was tinged with the soft scent of jasmine, which was not unpleasant. The doors opened. The man reappeared, closed the doors behind him, and regarded Black with the same bland, detached expression.

"Mr Cromwell will be with you shortly," he said. "Would you like a refreshment?"

"What's on offer?"

"Anything you want. Mr Cromwell has a wide selection."

Black had sampled the whisky belonging to the man he'd encountered in the lobby bar, and had a notion for more. "Glenfiddich would be appealing."

"Of course." The man went to an oak wood cabinet in a corner, opened it. Inside, an array of bottles and glasses, sparking like a trove of treasure. He selected a bottle, poured the contents into a crystal glass. "Ice?"

"Neat, thank you."

"Please, have a seat, Mr Black." The man gestured to any number of chairs.

Black sat on a leather chair, facing a large rectangular window. They were seven floors up. Not high enough for panoramic views of Glasgow in the summer sunshine. Instead, the view was of the stone and glass structure of the building opposite – Glasgow Central Train Station.

The man handed Black the glass of whisky.

"Enjoy."

"I'm sure I will."

The coffee table in front of him was low, glass-topped, devoid of any ornamentation, except for a single object, the likes of which Black had never seen before. A contraption maybe eight inches long. Polished red metal on a stepped mounting. An open half-cylindrical groove running along its length, culminating in vertical gold plating an inch high, in which was a space in the shape of a perfect circle. Above it, red metal housing, with a lever on one side. Reminiscent of a guillotine.

The double doors opened. A man entered. Black turned towards him. There was no doubting who he was. His face was unmistakable. It was advertised on posters, billboards, TV, internet. Everywhere. Probably every country in the world. Dressed in black loose-fitting jogging trousers, black long-sleeved gym top, collar up.

"I think I'll have one of those too. I'm out of bed, after all." He gave Black a gleaming smile, revealing California-white teeth, shot a glance at the man at the drinks cabinet, who immediately poured him a glass.

"Thank you for meeting me, Mr Black," said Victor Cromwell. "I see Mr Dalrymple has been looking after you. He is... how can I put it... my man Friday. I don't know where I'd be without him. Where would I be without you, Dalrymple?"

The man introduced as Dalrymple reacted with the slightest shrug. The easy smile never left his face.

"He doesn't talk much," said Cromwell. "Then I suppose I don't pay them for their loquacity."

He sat on a wide leather chair opposite Black. Dalrymple handed him the whisky. Cromwell sipped it.

"Good choice. Cigar?"

"No, thank you."

"Quite right. The healthy option. You don't mind if I..."

"Not at all."

Cromwell raised a finger, gestured to Dalrymple, from which he appeared to derive exact information. He lifted a box from a table, brought it over. Cromwell opened it, took out a cigar.

He held it up to his nose, running its length under his nostrils.

"These are from the Dominican Republic, where, in my humble opinion, you find the finest cigars. It's wrapped in the Corojo leaf, which sets it above the rest. Gives it the mellow blend that every other cigar lacks. But you have to get the cut right, Mr Black. Otherwise, you've wasted a fine smoke. And four hundred dollars."

He placed the cigar in the groove in the little contraption on the coffee table, the tip of the smoking end through the circular space.

"You only cut a tiny portion. Amateurs will cut into the body of the cigar, and thus lose the consistency. A common mistake."

He pushed the lever down. The blade fell. The tip of the cigar dropped into a tiny silver tray.

He lifted out the cigar, and produced a miniature revolver from his pocket, pulled the trigger. A flame appeared from the barrel. He lit up, inhaling, puffing, until the end glowed.

"I hope you don't disapprove," said Cromwell. "Smoking is banned in most places in Scotland, which to me is downright uncivilised."

"But the Radisson permits this?"

Cromwell leaned back. "We have an arrangement. I pay their exorbitant prices, and then a little more. In exchange, they allow me my peccadillos."

"It's the way of the world."

"So it is. It was kind of you to come at such short notice."

"The call intrigued me. I had to see if it was true."

"And is it true?"

"You're sitting opposite. You say you're Victor Cromwell. You look like him. It adds up. What doesn't add up, is why you called me in the first place."

"Did you enjoy my movie?"

Black sipped the whisky. "Yes. Very much."

"I'm rather pleased with it. I think it turned out okay. And it's making a ton of money, which pleases the studio. And it's given me... kudos." He puffed on his cigar, watching Black with a glittering gaze.

"Kudos?"

"Starring in movies, Mr Black, is the equivalent of living life like a butterfly. It's ephemeral. It lasts for a blink of an eye. The money's cool, don't get me wrong. But to increase your longevity in the film world, you need to be treated seriously, and that's a plain fact. Now, starring in a film which not only makes a pile of money, but also makes people realise you can act. Well, there you are. You've cracked both ends of the nut. The public love you. The critics love you. Where can it go wrong?"

He smiled at Black through coils of smoke, teeth sparkling like a row of white pearls.

Black shrugged. He couldn't have cared less about either kudos or money. He studied the man before him – tanned, slim. About the same height as Black. Six-two. Forty or thereabouts. Slate-grey eyes. Thick brown hair, swept back from his forehead, over his ears. Stylishly long. Strong chin, thin lips, chiselled features. A face which looked good from any angle. The face of a hero. A face the cameras would love. The guy was reputed to be Hollywood's most bankable movie star. Black could see why.

"I'm glad you're happy," said Black. "Your accent. I can't pick up where exactly you're from."

Cromwell gave a silky laugh. "Blame all that on RADA, darling. Royal Academy of Dramatic Arts. They knock out any accent pretty fast. I was brought up in faraway places." He pursed his lips. "Though I lived in Scotland for many years, as a younger man. Hope you don't hold that against me." He laughed, though the sound had a tinny undertone.

"Whereabouts?" asked Black.

"Here and there."

Black raised an eyebrow. "A big place."

"We moved about. But it's part of the reason why this is so important. A man should never forget his roots, don't you think?"

"I don't know what to think. I'm still trying to work out why you asked me here. Why *did* you ask me here?"

"Straight to the point," replied Cromwell. "Quite right. Let's get down to business. Top-up?"

"Why not."

Cromwell gestured to Dalrymple. "Refills. Plus get me an ashtray."

Dalrymple got the bottle of Glenfiddich from the cabinet, came over and poured whisky into each of their glasses. He placed an ashtray on the table, fashioned from a lump of blue crystal. Black watched him. Thick wrists, strong hands. His suit couldn't hide his muscular physique. He moved with the suppleness of a cat.

"We're shooting a new movie," said Cromwell. "I'm a co-producer. Which means I'm putting up a sizeable chunk of my own money. The opening scenes are going to be based here. Right in Scotland. I thought I would visit for a few days, try to tie up some loose ends, so to speak. Shooting starts formally in four weeks. It begins at Loch Lomond, then we head to Dundee. Then to other locations in America."

Another puff, another sip. Black waited. He had no idea where this was going.

"It's a thriller. Serial killer. Good and evil. Cat and mouse. Edge of the seat stuff. You know the type of thing, Adam. May I call you Adam?"

Black nodded. "Sounds interesting. I'm not sure how I fit into all this."

"He didn't tell you?"

"Who didn't tell me about what?"

"Strange. Here's the thing. We need a hotel. We know the one we want. It's ideal. It's perfect. It sits right on the lochside. The film begins there, and ends there. Like I said, revisiting my roots. But we have a problem. The owner is proving difficult. He says the only way we can use it, is if we buy it. And we definitely want to buy it."

Black drank his whisky, savouring the taste. He thought he knew where this was going.

"Let me guess," he said. "You need a lawyer to complete the deal. To carry out the land transaction. Why me, Mr Cromwell? You could have chosen a thousand lawyers out there, from the biggest and best law firms. Instead, you chose me, and telephoned my mobile on a Sunday night. Which I don't understand."

Cromwell frowned, eyes narrowing to slits. The sunny disposition slipped for a second. "You don't understand? How can you not understand? It had to be you. Who else could it be? Given the circumstances."

"What circumstances?"

"The owner gave us your name. Said we could only deal through you."

Black took a deep breath, finished the whisky. None of it made sense.

"Who said this? Who is the owner?"

37

"Hasn't he spoken to you?"

"Hasn't *who* spoken to me?"

Cromwell took a deep drag of his cigar. The smoke weaved about him, like serpents' tails.

"The owner of the hotel. Your father. Who else?"

10

The Farm.

A place where no farming took place. At least not in the conventional sense. It consisted of a large house and a cluster of barns and sheds around a centre square, all enclosed by a high stone wall, entrance gained through a double gate, always locked. No tractors, no combine harvesters, no ploughs. No crops, no animals. Still, it was known as The Farm.

These thoughts passed through the mind of Besnik Wajda, as he sat in the kitchen. It was not luxurious. Big, square. Peeling wallpaper. High ceiling, and across the top, an old-style pulley for drying clothes. The weather was warm outside. A washing line could easily have been stretched. But orders were orders. Clothing was to be dried inside.

An ancient free-standing cooker, with four rings. Beside it, two large fridge-freezers. Well stocked up. It had to be. At any given time, the Farm could play host to up to twenty people, not including himself, his brother, and the guards. In a corner, an industrial-sized washing machine. Cupboards on the walls, some with doors askew, containing pots, pans, other kitchen stuff. A sink. Some drawers. The floor was flowery green linoleum, probably laid fifty years ago. Warped and rippled in places. Across the top of one wall, a black stain. Mould. Dampness from a leak somewhere in the roof. Loose slates, probably. He'd been told to fix it, weeks ago. But what was he? A fucking roofer? It would do, until the winter. Then, maybe he'd see to it.

He sat on one of six plain wooden chairs around a plain wooden table. He was smoking. There was nothing on the table, except a saucer, where he flicked the cigarette ash. He smoked thirty a day. Rolling tobacco. Golden Virginia. Strong. When inhaled, it bit the lungs, made you feel every particle. The single window in the kitchen was open. It was July, and hot. But here, on the moors, there was a constant wind, reduced to a breeze in the summer. Wajda leant back in the chair, the wooden legs creaking under his gross weight. He let the breeze play on his face. He half closed his eyes, thoughts drifting.

He liked this particular time. Between shifts, as he described it. A batch had been sent out the previous night, late. Another batch was due in that evening. He had to clean the sheets, the pillow cases. Have food prepared. He had eight hours before they arrived. Plenty of time to do nothing.

He took another deep drag of the cigarette. His hand drifted to the crotch of his jogging pants. His mind played through the sequence of events to follow. He stroked his dick.

They would arrive. They would be scared. He could imagine the stark terror on their faces. He'd seen it a hundred times before. It never changed. But also defiance, possibly. There was always one or two. His job – to crush any thoughts of hope. Crush their souls. Make them understand the reality of their situation.

He licked his lips with the tip of his tongue. They'd get herded through to another room of the house. The Big Room. An internal wall had been knocked away. Two rooms converted into one. They'd be lined up, back against the brick. Wrists bound. He would inspect, consider, decide. His brother would stand behind him, carrying a shotgun, and explain in his perfect English, that they were to be good. No screaming. No attempts at escape. But if they were badly behaved then...

He was allowed to choose one. One which he could pick. He was good at picking. He could smell out the rebels.

He pulled down the front of his jogging pants, lifted up the front of his sweater, revealing a large white belly. His dick was brick hard.

He would untie one, pull her to the centre of the room, to a mattress on the floor. He would take his dick out, just as he was doing now, and let her see what was to happen. Let them all see. Then, with a captive audience, he would push her down, lay his massive weight upon her. All the while, his brother would explain that this was the fate of those who refused to accept the new order.

Screams, and then the screaming would stop.

Besnik Wajda pulled his jogging pants back up.

He needed his strength. He took another drag, savouring the flavour of the tobacco. Savouring the moment.

This was The Farm.

And he was The Beast.

11

Most people exist. We men of the Special Air Service live.

*Observation raised by Staff Sergeant to new recruits of the 22nd
Regiment of the SAS*

"That's interesting." Black finished off the whisky. "I'll have
to speak to my client."

"You mean your father," said Cromwell.

"I think a mistake's been made. Perhaps you picked him up
wrong. My father died over twenty years ago. Unless there's been
a resurrection, the man you spoke to could not possibly be my
father. What did he say his name was?"

"I didn't get it wrong, Adam. I drove up to the hotel to meet
him personally, last week. Spoke to him face to face. He lives in
the hotel. That's the real reason why I'm still here. To get this
over the line. And he was most specific. He wanted you to broker
this deal. His son."

"What did he say his name was?"

Cromwell gazed at Black for all of ten seconds.

"Is this some sort of joke? Time is money, Adam. I'm catching a flight in a few days, and I need certainty. I was hoping we could shake hands today."

"I believe we both need certainty. What was his name?"

"He said his name was Robin. Robin Black. The hotel is called The Raven's Crown. What the hell is going on?"

Black stood.

"Honestly? I have no idea. But someone's claiming to be my father, and given you my number to contact. I would describe the situation as bizarre, at best." Black reflected. *Mysterious* was also a good description. Black didn't like mystery in his life. It usually ended up with people dead.

Cromwell also stood, glass of whisky in one hand, cigar in the other, perfect features creased in a combination of anger and confusion.

"What happens now? You just walk out, and I have to what? Wait about, while you guys sort out some family issues? I offered him $2,000,000 for his hotel. Which I reckon is about five times more than it's worth, given the state it's in. The offer still stands. But it won't stand forever. If you don't get something sorted soon, then I'll look elsewhere. And then we all lose out. Me, you, your father."

"He's not my father."

"Call me when you've sorted this." Cromwell nodded to Dalrymple, who handed Black a card. "That's my mobile. Call me any time. I'll pick up."

"This individual who claims to be my father – did he give you a number to contact him?"

"He didn't. Why should he? Like he said, all dealings have to go through you. Isn't this a lawyer–client thing?"

His features softened into a smile. Suddenly the Hollywood movie star was back again.

"I don't mean to be abrasive, Adam, but this film means a lot to me. To see *Dreams* get to the big screen would be... well... a dream." He held his hand out. Black shook it, hesitated.

"What did you say?"

"I didn't mean to be abrasive."

"No. You mentioned *Dreams*."

"Of course. It's the name of the new film. Or a shortened version of it."

"What's the full version?"

Cromwell sucked on his cigar, the brown leaf turning to ash. He leaned forward, like some fellow conspirator relaying a deadly secret, and spoke in a low, soft voice. "Promise not to tell?"

Black smelled the heavy scent of cigar from his breath. "Wouldn't tell a soul."

Cromwell's smile broadened.

"The Book of Dreams."

12

B lack had parked his car a short distance from the hotel. A walk of about five minutes. As he left the main foyer, he happened to look over, to the corner where the woman called Elena had been sitting. She and the man were gone. He felt a mixture of emotion. Where was she now? He had intervened. An instinctive reaction. Perhaps he should have left it. Maybe he'd made it worse for her. Perhaps he shouldn't stick his nose into other people's business. But he would never change, and he knew it. If Black saw it happen again, he would simply repeat the process. He felt a tinge of disappointment. He'd wished he'd broken the guy's jaw. Made him feel it. No point dwelling on the matter, he thought. He would never see her again.

He got to his car – a BMW 4 Series Coupe – drove off. He headed back to his office, on the south side of Glasgow. He took the motorway, the M77. A twenty-five-minute journey. He pondered the last few days. Black was no stranger to the mysterious. The recent events had cranked *mystery* up to a new level.

The Raven's Crown. A hotel on the Banks of Loch Lomond, so Cromwell had said. Black had never heard of it. Someone claiming to be his father was the owner. Robin Black. Same name. His father had died twenty-two years earlier. Throat cancer. A strong, robust man, dwindled down to a skeleton. In pain for weeks, the morphine eventually ineffective.

Black thought back. He was in his mid-twenties at the time. He'd already lost his brother to a bomb in Northern Ireland, and his mother three years before that. To skin cancer. That had been quick. She was dead within four weeks. So quick, one second she was there, and then gone. Her life extinguished, as quickly as the snuffing of a candle. His father on the other hand... his thoughts drifted. The prolonged horror of watching his father dying on a hospital bed before his eyes had replaced any earlier memories. When he thought back, all he saw was his pain. His father's pain. His own pain, at witnessing such suffering. And after all that pain, nothing. No family. An orphan. His family snatched away.

He was on his own.

Someone was claiming to be his father. A mistake? Perhaps. Black took the next turn off. Change of plan. He had no appointments. Even if he had, he wouldn't have cared. He changed his route, heading north.

To 'The Raven's Crown'.

To pay a visit.

To his dead father.

13

K osice, Slovakia.

Danika Biskup thought back to the place of her birth, her home town, as she and the others waited in the minibus. A distant dream. But not so distant. The memories were still fresh. The horrors still vivid.

Kosice, a city she knew and loved. She lived with her parents only a five-minute walk from St. Elisabeth Cathedral. She remembered cursing the never-ending peal of its church bells, as they rang through the streets and narrow lanes. She gave a humourless, frightened smile. How she would give everything to hear the bells again, see the shops she knew so well, the pubs where she and her fellow students laughed and drank, spilling onto the cobbled courtyards in the early hours, smoking cheap cigarettes on park benches and somehow, miraculously, always managing her early lectures the next day, despite the hangovers. Laughing. Lots of laughing. She shuddered. The laughter had left her life. Beaten out of her. It didn't look like it would ever return.

She was studying economics at university. In her third year, and just turned twenty-one. It was in an Irish themed pub called

Donovan's, popular with students, where she'd met a young, handsome Englishman. From London. She loved his accent. He spoke her language, fluently. The name he had given her was Patrick Friel. He told her he was a student, studying languages at Westminster University, staying in Kosice for a few weeks' holiday. She fell in love. She believed he was in love with her. She remembered the first night she'd given him everything. His tenderness.

She fought back a wave of nausea, remembering.

He'd invited her to Britain to stay with him during the summer. They would travel. For nine weeks, visiting places throughout England and Scotland, then back to Kosice, in time to resume her studies for her graduation year.

Her parents remonstrated. They weren't happy. She'd never left home before. Not for an entire summer. Not to another country. They'd never met this young handsome man. Didn't know anything about him. She'd never given it any thought, his reticence towards meeting her mother and father. But she understood now. Everything had sudden sharp, brutal clarity. She thought about her parents every minute of every day. They would be unaware of her desperate situation. But in time, when she didn't contact them, their bewilderment would turn to anguish. Anguish to despair.

He owned an old Honda Civic. The intention was to drive to Calais, take the ferry across the English Channel. Disembark in Dover. Then to London, to meet his parents. So he said.

Danika looked out the minibus window. It was a dismal grey morning. Outside a warehouse, somewhere in England. She didn't know where she was. She shared the bus with other girls. They looked like she looked. Confused. Terrified.

Term had finished. The summer was starting. They had driven a hundred miles from Kosice. She was alive. Joyful. They chatted. She couldn't stop talking. Him smiling at her. Laughing with her. The world was fine. Then the world changed.

He had to stop, at a layby on some country road. *To relieve myself*, he had said, and she found that funny at the time, for no particular reason other than she believed she was in love. A van was parked there. She didn't give it a second notice. Why should she?

She didn't want to remember what happened next, but each moment of the events to follow was lanced into her brain, running on constant replay. Patrick got out. He went behind some trees. She waited. A man, heavily built, got out of the van. He approached the car. He tapped on her window. She wound the window down. *Perhaps he's lost*, she thought. The man was smiling. She looked up at him. He was unshaven. Smelled of garlic and cigarette smoke and sweat. She smiled back.

With both hands, he grabbed handfuls of her hair, dragged her through the open window. She screamed. The movement was quick and savage. She had never experienced such strength. He pulled her clean through. She fell on the ground. He slapped her hard across the face. The blow was mind-numbingly hard, shocking her to instant silence. Her head spun. He hoisted her up, rough hands under her armpits. She was weak, her legs unstable. He half marched, half carried her to the back of the van. Patrick appeared. Her salvation! He was smoking. Her vision was blurred. She moaned. *Help*, she said. But Patrick didn't help. Instead, he opened the van door. He was saying something, but she couldn't make out his words. She was bundled into the back. It smelled of diesel and dirt. She saw Patrick. Watching her. He gave her a little wave. Darkness, as the van doors closed. She heard drifts of conversation. The van moved.

She screamed, thumped her hands against the sides. Eventually, she sensed the van stopping. She held her breath. The driver's door opened, closed. Suddenly, the back doors swung open. She shrank into a corner. The big man clambered in, loomed over her. He crouched down, a dark presence only inches from her face.

"If you make another sound, I'll kill you." He spoke in broken Slovakian, his voice thick, low. He slapped her again, across the face, the blow powerful. Her vision darkened. She lost consciousness.

~

She awoke. She was in another vehicle, larger, with other women. They were bound together by the wrists with chains, sitting on rugs. Pale frightened faces watched her. A series of stops. No one dared speak.

Time passed. The doors opened. Night time. Impossible to say where they were. She needed the toilet. They filed out, one at a time, linked by shackles. They were pushed and shoved towards trees by the side of the road. Four men. They had sticks.

"Toilet," said one. The men spoke with each other. Casual conversation. Sounded like Romanian. A girl collapsed on her knees, bringing another down with her. The sticks were used to beat them until they got up. Danika squatted, relieved herself, the men watching, smoking, laughing. Back into the van. They were each given a bottle of water.

More driving. For hours, perhaps. The heat was unbearable. Maybe she dozed, maybe she didn't. The van stopped once again. A disused garage. It was still dark. They were taken to a room. In the middle of the room was a chair. Like a dentist's chair, she remembered thinking. She would never forget it.

Another man was there. He sat on a swivel stool. He was thin and old, his face a mask of wrinkles. He wore a blue boiler suit. He gave a gap-toothed grin when the girls entered. Next to him, on a trestle, were small plastic bottles of coloured liquid, towels, paper tissues, a basin, antiseptic cream, a bar of soap. In his hand he held a strange metal object, the likes of which she had never seen before. Something between a gun and a drill. It was connected by a length of cable to a socket on the wall.

One at a time, they were tattooed. On the back of the wrist. Each given a number. Hers was *61*.

Branded. Like cattle.

More travelling. Stops. Food, water – until this moment, when the chains were removed, they were ushered into a minibus, and told where to sit. The four men remained with them, one of them driving.

The vehicle rumbled into life.

"We're taking you to a special place," announced one, in good clear English.

"We're taking you to the Farm."

14

The drive to Loch Lomond took just over an hour. The traffic was fairly light. It was early afternoon. Most people were working. Black hadn't been in this part of Scotland for years. The last time, they'd hired a lodge for a long weekend, only a hundred yards from the banks. Himself, his wife, his daughter. He remembered fleeting images. It was cold, he remembered. The timber lodge taking a lifetime to heat up. Buying cheap cane-handled fishing nets. Searching for tadpoles in the tiny pools and puddles formed between the rocks and stones. Skimming stones across the surface of the water. Buying fish and chips for dinner. Watching stuff on a small television, the reception poor. Listening to the patter of rain on the flat wooden roof, as their daughter slept. Laughing, planning their lives. Enjoying the moment. When life was uncomplicated.

Black took a deep breath. He had killed the men responsible for the murder of his family. He had killed many others. He wondered if the killing would ever stop. Death seemed to tail him. Where he went, it went. He *was* death.

Black had googled the name *Raven's Crown, Loch Lomond,* on

his mobile. Nothing came up, of any relevance. It seemed he would have to find the place the old-fashioned way.

He drove to Tarbet, and parked at the Tarbet Hotel. A large castle-like structure, complete with turrets and embrasures and sharp Gothic slate roofs. It cut an impressive outline from a distance. Also, it sat at a junction. Turn right, and you travelled a road which hugged the shoreline. Straight on, and you travelled west, towards Loch Fyne. He made enquiries inside. The receptionist was young, and claimed to have never heard of the place. An elderly man, sitting at a table, reading a newspaper, overheard the conversation.

"Past Ardlui," he interrupted. "Though you won't find much."

Black turned to the man.

"Past Ardlui?"

"Maybe a mile past it. It sits just off the main road, yards from the shore. You can't see it from the road. Hidden by trees. There's a single lane, leading down to it. Blink, and you miss it."

"I won't find much?" said Black.

"It's been years since it was a hotel. Closed down maybe ten years back. Maybe more. Now just a big, derelict, rambling house." The man squinted at Black. "What takes you there?"

Black smiled. "I like the sound of the name. *The Raven's Crown*. It has a ring to it. I'm curious."

The man gave a wheezy laugh. "It killed the cat."

Black left the hotel, and drove the winding road to Ardlui. A distance of about fifteen miles, the loch to his right, shimmering still as a mirror in the afternoon sunshine. Serene in the summer. Treacherous in winter. Swimmers underestimated the cold and the swift current. Loch Lomond had taken more than its fair share of lives over the years.

Black reached Ardlui – a hamlet comprising little more than a hotel, a marina, and a cluster of houses perched on the slopes.

Black drove through, concentrating to his right. There! As the man at the hotel had said, a lane branched off from the main road, heading down to the banks of the loch, wide enough for a single car. Black turned in, and down, heading back on himself. He drove a hundred yards, trees blocking any view from the road. Ahead was a substantial stone building. He parked in a courtyard of uneven slabs, grass and weeds growing through the cracks in between. It stood close to the water, separated by a narrow strip of beach and moss-covered rocks.

He parked, got out. A three-storey building, wide bay windows on each side of the main entrance. It was solid, the walls of heavy grey stone. Medieval-style turrets on either end, the roof sectioned into points and flat surfaces. The entrance was a yellow double Victorian door. The paint was peeling. There were cracks in the windows. The guttering was hanging and clogged with vegetation. The window sills were rotten.

This was it. *The Raven's Crown.*

The man at the Tarbet Hotel was right – it looked abandoned.

Black gazed at it. Victor Cromwell felt the need to spend $2,000,000 on this shithole, all for his movie. Probably a fraction of the budget. Nice to have money to burn.

Black approached the front doors. The windows were blanked out by drawn curtains. There was no doorbell, no door-knocker. He rapped the wood with his fist. No response. The door was locked, and solid. He tried again. Nothing.

He sauntered round the side of the building. He opened a hanging wooden gate, entered a garden, maybe a half-acre in size. Once, perhaps, it would have been pretty. Metal chairs, benches, half rotten wooden picnic tables, all sitting scattered in grass a foot high. In the centre of what was once the lawn, a large patio had been laid. Black gave it a cursory glance. The slabs were decorative, depicting shapes coloured and fashioned into the stone, barely recognisable through time and weather.

One shape was distinct, however, unaffected – a striking image of a galloping white horse, in clear and vivid detail. Even amongst the ruins, it was an impressive piece of stonework, involving effort and money.

At one end of the garden, a wooden gazebo, its latticed framework broken, overgrown with thorny brambles. Stone figurines lurked in the bushes, rendered smooth by the elements. The place was dilapidated. Black made his way round, to the back. The lochside was only yards away. Stretching into the water was a narrow jetty, comprising pale bleached planks of wood. Moored to a cleat was a large speedboat, swaying with the current.

Black got to a storm door. It was open. He stepped through, into a vestibule. It smelled damp. Another door with frosted-glass panels. Black peered in, making out images and shapes, but nothing distinguishable. He knocked on the glass. A sound? Perhaps. He knocked again. Silence. But he'd heard something. He was suddenly wary, senses heightened.

He could turn back, walk away. Something told him, perhaps a lifetime of experience, that danger lurked close by. But walking away was not Black's style.

He turned the handle. The door was not locked. Black went in.

And entered a nightmare.

15

She had been drugged. When she came to, she found her arms hoisted wide above her, and fastened to a wooden beam. She was upright. She was naked. A fog clouded her brain, clogged her mind. Her tongue felt thick, her mouth dry. Gradually, she gained awareness. A dull ache spread from her hands, through her wrists, her forearms, seeping through her bones. Her vision wavered. Images floated.

She closed her eyes, swallowed, the pain intense. She stretched her neck round, looked up. Focused. She saw what had been inflicted upon her, and couldn't believe what she was seeing. It took several seconds for her to rationalise the situation. She decided she must be dreaming. That this was happening to someone else. But the pain came in great racking waves. The pain made it real. And with the pain, the horror.

Nails had been driven through the palms of each hand, deep into the wood. Blood streamed from the wounds. Her blood. She tried to scream. Her mouth was too dry, her throat throbbed. The pain. It flooded through her. She tried to move. Her hands were nailed tight, the tops of each nail twisted to one side, preventing her from pulling free.

She tried to take in her surroundings. The place was illuminated by a soft glow, to one side. She concentrated on its source. A single lit candle, standing upright on its own wax on a saucer. Its light made the air around it shimmer. She made out vague images, silhouettes. Boxes, crates. Indeterminate objects. No windows.

She began to sob. The effort made the pain worse.

"Is there anyone there?" she croaked, her voice brittle.

She detected movement. A shift in the air. Something had been standing in the shadows, quite still. Just on the periphery of the candlelight. Like a statue. Now it stirred. She gasped. A figure stepped towards her, to stop four feet away. Her breath caught in her chest. Her eyes regarded the thing before her. The pain was forgotten. Vanished. In its place, terror.

She tried to speak. She was unable to articulate.

It shuffled a little closer. If it reached out, it could touch her. She shrank back, contorting her body, restricted by the nails driven through the palms of her hands.

The thing before her was a man. Barely. His face was incomplete. His left eye was missing. Instead, a black empty socket. No skin or tissue on his left cheek and lower jaw. The bare bones gleamed yellowy-white in the candle flame. The nose had been split in two, a clean deep cut through cartilage and bone, creating two separate protrusions of flesh. His left ear was missing. His lips were also missing, both upper and lower, the skin drawn back, displaying red gums and long teeth.

The skin on the remainder of his face was ghastly white. As if he'd applied make-up for the effect. Long thin hair trailed from his scalp, down to his shoulders. He was tall. He stooped over her. He wore a shapeless gown. He came closer still. She felt his breath on her face.

She screamed. The noise echoed. He opened his mouth

wide, his teeth sharp. He stretched out his arms, imitating her own outstretched arms.

He loomed in close.

"Please," she whispered, turning her head away.

He flicked his tongue in and out, like a lizard, then leaned in, and licked the length of her cheek.

She screamed again. Then, a sudden movement – he had her by her throat, angling her face, so she was looking directly at him. She kept her eyes tight shut.

His voice was a dry rasp. Like dead leaves in a breeze.

"Look at me," he said. He squeezed long fingers round her neck. "Look at me."

She opened her eyes. He nodded.

"Good girl."

He brought his face in, to kiss her. She felt a burst of blood. She groaned. He wasn't kissing. He was biting. He bit her lips, her tongue. Bit deep. He hovered his mouth over her face. Her nose, her cheeks. Biting. Removing. Chewing. Spitting. She tried to shake her head, but he was clamped on, teeth hooked into her skin.

The process continued, the man undeterred by her screams. He withdrew, reached to something placed flat on top of some wooden boxes.

A mirror.

He was smiling, his lipless mouth bared back.

"Look," he said. "Look, my pretty."

She glanced at her reflection. Her face was gone. She sobbed.

He picked up something else. A long-bladed sawing knife with a yellow plastic handle. He shuffled behind her, started working on her back, cutting, pulling.

"Playtime," he whispered.

16

Black entered a narrow hallway. The wallpaper was peeling, the carpet underfoot thin, threadbare. He got to another door, entered a kitchen. It was large, sunlight streaming through a window. In the centre, a marble-topped island for working. Cupboards, a double sink each filled with dirty water. A range-style cooker, the burner covers rusted. The place smelled of dampness and rot. Crockery still stood in a plastic dish dryer. The kitchen hadn't been used for years.

Another door, to the interior of the building. Black hesitated. He had entered the house because he thought he'd heard something. Maybe his imagination. He thought not. Maybe kids, fooling about. Maybe. He was unarmed. He should turn round, walk back out the door.

He went through, emerged into a large room. Once, possibly a dining room. He could imagine people sitting here, chatting, laughing. In better times. High ceiling, bare white walls. In a corner, stacked in a pile, broken furniture. A stone fire surround, the hearth empty and cold. Above, a mirror, hanging askew, cracked down the middle. One end, wide bay windows, curtains drawn. A great view of the loch, had they been open. The sun still got in, through the edges and holes in the fabric, sending slants of light across the room. The carpet, once red, was a patchwork of stains.

In the centre sat a man. His arms and legs were bound to the chair by rolls of industrial sealing tape. A piece of tape had been placed over his mouth. He stared at Black, straining against his bonds, the veins on his neck bulging. He wasn't wearing socks and shoes. They had been placed neatly to one side. At his feet was a pair of hand-sized metal shears. Three of his toes had been removed. The carpet was saturated in blood.

Black sensed movement. He spun round.

A man stood framed in the doorway. In his hand, a pump-action shotgun, sawn down. Pointing in Black's general direction. From that distance, he couldn't miss. A twitch of the finger, and Black was a dead man.

Black did exactly as he'd been trained. He ignored the point of the gun. Instead, he levelled his stare at the man's face, his eyes. Personalise. Bring him in. Bring his guard down, if possible. Then kill. As he'd been trained.

"We meet again," said Black.

The man gave a wide smile. "What a pleasure. I am truly blessed."

"It looks as if I'll be keeping my promise earlier than I thought."

"What promise is that."

"My promise to kill you."

The man's lips curved at the edges into a crooked smile. "I've got the fucking gun. We weren't expecting you this early. But here you are."

Black returned the smile. Keep him talking. "Here I am. You were expecting me?"

Black kept his eyes locked on the man's face. The same man

he had met earlier that morning, briefly, in the bar at the Radisson Blu. The guy who liked to slap women.

"Move." He gestured with the gun. Black turned and walked slowly towards the centre of the room, to stand next to the man sitting on the chair.

"Andreas! Where the fuck are you?"

Another man appeared, flustered, in the process of tying the cord of his trousers. He was small, round shouldered, belly flopping over a pair of loose tracksuit bottoms, pale green T-shirt. Like his friend, he looked Eastern European, hair bleached unnaturally white, beetling button-black eyes, heavy jowls.

"Christ, Luca, I was having a fucking shi–" He stopped when he saw Black. "Is it him?"

"Shut up," said the first man, Luca. He scrutinised Black. "It's good to catch up. Elena passes on her love."

Black's eyes glittered. He didn't respond.

Luca nodded, his round flat face expressionless, the only sound in the room the grunts and groans of the man strapped to the chair. Eventually Luca spoke, his voice soft.

"Where is it?"

Black stared, thoughts racing. He had no idea what Luca was talking about. But he needed time.

"A safe place."

"Where?"

"Your boss already has it. That's why he sent me here. To clear up loose ends."

Distraction, thought Black.

The man sitting tied to the chair squirmed, straining against the tape, causing the chair to rock back and forwards.

"Keep still!" snapped Andreas. From a pocket in his tracksuit trousers, he pulled out a six-inch serrated blade.

"What the fuck do you mean?" Luca said, addressing Black.

"I was sent here to kill you. Looks like you got here first.

Perhaps we were meant to kill each other." Black glanced at the man tied to the chair. "After you'd taken care of him, I was to take care of you. No loose ends. Those were my instructions. No loose ends."

The man with the gun licked his lips with the tip of his tongue. *He's thinking*, thought Black. Uncertainty had been introduced into the equation. No one liked uncertainty.

"Cut their fucking eyes out, both of them," said Andreas.

"Shut up," said Luca.

Black continued, bombarding him with more information. Confusion. Disorientation. "I have proof. I can show you a text. Telling me precisely where you'd be. At this rundown shithole. £50,000 has been transferred to my account. The next fifty I get after I kill you. We've both been played."

"He's a fucking lying scumbag," said Andreas. "Kill him, Luca. Kill them both."

"Shut up, Andreas. You don't get paid to think." Luca took a deep breath, straightened. "My friend wants me to kill you. He's got a quick temper. I'm inclined to agree with him. Tell me this – who sent you? Give me a name? Then I'll know whether you're bullshitting."

Black spoke quickly. His pulse raced. To die here, in this place, at the hands of such men, was unthinkable. Still, every man died. Most didn't choose the location, or the manner. Seconds were slipping by. He heard a sound in his ears – his heart.

"No names. Never. All communication by email or text. I can show you." He slowly moved his hand to his trouser pocket.

"Don't fucking try it!" Luca jerked his head round to Andreas. "Get his phone. Don't you twitch as much as a fucking muscle, Black, or I swear to Christ I will blow the top of your head off."

Andreas lumbered forward, knife bristling.

Black remained still. At such moments, in the raw heat of confrontation, a calmness settled in his mind. He watched the scene unfold with detachment, with bright clarity, almost an out-of-body experience.

Andreas was close. Black could smell his breath. Heavy, rancid. Also, a sour mix of sweat and cologne. He squared up to Black. He was all of eight inches shorter. Black could have laughed. The man called Andreas was exactly where Black wanted him to be. In the line of fire. Amateurs.

Andreas raised his knife to Black's face, pressing the tip into his cheek. "I'm going to cut your fucking eyeballs out," he whispered.

"Get the fucking phone!" shrieked Luca.

Black leaned his face into the blade, causing the tip to burst the skin on his cheek. He felt blood dribble. Andreas gasped in surprise. "Get your friend the phone," Black said. "You fat fuck."

He used his fist, struck Andreas hard on the testicles. Andreas grunted, collapsed into Black's chest.

Luca screamed. Still, he wavered. If he fired, he'd hit his friend.

"Out the fucking way!"

Black leant back, raised himself up, arching his back, brought his head down, slamming it into the bridge of Andreas's nose. He felt bones crunch. Andreas wobbled on his feet. Black held him up, using his body as a shield. Black seized his arm in a lock, pushed the bone above the elbow, felt the ulna snap. Andreas howled. The knife fell from limp fingers.

"Out the fucking way!" Luca screamed again, his voice shrill.

Black propelled Andreas towards Luca, stooped down, snatched up the knife, lunged forward, his weight balanced on his outthrust leg, hurled the blade. It plunged almost to the hilt into Luca's throat. Luca stood, transfixed, mouth gaping, and for a grotesque moment stared at Black in horror and accusation.

He sank to his knees. His finger spasmed on the trigger of the shotgun, a reflexive action, and blew a hole through the curtains, and the window beyond. He sagged forward, onto the floor. His body weight pushed the knife clean through his neck.

Andreas staggered towards the dropped gun. He was slow and in pain. Black was on him, swivel-kicking him on the chest. Andreas flew back onto the floor. Black picked up the gun.

He regarded Andreas for several seconds. "Get up."

Andreas groaned, clambered to his feet. Blood oozed from both nostrils. His nose was broken, his arm hung at an ugly angle. He wavered, trying to keep his balance. "Please," he croaked. "We were never going to kill you. You have to believe me."

"Sure," said Black. "When your pal Luca had his shotgun pointed at my head, I knew deep down it was just for show."

Andreas looked at Luca's body, on his stomach, the blade of the knife issuing six inches from the nape of his neck. "I've never seen anyone do that before."

"There's always a first," said Black. "Look at me, Andreas."

Andreas shifted his focus to Black, eyes glassy. The pain was turning to shock.

"Luca asked me where it was. What was he talking about? Where what was?"

Andreas swallowed, chin wobbling, as he tried to formulate words. "I dunno. I swear."

"I understand."

Black took three steps, bent over, flipped Luca's body over onto his back, grasped the hilt of the knife, pulled it from his neck.

He approached Andreas. Andreas half hobbled, half shuffled, trying to retreat. He got to a wall, and could go no further. Black loomed over him.

"Look at me, Andreas," he said softly.

Andreas raised his head.

"You were very keen to cut my eyes out. With this very dagger. It must be a kind of turn-on for you. Is that what it is – a turn-on? My go now."

His arm darted forward, hard, fast. The point of the blade popped Andreas's left eye. Andreas shrieked, fell on his knees, one hand clutching his face, blood pulsing in spurts.

"Jesus. You've fucking blinded me!"

Black stepped back.

"Not quite," he said, his voice a flat monotone. "You have another eye. If you don't start talking, I'll take that one out too. I'll ask again. What is it you're looking for?"

Andreas sobbed. "I swear, I don't know anything. I do what I'm told. Andreas – do this. Andreas – do that. I don't ask questions."

Black took a deep breath. "Who sent you?"

"Please," he moaned. "You don't understand. They'll kill me if I tell you."

"Wrong answer."

Black moved towards him, knife in one hand, shotgun in the other.

Andreas shifted his weight, so that he was facing the wall.

"I don't know his real name. I've never met him. He's known as something else."

"What?"

"I need to get to a hospital," he muttered.

"Sure you do. Who sent you? You have three seconds to answer."

Andreas squinted round, one hand covering half his face, blood soaked. "You're the devil."

Black allowed a steely smile. "The devil? I am far worse. Talk."

Andreas's shoulders slumped. "The Blood Eagle," he said. "We call him the Blood Eagle."

"And after you got what you came for, what was to happen?"

Andreas sobbed.

"You were to kill me," continued Black. "You can see why the quality of mercy is running a little dry. What would you do if you were me, Andreas?"

"Please... it was a job. I didn't..."

Black shot him through the head. He shot him again, through the chest, for good measure. When Black killed, he liked to make sure.

The Blood Eagle. These men had been waiting for him. They had been given a task. To get something, then kill him.

A noise. Black turned to the man sitting bound to the chair. He would have witnessed the entire scene. Black strode over to him, and pulled the tape from his mouth.

The man gasped, and spat lumps of pale gristle onto the floor. It took five seconds before Black understood.

They had cut off the man's toes.

And fed them to him.

17

D anika had a window seat. Beside her sat a woman dressed in a stained floral dress, her face deathly pale, her eyes dull and blank. Probably in her late teens. Danika attempted a weak smile. The girl's lips twitched. There were thirteen other girls on the bus, each dishevelled, shocked, frightened. The men sat at the front, chatting to each other, like it was business as usual. The rumbling noise of the engine drowned out their conversation.

"My name is Danika," she whispered.

The girl stared back at her with a glazed look. Suddenly, as if just comprehending a conversation had been initiated, her features came to life. She bit her bottom lip. She glanced at the men at the front, then back to Danika.

"Don't worry," said Danika. "They can't hear us if we talk quietly. What's your name?"

The girl was in a daze. Danika took her hand. "What's your name," she asked again, squeezing her fingers gently, as if the act would somehow penetrate her shock.

"My name?" she muttered. "Monica. My name is Monica." French accent.

Danika gave a tight smile. "Where are you from, Monica?"

The girl called Monica shook her head. "Travelling. I was travelling."

"Okay."

"Two of us. We were leaving a hostel in Berlin." Her eyes lost focus. *She was looking back, remembering*, thought Danika. Just as she had done, a thousand times, no matter how she tried to block it out.

"You're from France," said Danika. "Whereabouts?"

Monica replied in a flat voice. A single tear trickled from the corner of her eye, down a pale cheek.

"We were leaving the hostel. It was early. We had breakfast in the dining room. I had coffee and croissant with marmalade. Frances had a chocolate pastry." Her bottom lip wobbled. "She loved chocolate."

"Your friend is called Frances?"

"We left early because we had to catch a train. 8.30am. The station was a half hour walk from the hostel. Frances thought the manager was so sweet."

"The manager of the hostel?"

"He said his name was Freddy. He gave us a lift. His car smelled of cigarettes."

She lowered her head, staring at her lap.

"He didn't take us to the station. He took us to a different place."

"You don't need to tell me," soothed Danika.

"He took us to a warehouse in the middle of nowhere. All the windows were smashed. A van was waiting. Five men got out. They were laughing. They knew Freddy. We were sitting in the back seat. We knew something was terribly wrong." She swallowed, took a small shuddering breath. *She needed this out*, thought Danika. Like pus from a sore.

"Freddy shook hands with one of them, and pointed to the car. To us. They came over."

She paused. She lifted her head, and turned to look at Danika.

"Freddy hadn't locked the car. Frances opened the door, and ran. But there was nowhere to go. They ran after her. Two of them. I watched. I saw everything. You understand? I saw everything."

Danika rubbed the back of her hand. "You don't need to tell me," she whispered.

"She didn't get far. They caught her. She struggled. She screamed. She scratched. But they were too strong." A small smile played on her lips. "But she didn't give up. She clawed at their faces. One of them shouted. He took a knife from his trouser pocket. I watched him shove it through the side of her neck. Then he pulled it out, and stabbed her in the chest. Again and again. He didn't stop."

Danika was silent.

"They came over to the car. They dragged me out, and took me over to her. She lay there, her eyes wide open, in her own blood. Freddy grabbed me by the hair, forced me to look at her. *See*, he said. *See what happens to naughty girls.* I screamed, and screamed. Then one of them hit me. I lost consciousness. Now I'm here. With you. In a bus. Going to a place called The Farm."

Danika reached up, stroked away the tear from her face. "We have each other now. If we think and work together, we can get out of this. You have a mother and father, yes?"

Monica nodded.

"Then think about them. Think about everything you love, everything you hold dear. That's what will keep us sane. That's what will get us through this."

Monica managed a weak smile. "Promise, Danika?"

"I promise."

Danika looked away, at the passing scenery. She saw houses, and people walking, and streets and shops. Ordinary life. A group of kids laughing, on their summer holidays. She could scream, bang the windows. But what would happen then? She had no doubts. The same fate as Frances. The sun was shining, in a near cloudless sky. On any other day, she would be enjoying the thrill of another country. She had to keep her courage, what was left of it.

The familiar panic rose up from the pit of her stomach.

She had no one. No rescuer. No knight in shining armour. No prince to scale the tower.

In that moment, she gave a silent prayer, for something she knew, deep down, couldn't happen.

A miracle.

18

The man had finished his work. The woman hung before him, limp, dead, the remnants of her face and neck scattered on the floor. He sat on a wooden crate. He picked up a plastic bottle of mineral water, drank deeply, then poured the rest over his head. Tossed in a bundle was the gown he had worn. He preferred being naked when he performed. He reached down, picked it up, retrieved a mobile phone from a pocket. He dialled a number. A voice responded.

"Finished?"

"Yes."

"I'll arrange for you to be picked up. Five minutes."

"She was disappointing."

"How could she be disappointing? She was beautiful. She was what you asked for."

"She lacked spirit. Don't disappoint me again. You need to improve your game."

He switched off the phone. He pulled the gown over his head, stood, appraised the dead woman. He reached over, gripped her by the hair, tilted her head up. He stared at his work. The woman stared back, eyes empty and dead.

"When the beauty's gone, what's left?"
He stroked the side of her head.
"I have to go. Be good."
He turned and left the room.
He had appointments to keep.

19

"You saved my life. I've never seen anything like that."

"You should get out more."

Black was standing over the man. Black hadn't yet removed the tape strapping his arms and legs to the chair. He needed answers first.

The man had been worked over pretty badly. Swollen eyes, burst lip, bloodied nose. He had been stripped of his clothing, down to his underwear. His chest was a tapestry of bruises. With his injuries, it was difficult to ascertain the man's age. Possibly in his thirties. He was thin. Too thin. Gaunt. His chest skeletal, ribcage clearly defined. Sharp cheekbones, shrunken face, pointed jaw. The skin, where it was unmarked, was sallow, with an almost bluish tint. A metamorphosis from health to decay. All the hallmarks of a serious heroin user, when, after a prolonged habit, the physiology transforms.

"Aren't you going to help me?" said the man.

"Soon. What's your name?"

"Why do you need that?"

Christ, thought Black. *No one wants to talk today.*

"It's not a difficult question."

"It's not important."

"Fair enough."

Black took out his mobile phone.

"What are you doing?"

"I'm calling the police. And an ambulance."

"No police. I don't need an ambulance."

"These friends of yours cut off your toes. You need help."

"I don't want the cops. My name is Davie. Davie Gillon."

"What happened here, Davie?"

"Let me go."

"Tell me first."

The man called Davie Gillon took a wheezing ragged breath.

"You don't get it. Cut me loose and get the hell out."

Black shrugged. "Your call."

He made to start pressing numbers on his phone.

"This is where we meet," said Gillon. "Where we do... business. Transact – you know? No one ever comes here. It's quiet. No distractions. At least not normally. I got here. These two guys turned up. They came by boat. I never heard them come in." A crooked smile played across his mashed face, revealing a row of rotten teeth – another heroin trademark. "They were as surprised as I was. The look on their fucking faces! They bound me up, started asking me questions. Just like you're doing now. Don't think they believed me. Starting feeding me my fucking toes!"

"Maybe they did believe you, but just enjoyed what they were doing."

"Let me go. I've told you what you wanted."

"You've told me nothing. How did you get here?"

"Taxi."

"Taxi? From where?"

"What the fuck do you care?"

Black waited.

"Glasgow," said Gillon sullenly.

"You must have money to burn." Black gestured to the dead men sprawled on the carpet. "You weren't expecting them?"

"Not them. They just came at the wrong time." A sly grin creased his features. "Looks like they were expecting someone else. Looks like maybe you were the man they wanted."

Black ignored the remark.

"You still haven't explained what you're doing here. Talk, then I let you go."

Gillon cocked his head to one side. Through the swelling, his eyes were like two pinpoints of darkness.

"Too late," he said. "You are now officially fucked."

Black hesitated, spun round.

Gillon was right.

20

The Oyster Bar on Royal Exchange Square was, arguably, the most expensive restaurant in Glasgow. The exterior was unremarkable. Glossy black marble walls. Darkened windows. Outside, straddling the pavement, seats and little circular tables arranged in no particular order, under a netted awning of sparkling white fairy lights.

The interior was subtle elegance. A bar of age darkened wood, behind which, a frosted mirrored gantry of every conceivable liquor. The walls were painted sceneries, of fields and woods, and distant mountains in dark, earthy colours. At night, candles flickered from intricate wooden candelabras suspended from ochre ceilings.

Beyond the bar area, the dining room. The same remarkable landscaped walls, burning candles set in brass sconces creating a strange, witchy cast. Waiters and waitresses darted like silky wraiths from table to table. One wall was made up entirely of champagne bottles, perfectly arranged, creating a hundred subtle reflections.

It was mid-afternoon. The place was not yet busy. In a dark corner booth sat a man, on his own. On the table before him was a wide cup of frothy coffee on a saucer. Beside it, on a little plate, was an almond cake and a silver knife.

He was perhaps seventy. Lightly tanned. He wore a pale cream cotton suit, blue open-necked shirt. Thick white hair, swept back from his forehead. Strong jawline, prominent cheekbones.

He sipped the coffee. It was 3.30pm. He glanced at his watch. A silver Rolex. Exactly on cue, a man appeared, sat opposite. He wore a loose T-shirt, track bottoms. The top part of his face was hidden by a baseball cap, worn low.

The man with the white hair attracted a waiter's attention, who came scurrying over.

"You have Jamaican Blue Mountain coffee?"

"Yes, sir," said the waiter.

"A small cup for my friend." He raised an eyebrow. "No milk?" Baseball cap nodded.

"Anything with the coffee, sir?"

Baseball cap shook his head, keeping his face down.

"Very good, sir."

The waiter left.

"I believe this is the only place in Glasgow that sells Blue Mountain," the white-haired man said. "I dare say there's no great demand, at £9 a cup. And a small cup, at that."

"The price isn't important."

"Of course it's not. Especially when someone else is paying. Though you can afford it."

"This is true."

The white-haired man cut a slice of the almond cake, and placed it in his mouth.

"This is delicious. Would you like a taste?"

"No, thank you."

"Your loss."

A silence fell between them – in the background, the low

murmur of conversation from those around, blended with classical music, playing just on the periphery of the senses.

"Aren't you going to take that silly hat off. No one's going to trouble you here. You look ridiculous."

The man shrugged. He took the cap off, and laid it on the table. He smiled, showing his perfect whiter than white teeth.

"It's been a while, Victor," said the white-haired man. "You look well. Wealth and fame agree with you."

"As they would with most people, I imagine."

"Everywhere I look, I see your picture. Everyone loves you."

"Not everyone."

"We can't have it all."

"Why not?"

"Because we're not gods, despite our best attempts."

The waiter returned, placed a cup and saucer on the table. Cromwell kept his head down. If the waiter recognised him, he didn't show it, remaining impassive.

"Anything else, sir?"

The white-haired man smiled. "We're fine, thanks."

The waiter left.

"You've kept yourself fit," said Cromwell.

"I try. I still run. Or jog. Or perhaps shamble. Two miles every day. I don't have the luxury of a personal trainer. I'm getting old, Victor. With age, there's a price."

"Like death?"

"There's that. And other things. The past, for example. The longer you live, the greater it becomes. Somehow, the past always finds a way to meet the present. You know the worst thing about getting old?"

"What?"

"Remembering what it was like to be young."

Cromwell took some coffee.

"Good?"

"Bitter," said Cromwell. "The fucking barista should be shot."

"You were never satisfied."

Cromwell ignored the comment. "I don't want to be here any longer than I have to be, Lyle. So let's put the coffee, and the fucking running, and how well we're both looking, and all the fucking pleasantries in the place where they belong. The fucking bullshit bin. You asked me here. I'm here. I did what you asked. I'm now hoping that you can handle this situation."

The white-haired man referred to as Lyle took another sip of his coffee, and cut another slice of almond cake.

"Is that all you've learned in Hollywood?"

"What?"

"How to be impatient."

Cromwell gave a thin-lipped smile. "Not at all, Lyle. I've learned much more."

"And is Mr Dalrymple looking after you?"

"He seems a capable man," replied Cromwell.

"And resourceful. He's been working for me for ten years. He'll look after you while you're here, make no mistake."

Another sip of coffee.

"You still have your hobbies?" he asked suddenly.

Cromwell said nothing.

"I understand," said Lyle. "Old habits die hard."

"You asked me to come. I'm here, drinking crap coffee in a pretentious shithole."

"Tell me about Adam Black."

Cromwell frowned. "There's nothing to tell. He came to my hotel. I told him what you wanted me to say. His father. The Raven's Crown. He left the hotel. That's it. You know this already. What more is there?"

Lyle leaned closer. "*What's he like?*"

Cromwell compressed his lips, considering the question. "What does it matter?"

"It matters."

Cromwell sighed. "He's a physically big man. I reckon about six-two, maybe six-three. Looks like he can handle himself. Even your man Dalrymple might have a hard job putting a guy like that down." Cromwell stared briefly at nothing, thinking back. "His eyes. They creeped me out a little. He's intense. He looks at you, but he also *sees* you, if you get my meaning. He sees you, right to the core. His eyes are old. I reckon they've seen a ton of shit." He gave a short, humourless laugh. "Who gives a fuck. At the end of the day, he's just a fucking lawyer."

"Just a lawyer," repeated Lyle softly. "Oh, Victor. He is so much more. He's an interesting man, is Mr Adam Black. Captain in the SAS. War hero. Recently, he rescued the Prime Minister's daughter from death at the hands of a psychopath. You couldn't make it up. Don't you read the papers?"

Cromwell remained motionless. "I've been busy."

"Of course you have. You've been in Hollywood, while the rest of us have been in the real world."

Cromwell grunted, but didn't reply.

"Since we've been aware of his involvement," continued Lyle, "I've taken a special interest in him. I've come to a conclusion."

"What?"

"That Adam Black is a man who doesn't care."

"What does that mean?"

"Everything. He's like a dog. A hound. Once he has the scent, he will not stop. And he won't care. He won't care who he destroys, even if it's himself, as long as he achieves his mission."

"Even if he dies trying?"

"I believe you've just captured the essence of the man. I believe that's exactly what he desires. To die. And that, my dear old friend, is the very worst type of enemy."

"It doesn't matter," said Cromwell. "You've got this sorted, yes? Like you sort everything?"

Lyle smiled. "I knew his father. He died years ago. Cancer."

"So?"

"I'm reminiscing, Victor. And wondering if there really is a God, who can create such exquisite coincidences. First the father, now the son."

"I don't understand. You're talking in riddles."

"Put it this way, Victor," said Lyle, his voice hushed. "If Black's father hadn't died of whatever cancer killed him, I would have killed the fuck myself. I hope that's a little clearer for you."

Cromwell clapped his hands. "And now, the true Lyle Taylor is revealed! The veneer has slipped, and we see a glimpse of the monster beneath."

"Maybe. But this monster can break you, if he so chooses. Let's not forget."

"As if I would. You asked me here – why? So I could tell you about Adam Black?"

"Yes. And to advise you."

"About what."

"Be discreet."

"What do you mean?"

Lyle Taylor gave him a reproachful look. "You know."

"Fuck you. Take care of Black. Like you promised. Or we're both fucked."

Cromwell made to go. He slipped his baseball cap back on, positioning it low over his face.

"Aren't you going to finish your coffee?" said Lyle.

"It was shit. Keep in touch."

He left. No one had noticed, apparently, that the world's biggest movie star had exited the stage.

Lyle put the last piece of almond cake in his mouth, sat back, reflected –

Once they had Adam Black, then getting the book would be easy. His partners could be very persuasive in the art of torture. And despite his impressive record, Adam Black was only human. Then, once Black was dead, only one more thing remained to be done.

Lyle gave a small sad smile.

His own brother had betrayed him, and as a consequence, his brother had to die.

21

F our men had entered the room. Casually dressed, jeans, collared T-shirts. Each carried a pistol. Glocks. Powerful armoury. They looked like men who knew exactly how to use them.

"What the fuck's going on here!" exclaimed one.

Davie Gillon spoke, still strapped to the chair, the words rattling out like machine gun fire. "I swear to Christ I don't have a fucking clue! The two guys on the floor tied me up. Then this guy comes along from nowhere, and takes them both out. I swear, Tommy, this has nothing to do with me!"

The four stood in a row, all big men. They faced a remarkable sight, thought Black. Two dead bodies, bleeding on the carpet, a third man tied by tape to a chair in the centre of the room with his toes scattered on the floor. And Black, in the middle of it all, with a sawn-off shotgun. Dante's *Inferno* didn't have a patch on this.

"Drop it," said another, gesturing to Black's gun. Black let it fall.

"And the knife."

Black dropped it.

"Good boy. What's your name?"

"Adam Black."

"What's happening here, Adam Black?"

Black nodded towards Gillon. "He's summed it up nicely. I came in. He was tied to the chair. Two guys were giving him a rough time. I killed them both. End of."

The four men could have been made of wood. No facial reaction, dead-pan expressions.

Then one said, "You a cop?"

"No."

"What the hell are you?"

"Unlucky."

One of them laughed.

"Too right."

Gillon squirmed against his bonds, using his body weight to bounce the chair up and down.

"Get me the fuck out of here!" His voice was raised to a high-pitched soprano, his face livid.

"Settle down, Davie," said one of the men.

"Settle fucking down! What the fuck does that even mean! I need to fucking score! Have you got the gear?"

A momentary thought entered Black's head – a man with his toes sheared off sitting strapped to a chair was more concerned about his next score. It said everything.

The four men, in unison, turned their attention to Gillon, like four birds attracted by the same worm.

"You got the money?"

"Of course I fucking have. It's in the usual place."

One of them ambled to the fire surround. The other three kept their guns focused on Black. The fire was a space full of litter, set beneath a flue running up behind the wall. It looked like it hadn't been used in years. The man reached up, groped about, retrieved a polythene bag. He opened it, pulled out a wad of paper money wrapped in an elastic band.

He thumbed through the notes.

"It's all fucking there, for Christ sakes! When have I let you down before? Now get me the hell out of this and give me the fucking drugs!"

The man finished counting, replaced the money in the bag, nodded to the others. One of them produced a mobile phone, made a call, spoke in a low murmur, occasionally glancing at Black. The conversation lasted two minutes. He hung up.

"It's all a bit strange, Davie," said another. "I mean look at it from where we are. It doesn't add up. We'll need to take you back. To answer a few questions." He concentrated on Black. "You don't add up either, Mr Black. Afraid you'll have to come back too."

"Do you mind if I ask where we're going?"

"I don't mind at all if you ask."

Gillon rocked the chair harder, screaming profanities. One of the men strode over, pulled a short leather cosh from a side pocket in his jeans, and whipped Gillon across the side of the head, rendering him unconscious.

"Thank fuck for that," said another. "The only thing worse than a junkie, is a screaming junkie. We'll put him in the boot. We trust we won't have the same issues with you, Mr Black?"

Black thought through his options. Unlike the two he had just killed, these men emanated an air of discipline, competence. They acted as a pack, each aware of his role. Hard men, thought Black. Armed, and eminently dangerous. If he tried anything, they would kill him without compunction.

"No issues," replied Black.

"That's your car outside?"

Black nodded.

"Keys. And mobile phone. Please."

Black fished them out of his trouser pocket.

"Toss them on the floor."

Black did as he was told.

One of the men reached down, scooped them up. "We're taking your car. What's the correct expression – *commandeering?* Any problems?"

"None."

"Now pick up the knife, and cut Davie free."

Black retrieved the knife. All four had their pistols trained on him. From that distance, it would be harder to miss than hit.

Black sliced away the tape. Gillon slumped to the ground.

"You know what to do, Mr Black."

Black took a deep breath, picked Gillon up, hoisted him over his shoulder. He was light, all bones and skin, and nothing much else.

"You first." One of the men gestured him to the door. They followed Black out, through the hall, the kitchen, out the back door, and through the side garden, to the front of the building, to Black's car. And beside it, a silver BMW X5.

"Beautiful view, don't you think," one said.

"Difficult to take in," Black replied, "carrying someone over your shoulder, with four guns at your head."

Quiet laughter. "You've got a pair of balls, brother."

One of them pressed a button on Black's car key. The boot popped open. Black dropped Gillon inside, closed the boot door.

"You're in the back, Mr Black. Hope you're not one of these 'back-seat drivers'."

"I get car sick," said Black.

"Puke on your lap. We don't have any problem with that."

"That's reassuring."

Black slid in. He was joined by three of them, one driving, the others in the back seat, one on each side of him. He felt the muzzle of a Glock at his waist. The fourth man got in the silver BMW.

"Let's hope we don't have a bumpy ride," Black remarked.

"I'm a very careful driver," said the one in the driver's seat, glancing at Black in the rear-view mirror.

"Where are you taking me?"

One of the men at his side answered. "Better we don't tell you. You won't only be puking. You'll be fucking shitting yourself."

"Try me. Actually, I have a strong constitution."

"I tell you what you do now," said the man on his other side, his voice quiet. "You shut the fuck up, or we'll kill you, and dump your body in the fucking loch for the fucking fish to eat. You clear on this, Mr Black?"

"Crystal."

Black sat still. He had no doubt the threat would be carried out. Fear, when he confronted it, came strangely to him. He felt detachment. He could place it in a compartment in his mind, and then step back, consider, rationalise, like an observer witnessing a distant scene. How this would pan out, he had no idea. He seemed to have landed from one situation to another, and still had no clear picture what was happening.

A thought crossed his mind, as they were leaving the house, the silver BMW following. Something was missing, which only occurred to him at that precise moment.

The motorboat docked at the jetty was gone.

22

Lyle never took the car for his visits to Glasgow city centre. Parking was a nightmare, traffic was congested, the road system designed to infuriate and frustrate. Instead, he got the train. Central station was a ten-minute walk from the Oyster Bar. The journey would take all of twenty-five minutes, and then a relatively short walk to his suburban mansion in Newlands, a district four miles from the centre.

It was during his walk to the station when his phone buzzed. He answered, listened, hung up. Cold wings fluttered in his stomach.

The Raven's Crown had turned into a disaster. Two men dead. And Adam Black was still alive. He'd been seen leaving the hotel with others, their identity unknown. The situation was blossoming into something far more than an irritation. Black, it seemed, was proving difficult. Lyle adjusted his thoughts. Attack from a different angle. Black had his vulnerable spot. The journalist, Black's girlfriend.

He made a call, as he emerged into the vaulted glass and stone structure of Glasgow Central Station. He would need to use, once again, the movie star charm of his old friend Victor Cromwell. And he knew Cromwell would obey, because he had no choice.

Cromwell, like himself, had too much to lose.

23

"Am I dreaming?"

"If you are, then I'm having the same dream. Which would be just plain odd."

As soon as Rachel Hempworth got the call, she went to her boss. Billy Cosgrove was, as per usual, glued behind his over-large desk, drinking fresh roast coffee he made himself from a percolator his wife had given him for Christmas. On his desk was a computer screen, keyboard, a mess of papers, and an open packet of Marlboro Reds. He had one perched in the side of his mouth, unlit, bobbing up and down as he spoke.

"Why do you do that?" asked Rachel.

"It provides me with significant comfort," he replied in a dry voice. He regarded her over the top of thick varifocal spectacles, which had the effect of enlarging his eyes. They gazed at her now with unsettling concentration. "I have been stripped of my right to smoke in my own office by those in authority, which is, in my estimation, reminiscent of Nazi Germany. I have not, however, been stripped of my right to pretend to smoke. This is about the most rebellious act I can think of at this moment, where I am a hair's breadth away of committing a crime, without ever actually committing it."

"I'm glad I asked."

"You'll learn, one day. What do you want? You entered my office with the words 'am I dreaming'. A novel approach to get my attention. Which you have."

Without being asked, she sat on one of the two chairs on the other side of the desk.

She placed a yellow Post-it on top of the landscape of paperwork.

"What do you see?" she said.

Cosgrove picked it up, scrutinising the name she had written on it.

"I see a name."

"Well observed."

"Not just any name." The cigarette nodded with every twitch of his lips, as if it had a life of its own, capable of independent thought.

"This is true."

"What exactly am I to make of this. Full marks for spelling. Zero for handwriting."

"The person who belongs to that name has just telephoned me. At least his PR person has."

Cosgrove cleared his throat, pushing his glasses up to the bridge of his nose. He stared at the name for several seconds, then placed it back on his desk.

"So that I don't have this wrong, Victor Cromwell's PR person has just telephoned my senior reporter. That's a story right there. Why?"

"He wants to give an interview. He's chosen this very paper. He's chosen me. I am to meet him tomorrow, for lunch at the Princess Hotel. 1pm precisely. So, I repeat – am I dreaming?"

"Who's paying?" Cosgrove asked in a gravelly voice.

"Not you. So don't have a cardiac arrest. At least not in front of me."

"That's the best news I've heard this month. So, my turn to repeat – why? The biggest super-duper star in the western hemisphere wants to be interviewed by Rachel Hempworth, unknown reporter for an obscure newspaper he's probably never heard of. I suspect there's more to this."

Rachel gave a wry smile. "I'm a film buff. He likes people who likes films."

Cosgrove waited, giving her his unflinching gaze. She shrugged.

"He telephoned Adam last night. They were meeting earlier today. He said he needed Adam's help. I suppose it's entirely possible Adam mentioned my name."

She watched, as Cosgrove placed the cigarette in his fingers and pretended to smoke.

"You know it's not lit," she remarked.

"A minor inconvenience. I wonder what he wanted with the invincible Mr Black. Now that could be an altogether different story. If your Adam Black is involved then cue a whole saga of mystery and mayhem. Yes?"

She found she couldn't disagree.

"Do you know why Cromwell wanted his help?"

"I haven't spoken to Adam yet. I dare say I'll hear all about it this evening. Unless client confidentiality..."

"Please, Rachel. Confidentiality doesn't exist in the journalist's dictionary. As you have proved countless times. Tomorrow at one?"

"Yes. Aren't you excited? I might be late coming back. Depends on how many bottles of Bollinger I can pour down my neck. Should I get you his autograph?"

"Another time, perhaps." Cosgrove sniffed. "Pass on my regards to Adam. Tell him, if he's going to blow any buildings up, or shoot any bad guys, then as a matter of basic courtesy, he should provide us with advance warning. That way we can get the story as it happens."

"I'll be sure to do that. Though his days of destruction are well behind him. So he assures me."

"Shame. He knew how to liven life up a little."

"A little?" Rachel smiled. "Now there's an understatement. I'll pass on your regards."

She stood. Now that they were on the Adam Black topic, she knew he would ask the same old question, which he did, for the millionth time. "I would be more excited if you told me what happened," he said. "That could be a great story, Rachel. The final piece in the jigsaw."

"The jigsaw. Is that how you'd describe Adam Black's life? A jigsaw? Perhaps it's as good a description as any." She winked at him. "I'll give Victor Cromwell your warmest."

"The final piece!" shouted Cosgrove, as she left the office. "For my own curiosity! And everybody else's, for that matter."

She turned, and smiled archly, closing his door.

She mulled over Cosgrove's words. The missing piece of the jigsaw. Six months earlier, Adam Black had rescued the Prime Minister's daughter, Elspeth Owen. Sensational news. He'd found her, imprisoned in a house, on a remote island called Jura, off the West Coast of Scotland. In a last desperate effort, her captor had tried to kill Elspeth, on a cliff edge, the sea crashing on the rocks sixty feet below. Her captor was a female. A policewoman. Detective Inspector Vanessa Shaw. At the last moment, she and Black had struggled. They'd both fallen. Shaw was found two days later, washed ashore, dead. Black's body was missing. That is, until two months later, when he appeared at Rachel's office, healthy and very much alive.

His survival was, at the very least, miraculous.

He'd told Rachel what had happened, his fall broken by a

narrow ledge, how he'd woken in a rather secretive health resort in the north of Scotland, courtesy of the mysterious department he worked for. And how he'd retired from their service, turning his back on a world where there was nothing but darkness and death. His words. *I've had enough*, he'd explained to her. And she believed him.

She mused over Billy Cosgrove's expression – *the final piece in the jigsaw*. The final piece was Adam Black joining the human race, for which she was glad. The past was behind them, and they were looking forward, together.

Black had let the sunlight in, and by doing so, had chased away the shadows of his past.

24

L ittle was said in the car. They were heading back to
Glasgow, the silver BMW following. Black was conscious
of the Glock pressed into his ribs. The countryside slipped by.
They drove through Tarbet, passed the Tarbet Hotel, where
Black had asked for directions. It seemed like a lifetime ago.

Black was not scared of death. He'd met it many times, up
close. Before, on those occasions, there'd been a reason. He'd
walked, hand in hand with it, to reach the end of a journey. Now
it whispered in his ear, directing him on a journey not of his own
making. He had no idea who these men were, or where he was
going. He had a grim premonition. Adam Black. Shot in the
head without knowing why, and left in a ditch in some forgotten
field. He would die for reasons incomprehensible, and death
would get the last laugh.

They stuck to the A82, heading towards Glasgow. A noise
emanated from the boot. Davie Gillon had apparently gained
consciousness. This caused a source of merriment for the three
men. Black felt the back of the seat vibrate. Gillon was trying to
kick his way free. A remarkable feat, he reflected, for a man
minus several toes. They passed through a place called Renton,

which comprised little more than rows of grey concrete houses with flat roofs, and a car showroom. The noise and commotion from the boot subsided to a resentful silence. Gillon had either exhausted himself, or knocked himself unconscious again.

They drew nearer to Glasgow city, then veered west, crossed the Erskine Bridge, heading into Renfrewshire. They passed Erskine Hospital. Black wondered if perhaps that might be his final destination this sunny evening. Specifically the morgue. He took a deep calming breath, restraining the urge to wrestle his way out. Life and death were separated by the twitch of a trigger finger. Plus, even if he dodged the bullet, he still had the prospect of dealing with three capable men and escaping a moving car. Things looked bleak. His only comfort was that they hadn't killed him yet. Which meant they wanted answers first.

As did Black.

The scenery changed, became countrified. Houses slipped away to fields and woods. Black knew little about this part of the world. Black saw a sign – Houston Road. The road curved and twisted, reaching a smattering of houses. More turns. They got to a place called Houston, bigger than a village, smaller than a town. The main street was a hundred yards long. On one side, old terraced houses, narrow and cramped. On the other side a pub – The Thirsty Fox. A large building, two storeys. Mock Tudor. Steeply pitched roof, herringbone brick work, black timbering. Beside it, an entrance to a small car park to the rear. They manoeuvred in, parked. Two other cars were already there. A Merc, and a Range Rover. The silver BMW pulled up alongside them.

"We're here." The man driving caught Black's attention in the rear-view mirror. "No smart moves, Mr Black. You can either play it cool, or have your brains decorating the tarmacadam. The choice is yours."

"Difficult to play it cool with pistols stuck in my ribs."

"I'm sure you'll manage."

"I'm sure I will."

The driver got out, stepped back. The men on either side of Black got out in unison, also stepped two paces back, waited. The fourth man, the silver BMW driver, had left his car, and stood several paces away, watching.

If Black made a break for it, he'd be shot like a dog in two seconds flat. No one would come to his rescue. The car park was secluded, hidden from the main street by a high thick hedgerow. He'd be shot, his body dismembered, then dumped.

Black got out. The men were openly displaying their handguns.

A back door to the pub was open. A man waited.

"Please," said one of the men.

Black walked to the entrance, the four men following. The man at the back door disappeared inside. Black entered a seating area. Tartan carpet, a couple of couches, a couple of patterned chairs. The walls were decked with framed newspaper clippings going back a hundred years.

"Keep going. Through the doors. Up the stairs."

Black did as instructed. Through swing doors at one end, leading directly to stairs. A man waited at the top.

"This way," he said, waving him up.

Black got to the top, the four behind him. They got to a large, well-stocked kitchen. There was no sign of activity. Black made his way through another set of swing doors, emerged into a restaurant, with a bar and a small stage at one end. Each table was decked out with white tablecloth, silver cutlery, wine glasses. At one, in a corner, sat a man on his own. Before him was an open bottle of red wine, and a full glass. At another table sat two men, opposite each other. Both sported shoulder holsters over their shirts, complete with pistols. Another two sat at high stools at the bar, similarly armed. Otherwise, the place was deserted.

Black entered. He was ushered forward, to stand in the centre of the room.

He was surrounded by eight armed men. He had nowhere to go. If he tried to leap through a window, he'd be gunned down before he got two feet. Plus, the fall would probably break his neck.

"This is Adam Black," said one of the men behind him.

The man sitting in the corner raised the wine glass to his lips, sipped, pursed his lips as he savoured the taste.

"Are you fond of wine, Mr Black?" He spoke clearly, and precisely, with just the hint of a Glaswegian accent.

Black appraised him. Mid-sixties. Burly. Full head of dyed black hair, a pair of thick-lensed spectacles wrapped round his face. Thick bull neck, heavy shoulders. In his day, a real handful, thought Black. Probably still was, he reflected. He wore a blue double-breasted suit with the faintest pin-stripe, a matching blue tie.

"I'm partial to it. I'm partial to anything alcoholic."

The man nodded slowly, as if the words spoken by Black carried great weight.

"This is Argentinian. Malbec. I'm... how can I put it... sampling. For tonight, you understand. The restaurant opens in about an hour. Do you know what Malbec is?"

"A type of grape, as I recall."

"You recall correctly. It's a particularly dark grape. It gives wine that full-bodied appearance. Rather like blood." He beckoned Black to an empty chair on the other side of his table. One of the men waved his gun. Black manoeuvred his way over, sat. Close up, he saw the man sitting opposite had pock-marked skin, probably ravaged by teenage acne.

"Do you know who I am?" asked the man.

"Someone who enjoys full-bodied wine."

"Actually, I don't. I hate the shit. Tastes like piss. Not that I've tasted piss before."

He nodded at one of the men at the bar. "Bring him up." The man left.

"Let me introduce myself. My name is Ronald Wilkinson. I'm known as Ronnie. You can call me Ronnie, if you like. Ronald is too formal. And you're Adam Black. We won't shake hands, Mr Black."

Black waited, no idea where this was going.

"Do you like my restaurant?"

"Love it."

"I bought this in 1991. The person who sold it to me wasn't intending to sell it. Like you, he hadn't heard of me either. I gave him a fair offer, but he said – *no, Mr Wilkinson, I don't want to sell to you, or anybody else.* These were his exact words, I swear. He spoke like a squeaky little mouse." This caused a current of laughter. Wilkinson continued. "He chose to keep things formal, and didn't call me Ronnie. But I knew he'd sell eventually. With a little persuasion. And lo! He did sell. At bargain price. Now, on the rare occasion we meet, he calls me Ronnie."

"Persuasion?"

"You get the gist, Mr Black. I like things to be simple. Straightforward. Which is why I need to know why you were at the Raven's Crown, armed up with a sawn-off shotgun, with a good friend of mine strapped to a chair, with the shit beaten out of him. In the company of two dead men. Explain, please."

One of the men approached, and held a pistol to the side of Black's head.

"More persuasion?" said Black. "Talking of blood, if you shoot me, there'll be a lot of it on the carpet. I think the paying customer might wonder."

"You don't need to worry about such small matters,"

replied Wilkinson. "You have more important things to think about. You think I'm joking? Show Mr Black how serious I am."

The man with the pistol spoke. "This is a Smith and Wesson Model 36. You heard of it?"

Black regarded him, face expressionless. "I've made its acquaintance."

"It's a five-shot revolver. Not six. The odds become less favourable."

Black remained still. The sound of his heart resounded like a hollow drum in his head. Suddenly, his entire world was focused on this single moment in time.

"If you shoot me, I can't tell you what you want to know."

"This is what's called a prelude," said Wilkinson, watching Black with the faintest of smiles. "I like that word. Fancy for a man like me, with no education. It sets the scene. The purpose is to give you a taste of what to expect if you don't do as I ask. It creates a foundation, upon which we can base our dialogue. And if you should die..." Wilkinson gave the merest of shrugs, "...then you're right. We have to clean the carpet super-fast." More laughter.

The man with the pistol spun the barrel chamber.

"You get the picture, Black," said Wilkinson. "One bullet. One in five chance your brains explode onto the tablecloth."

"Fuck you," said Black.

"Tsk tsk. Now you're just being rude."

The man straightened his arm. He pulled the trigger. The gun clicked. No bullet. No instant oblivion. Black swallowed, released a long breath. If he got the chance, he would kill them all. If he got the chance.

"Lucky you," said Wilkinson. "Now we have an understanding. Now you know this is a serious discussion. Tell me then, what were you doing at the Raven's Crown?"

Black blinked away sweat, focused on Wilkinson, keeping his voice neutral.

"I'm a lawyer. Someone wants me to represent them in the sale of the hotel. I thought I'd check it out. Plus, it's a nice drive. I went there. I didn't think anyone was in. The back door was unlocked. I went inside. In the dining room, I came across a guy taped to a chair. Your friend. Davie Gillon. Two guys appeared. I'd never seen them before. They pulled a gun. I killed them. Then your fucking goons turned up. Now I'm here, playing Russian roulette. That's it. End of."

Wilkinson finished off his wine, poured himself another glass.

"End of? Do you work for the police, Mr Black?"

"No."

"Who do you work for?"

"Nobody."

"Who is this man you represent?"

"I don't know."

"So the bullshit begins." Wilkinson sighed, then glanced at the man holding the revolver. A glance that meant everything.

"You obviously have a death wish," the man said, as he positioned the gun to the side of Black's head.

"You can pull that fucking trigger a million times," said Black. "My story won't change. The client was someone it couldn't be."

Wilkinson raised a finger. The man lowered the weapon.

"Explain."

"I was told that the person who wanted to use me as their lawyer was my father. That can't be."

"Why?"

"He's dead. Someone's having a bad joke. Or they were hoping I would pay the hotel a visit, to give me a warm welcome."

Another sip of wine. "You were set up?"

"The two men I killed were waiting for me. My guess is, your friend Davie Gillon was in the wrong place, at the wrong time. What was it? A drug deal? It's got nothing to do with me. Let me go, and you'll never hear from me again." Even as he spoke these words, Black knew how impossible his situation was. They would never let him go, unless they were dumping his corpse in a place no one would find.

"That's an interesting story. Let you go? I'll have to think about that. Here's my take. You found out that we used the Raven's Crown as our... *rendezvous*. You knew our little friend Davie paid us £50,000 every month for some of the pure white stuff. He's a rich kid with a rich daddy, who has lots of little rich buddies. You and your two pals thought you'd get the money first. You killed your pals, because maybe you're anti-social that way. Or maybe you're just a greedy bastard, and you thought you'd keep the money to yourself. Which I think is the more likely explanation. But Davie wouldn't tell you where the money was hidden." Wilkinson gestured to the man with the pistol. "Tommy told me on the phone that poor Davie had some toes missing. That wasn't very nice of you."

Black spoke in a cold tone. "For such an ugly fucker, you've a good imagination. Why don't you ask Davie? Then you'll see I'm telling the truth."

"The business we're in, I have to send a message. To stop others like you thinking they have the right to come gatecrashing to a party they've not been invited to. It was nice knowing you, Mr Black. No Russian roulette this time. And no chances with the carpet." He gestured to one of the men sitting at the bar, who immediately stood, went behind the bar, and came back with a roll of black plastic sheeting under his arm, which he spread across the floor, next to Black's chair. The man with the pistol stepped forward, raised his arm, pointed the barrel directly at the back of Black's head.

"Stand up slowly, and step on to the plastic sheeting, please," said the man.

Black had little choice. If he didn't obey, he'd be shot anyway, where he sat. At least, if he were standing, his life was extended by several seconds. Also, it gave him more space and time to think.

"Bon voyage," said Wilkinson.

Black slowly got to his feet, the man with the pistol taking a wary step back, firing arm straight and pointed at his head. Others, Black noted, had pistols out, aimed at him. These men were skilled and seasoned. There was no element of crossfire, hitting each other by mistake. The only target was Black, and from that range, none of them would miss.

Black held his breath. This was it, at last. His life ended, in a place he didn't know, to be executed by strangers who would kill him as casually as kicking off shit from their shoe. Not with friends. Not with loved ones. Not with anyone who counted. It could only be this way, he thought in the second he had between the trigger being pulled, and everlasting darkness.

This was it.

The end.

25

The minibus pulled into a car park next to a roadside petrol station. On one side, the pumps, and a store selling chocolate, newspapers, fizzy drinks. On the other, a coffee shop. It was late afternoon. The sun was still bright and warm, the sky blemished with a thin straggle of cloud.

Danika had no idea where she was. The miles had drifted by, and she'd hardly noticed. The scenery was just a passing collection of images. Houses, fields, buildings, trees, cars. Then more of the same.

One of the men stood. He was plump, stomach drawling over his belt, stubbly cheeks, heavy Eastern features. His hair was lank and flat on his head, like a wet bathing cap. Looked like it hadn't been washed for a month.

"Toilet." He pointed out the window, to the coffee shop. "In there. Two at a time. No funny business." His face broke into a leer, causing his round face to fold in on itself. "Or I cut your fucking tits off." He pulled out a flick knife from a pocket of his baggy jeans, pressed a little button, releasing the blade. "You understand, girls?"

Danika responded with a dull expression. But she

understood well enough, as did all the others. The guy was not kidding. Violence was commonplace and easy in this new world.

She watched, as one of the other men got out of the bus, and met someone at the front entrance. This other person wore a blue uniform with a logo on the top right of his pullover, which she couldn't read. A youngish man with red hair. It looked like he worked there. She saw cash changing hands. The youngish man laughed at something the other man said, then looked over to the minibus, still laughing. He was being paid to turn a blind eye to kidnapping and trafficking.

It looks like everyone's involved. From Patrick, her lover in Kosice, to a fucking coffee shop employee. She glanced around, at Monica, at the other girls. They were cattle, each of them priced only for their meat.

They got off the bus, two at a time, closely watched. One of the men from the bus stood outside the main entrance, another went inside, presumably to stand by the toilet door. From where she sat, Danika could see through the windows of the restaurant. It was empty, except for a solitary individual in a suit, sipping a coffee, reading a newspaper.

They went in and out. Pairs of girls. The man with the belly and the flick knife pointed at Danika and Monica.

"You two. Get up."

They traipsed out. She felt seedy, dirty, aware she hadn't changed or washed properly for many hours.

They went inside.

As she'd thought, a man stood at a door with the word *LADIES.* Tacked below, a temporary sign, scrawled in black felt pen – *Out of Order.* For their benefit, she thought. No unwanted guests in the next cubicles.

"Inside," he said, his voice low. "Ten minutes. Wash yourselves. Don't make a fucking sound."

They went in. It was basic. Along one wall, stretching the full length, a head-height mirror. Four sinks with inverted plastic bottles of pink gel with press dispensers, fastened to the wall. Two electric hand driers. Four cubicles in a row. No windows.

They each went to a cubicle. Locked the door.

"We can get help," whispered Danika, through the partition wall. She tried to keep the shake from her voice. "I saw a man. He's having a coffee in the restaurant. If we can get to him. He'll help us."

"Nobody will help us," replied Monica, in a flat, listless tone. "It's no use. We're going to die." She broke into low, soft tears. "Or worse."

"Don't say that! We have a chance." No response, except stifled crying.

They finished, hunched over the sinks, washing hands, faces, stripping their tops off quickly, washing under their arms. Danika pressed the hand drier on. It rumbled into life.

"I can run through," she said. "He can help us. Once he sees me. Once I tell him what's happened. He can call the police."

Monica stared at her for five seconds, hollow-eyed, hollow-cheeked, devoid of spark, of hope. "You'll die. Better to do nothing."

Danika took a deep, trembling breath. "No. This is our chance."

They finished. Monica went out first. Danika followed. The man acting as sentry was there. He gestured for them to get back out and to the minibus. Danika looked to her right. A glass double door. Beyond, the seating area. She saw lots of empty seats. One wasn't empty. The man in the suit was still there. He looked about forty, clean, respectable. He seemed deep in a newspaper. At the far end, behind a counter, was the red-haired man she'd seen being given money. He was busy stocking up a refrigerator. She captured all this, in a fraction of a second, terror bringing every detail into sharp relief.

Time was diluted to this one second. She gritted her teeth and summoned up what little courage remained.

Then ran.

26

Rachel Hempworth owned a flat in a part of Glasgow called Finnieston. On the periphery of the trendy West End, and being on the periphery, lacked the full bohemian kudos. But interesting, bijou coffee shops and quirky restaurants were sprouting up, like mushrooms in the dark, and the place was becoming popular with students, and Airbnb tourists.

She lived in a flat on the ground floor of a ten-storey tower block, a stone's throw from the River Clyde. An expensive place to live, but she had an expensive mortgage to go with it. She left work at 5.30pm. Unusually early. The two-mile drive to her apartment took an age, the traffic heavy. She vowed silently that sometime soon – but not too soon – she would start walking to work. Maybe even jog. She parked her Fiat 500 in a private parking space, at the rear of the building. She made her way to the front, to the main common door.

Three police cars were parked at the front entrance, on a slabbed, pedestrian area. Two uniformed policemen stood at the door, like sentries. Voices crackled from their radio receivers. A small crowd of people had gathered. Rachel skirted round them, suddenly anxious, approached one of the policemen –

"I live here," she said, breathless.

The policeman inspected her, unsmiling.

This is serious, she thought. Her journalistic nose was already twitching, despite it being so close to home.

"What's your name?" asked the policeman.

"Rachel Hempworth. I live on the ground floor, number 2."

The policeman regarded her quizzically. "Miss Hempworth. Number 2?"

"Yes?"

He half turned from her, angled his head, spoke into the radio.

"The occupant is here." A voice crackled in response.

He turned back to her. "Please stay here. Someone will be with you in a second."

"What the hell's happening?"

"Someone will be here in a second," he repeated.

She waited. The front door had no glass panels. Solid metal, painted glossy red. She couldn't see in. Whatever had gone down inside was a mystery.

The door opened. A man stood at the doorway. Rachel knew him. DCI Bob Wishart. One of her sources. If there was a particularly juicy story, then he was the man to contact. They'd known each other for years.

"Small world," he said. A man in his early fifties, balding with a classic comb-over, weary, hangdog eyes, jowls resting on layers of chins. He was wearing, head to toe, white papery-plastic forensic overalls.

"You live here?"

She nodded.

"You'd better come in," he said.

She entered. The common hallway, usually spotless, was decorated in a new vibrant colour. On the white walls, on the grey tiled floor. Crazy spots and wild streaks, vivid red.

The door to her flat was open. A man emerged, dressed in the same white forensic overall. He nodded at her.

"What's happening here?" Dark thoughts filled her mind. This place had witnessed violence. She was no fool. She knew that violence and Adam Black were close friends. She prayed silently to a God she had no belief in that the blood spattered in the hallway was not Adam's.

"Please don't touch anything, Rachel," said Wishart. He pointed to the open door. "This is your flat?"

"Yes," she mumbled.

"Okay. I can't let you in. You've got to understand, this is a murder enquiry. Your flat forms part of the murder scene."

"Murder scene? Who?"

Wishart didn't respond.

"What's happened, Bob. Speak to me."

"Someone's been killed, Rachel. And whoever did it, left their calling card on your living room wall."

"What do you mean?"

"A message, in blood."

"What message?"

"Four words."

"What?"

"The Book of Dreams."

She shook her head, bewildered.

"It means nothing to you?"

"Nothing." Her words faltered as she tried to focus. "Who was killed?"

"Let's talk."

27

What's it really worth to you
To shake the holy hand of fate?

Anonymous

Black was ready to leap, do damage, do *anything*. He knew the bullet would catch him within a millisecond. He turned, to look directly at the man standing closest, the man with the pistol pointed directly at his head.

He would end this with a smile. "Don't miss," he said.

"I won't," replied the man called Tommy. He was well built, a physique moulded from countless hours in a gym. Hair shaved close. Several days' stubble on a lean face. The face of a killer. The face of a man who would end a life, with a gun, a knife, anything that came to hand. Then order lunch.

A door suddenly opened. The one Black had entered. In barged Davie Gillon, followed by the man Wilkinson had sent to get him, apologetic, flustered. Gillon was still dressed in his underwear, and looked agitated. Everyone turned. His head was swollen and crusted with dried blood where he'd been struck unconscious, giving him an almost Halloween ghoulishness. His foot was a mess, lacking three toes, blood congealed on the stumps. His eyes were wild, staring. He swept his gaze around the room, ignoring Black and the man looming over him with a Glock pointed in his face, zoning in on Wilkinson.

"Where's my fucking gear!" he screamed.

The room stopped, frozen for a single moment.

Wilkinson stirred, assuming an easy smile.

"Don't get agitated, Davie," he said. "It's right here."

He glanced at one of the men sitting at the bar, who leaned over, retrieved a small white polythene bag.

"But first, seeing as you've made an entrance, tell us what happened."

Gillon raised his hands in a gesture of profound bewilderment. "What?"

"Mr Black was telling us a story. As you can see, he's in a predicament. Tommy has a pistol aimed into his face, and is about to pull the trigger. Maybe first, we should hear your side of things. To see if the stories match."

"Why the fuck should I care about him." He cast a hungry look at the polythene bag. "Give me my fucking gear. It's bought and paid for. It's mine."

The smile on Wilkinson's face evaporated, his chin puckering, the edges of his mouth drooping into a frown.

"Humour me."

"Just fucking shoot him. Why the fuck should I care?"

"I won't ask again," he said quietly.

"Tell him," said Black.

"Shut the fuck up." Tommy inched the Glock closer to Black's face. "You're not a part of this conversation."

"Christ!" said Gillon. "What the fuck does a man have to do to get some fucking heroin in his veins. So I was waiting for you guys. At the Raven's Crown. Like we always do. Two other guys appear. They came by boat. Sneaked up on me. They wanted to know who I was. Wanted to know what I was doing there. They tied me to a fucking chair, started beating the shit out of me. Then the fuckers got a knife, began cutting off my toes. One by fucking one. And then they stuffed them in my mouth! That was just fucking plain evil."

"I'm sure," said Wilkinson. "What did you tell them?"

"Not a fucking thing, I swear. Then this guy comes in," he pointed to Black with a skinny prick-marked arm, "and... well... it was like they were expecting him."

"Expecting him?"

"Not in a good way, if you get my drift. They wanted to kill him. Like they were waiting for him. But then..."

"Yes?"

Gillon stared at Black. He licked his lips. His voice was quiet when he spoke. "I've never seen anything like it. He killed them both. He threw a knife. Straight through the neck." He paused. "The other, he stabbed in the eye. Then shot him. Up close. Then your men turn up, to do the deal." He took a deep, angry breath. "And then I'm fucking clobbered over the head and shoved in a car boot. And I still don't have my fucking gear!"

"Clobbered," said Wilkinson. "I like that word." He motioned to the man at the bar, who tossed the little polythene sachet to Gillon.

"About fucking time. Now I need someone to drive me home."

Wilkinson ignored him.

"Look at me, Black," he said.

Black turned, stared at Wilkinson.

"I guess my story adds up," he said.

"Why were these men waiting for you?"

"No idea."

"Why did you kill them?"

"Because they deserved to die."

"Judge, jury, executioner. You're the complete package."

Black held his stare, heart beating fast, acutely aware of the gun pointed at the back of his head.

"It's a shame." Wilkinson sighed. "I actually believe you. But we've gone too far down the line. A man like yourself understands, I'm sure. It's a dirty business we're in. Que sera sera, yes?"

Gillon suddenly emitted a high-pitched hysterical giggle. "Looks like you're fucked, Black. Where's the fucking Blood Eagle when you need him!"

Wilkinson stiffened, blinked. "What did you say?"

Gillon's face creased in puzzlement. "The Blood Eagle. That's what the guy said at the hotel. Before Adam Black put a bullet in his head. He was sent by somebody called the Blood Eagle. To kill Black. Who the fuck cares? Get me out of here. Please."

Wilkinson sat, motionless, then turned again to appraise Black with a brooding intensity, eyes cold as stone.

"What do you know about the Blood Eagle?"

"Nothing."

"But these men..." He seemed to struggle with his words. Suddenly he snapped his head round to a man at the bar. "Give me your fucking gun!" All coolness had departed. His voice was a snarl, his lips twisted.

The man at the bar jumped to attention, removed the pistol from his shoulder holster, gave it to Wilkinson. Wilkinson stood, pointed it at Black's face.

"Now tell me, what do you know about the Blood Eagle?"

Black looked straight back at him. "Not one fucking thing."

Wilkinson swallowed. Suddenly, he was sweating. Somehow, a nerve had been touched. Wilkinson swapped the pistol into his other hand.

"I swear I'll kill you, Black. Unless you tell me what you know."

"I don't know anything. But I want to find out." Black decided to play a wild card. "Maybe we can do this together."

Wilkinson took a deep breath, another. "Twenty years ago," he said, barely a whisper. "Twenty years ago. Three young women were murdered. In the same year. In Glasgow. You remember?"

Black didn't respond. He was certain if he even twitched, Wilkinson would blow his head off. The man was on the edge. Let him talk.

"Three women. All in their early twenties." His eyes were glazed over. He was looking back. Lost in another time, another world. "What he did to them." He swallowed again. His voice was cold and flat when he spoke. "Let me tell you about the Blood Eagle. It was a form of torture. In days when imagination was allowed to flourish in such matters. Invented by the Vikings. The skin on the victim's back was split, then peeled away, displaying the ribcage. The ribs were then severed from the spine. The lungs were hooked out through the opening, over the splayed ribs, mimicking spread wings. Eagle's wings. You can visualise this?"

Black didn't move.

"I'm sure you can. Three young women were killed in such a manner. Twenty years ago. The man who committed these acts was given a nickname by the tabloid press. The Blood Eagle."

Wilkinson leaned forward, one hand pressed on the table, the other wrapped round the pistol aimed at Black's head.

"It conjures up a grisly picture, yes? Then imagine the pictures in your mind if one of these women was your daughter. Difficult. You try to shut the pictures out, but they creep in. She was twenty-one. She got up early one morning, put on her jogging gear, went for a run, and never came home."

Wilkinson took another deep, trembling breath.

"She was found two days later. Strung up. The Blood Eagle's last victim. You remember? Then nothing. A killer who was never caught. People move on. The name gets lost in time. Until five minutes ago. When the name reappears. Can you see why I'm interested, Mr Black?"

Black looked into Wilkinson's eyes, saw nothing. Dead eyes. His daughter had been murdered, as had Black's. They shared an old pain, which never really got old, but which was fresh and raw with every waking morning, with every drawn breath. Like a deep wound, opened anew with every sunrise. Black's daughter was four when she'd been killed. His soul had died with her.

Dead eyes, thought Black. Just like his own.

Wilkinson scrutinised Black for several seconds, then said, "I believe you when you say you don't know who the Blood Eagle is. I have a keen sense of truth and deceit, having lived with both sides of the coin all my life. Especially the latter. It's maybe why I've survived this long. Let me make a proposition."

He placed the pistol on the table, sat back down, and took another sip of the red wine. He held the stem of the wine glass delicately in his thick fingers. The same fingers could wrap around a man's neck, and snap it like a dry twig.

"I'm all ears."

"I'm going to let you walk out of here, get back into your car, and drive away."

Black gave a wintry smile. "That's very generous, but...?"

"There has to be a but," said Wilkinson. "Otherwise, what's the point? I'm giving you forty-eight hours. Reasonable?"

"Very. To do what?"

"Find me the Blood Eagle. It shouldn't be too difficult, seeing as he's eager to find you. Find him and bring him here."

Wilkinson leaned forward again, the table creaking under his weight.

"If you do, you live. If you don't, then I will fucking burn you, Mr Adam Black. And burn all you love and care for. Fair?"

"I can think of better arrangements."

"I'm sure you can. Tommy will see you out. It's been nice talking to you but I have a restaurant to run."

Black left the building the same way he'd come in, downstairs, through a back door, and into the car park. With him was Gillon, hobbling on one good foot, which didn't seem to perturb him. Someone had seen fit to give him a pair of jogging trousers, and a pullover. He was clutching his bag of heroin as if it were gold, which, in a way, it was. Behind them was the man called Tommy, pointing a revolver at their backs, accompanied by two others.

Gillon was ushered into the back of a waiting car, parked beside Black's BMW. He gave Black a thumbs up, face cracked open into a smile of stained teeth. The car drove off.

Black was given his keys.

"Clock's ticking," Tommy said. "Mr Wilkinson's not the type of man who likes to be disappointed."

Black faced him. Tommy was two inches shorter, but all muscle and hard bone and attitude.

"Ten minutes ago, you were all set to fire that pistol into the back of my head."

"And I hate to leave a job unfinished."

"Next time we meet, I'm going to introduce you to a very old friend of mine."

Tommy gave a smirking grin. "And who would that be?"

"Death."

28

R achel was taken by DCI Wishart to a place a quarter mile from her flat called The Applecross Coffee Shop, which sold speciality coffee and freshy baked Danish pastries. They walked. Little was said. Rachel had never been to the place. It was quiet, homely. It had a real hearth, the walls pale bleached wooden timbers, the floor a mosaic of coloured stone tiles of red, blue and green. In the winter, with a fire crackling, it would be nice, she decided. Wholesome. Sprinkled on the walls in no apparent order, were vintage black-and-white pictures of nameless people sitting in places she didn't recognise.

They found a table in a corner. Wishart ordered two lattes. Double shots. He knew what to order. This was not the first time they'd had little secret chats over coffee.

A man with a tired smile – the owner, Rachel guessed – returned after five minutes, placed the drinks on the table, with two pieces of complimentary shortbread.

"Enjoy," he said.

Wishart nodded. They waited until he was out of earshot.

"I hate shortbread," said Rachel, keeping her voice low.

"Two bits for me," said Wishart.

She waited. He sipped his coffee.

"Someone was bludgeoned to death," he said, matter of fact. Rachel listened, riveted to every word. "The weapon used was left at the scene. A crowbar. The one we think was used to jemmy open your front door."

"Who...?"

"A neighbour." His hand disappeared into his inside jacket pocket. He pulled out a notebook. He started leafing through the pages. "Doreen Pritchard?" He swivelled his drooping eyes up from the notebook to look directly at Rachel. "You know her?"

Rachel released a slow breath. It was bad. But at least it wasn't Adam. Small consolation for Doreen Pritchard.

"She lives on the first floor. On her own, I think."

"Here's my take on it, Rachel. The assailant was either trying to get into your place, or was leaving, when she came downstairs, maybe disturbed him. Forensics still need to give us a report, but from the blood spray, he struck her in the hall outside your door." Wishart took another careful sip of his coffee. "He struck, and he struck. Relentless." Wishart paused, regarding Rachel with his sad eyes. "I'm telling you this for a reason."

Rachel said nothing. His words frightened her.

"The assault was frenzied. Her face was flattened into her skull, and her skull was beaten almost into two halves. Split down the middle. Plus, she was stabbed. Multiple times. This was all done in a common hallway, when any number of people could have walked by. He didn't drag her into the flat to do the deed. Privacy wasn't a concern."

"Which means the guy didn't care," said Rachel.

"Which means he didn't care," repeated Wishart. "Which means he's either one angry bastard, or completely mad. But it doesn't stop there."

Rachel waited.

"So our man goes back into your flat, gets a dish towel from the kitchen, returns to Doreen, dabs the cloth in her blood, then goes back in to leave a message on your wall. We reckon he must have taken two trips to write it all down. He was enjoying the moment."

This time it was Rachel to echo his words, in a soft voice. "Enjoying the moment."

"If someone else had happened by," continued Wishart, "and stumbled across Doreen on the floor, and the perpetrator dipping from her blood, then..."

"He would have killed them too."

Wishart nodded. "That's my reading." Another pause, as Wishart took another delicate sip. Then he asked the question she knew he would ask.

"Any idea who this might be?"

She stared at Wishart, but her eyes saw the blood spattered on the walls and on the hallway floor and in her mind, imagined the words scrawled in blood on her living room wall.

"I don't know anyone who could do such a thing," she whispered.

"And the words? *The Book of Dreams*. Any ideas? You're a journalist. Are you writing a book about somebody? Somebody who might take exception?"

"No. It's crazy."

"That it is."

Wishart regarded her with his aged careworn eyes. For a fleeting second, Rachel didn't see DCI Wishart, but a weary bloodhound, resigned to a world of madness and mayhem.

"You got somewhere to stay?"

She nodded.

"Let me know where. I can arrange to have a police presence. Some protection. We'll have to take a formal statement, you understand."

"I've known Doreen for years," she said, swallowing the urge to burst into tears. "I can't believe this."

Wishart took her hand, looked at her, his face long and solemn.

"You have to be careful, Rachel. This guy doesn't mind killing. In fact, I would go so far as to say he rather enjoys it. Which is a rare thing. A rare thing indeed."

She couldn't think straight. Shock. His words penetrated.

"A rare thing?" she muttered.

"I believe," he replied slowly, "we're dealing with a unique type of individual."

She furrowed her eyebrows.

"A psychopath," he said. "Full on."

29

She ran. Too quick for the man standing guard at the toilet door. She dodged past him, before he could react. She hadn't eaten a proper meal for over three days, was dehydrated, hadn't slept. But adrenalin kicked in. She sprinted away, powered by sheer nervous energy. The man lunged after her, one outstretched hand grabbing the back of her T-shirt. She kept moving, broke free. The man lost his balance, toppled on his ankle.

"Bitch!" he bellowed.

She ran on, didn't stop, heading to the cafeteria. The man in the suit, sitting, looked up, disturbed by the commotion. Their eyes locked. She kept moving, barged through the double glass doors, ran to his table, sank to her knees.

"Please!" Her voice was a shriek, high-pitched, hysterical. "Help me!" The man in the suit stood, eyes wide, mouth gaping. He was clean-shaven, strong-jawed, short blond hair. She could smell his cologne.

"Call the police!" she screamed. "Please!"

She jerked her head round. Her guard was lumbering

towards the table, limping. From the counter, the red-haired employee approached, tentative, confused.

They both halted, on either side of her.

She looked up at the man in the suit. "They're going to kill me."

The man in the suit stood, transfixed, then switched ·his attention to the two men.

"What the hell is going on here?" The trace of an American accent, she noted.

The two men stopped up short, silent, unsure.

The man in the suit helped her to her feet. She collapsed into his arms. She looked out the window. There, in the car park, the minibus, pinched faces gazing back at her through the windows. Two more men were making their way purposefully from the bus to the entrance. She rested her head on the lapel of his jacket, sobbed.

"I asked you – what the hell is going on here?"

"Sorry for this," stammered the guard, his accent thick, stumbling.

With gentle fingers, the man in the suit eased Danika's head up. "What's your name?"

"Danika," she whispered.

More men had arrived, forming a little half circle round the table.

The man in the suit swept his gaze round. "Careless."

Danika stiffened.

"What...?"

The man in the suit suddenly gripped her hair, brought his face down close to hers, their lips only inches apart.

"Hi, Danika," he said. "My name's Eddie. You've been a naughty girl."

"Nooo..." she moaned.

He held her away, at arm's length, still clutching her hair, regarding her as if he were admiring a painting.

"You're a beautiful girl," he said. He spoke to one of the men.

"You're a fucking moron."

He was met by silence.

"When we meet, I do not expect this type of shit."

"Sorry..." mumbled one of the men.

Eddie turned his attention back to Danika. "I'm sorry, my pretty one. Bad luck. But a good effort."

Danika felt her legs give. She would have fallen, had she not got caught by the man called Eddie. Her world had shattered. He held her, then she was bundled into the arms of two of the other men.

"I like her," Eddie said. "She has spirit. You don't touch her, you understand?"

One of the men grunted an affirmative.

"Not one hair on her head. She's special. We'll use her later."

She listened, terrified, uncomprehending.

We'll use her later.

"Now," he continued. "Let me check the merchandise."

They all made their way out of the restaurant. Danika was propped up and half carried, half dragged back to the minibus.

One of the men was babbling. "Forgive me, please," he said. "This hasn't happened before. We tell them to be good. Obedient. But some stray, you understand?"

"You were complacent," said the man in the suit. "What would have happened if there were other people there. It was a fuck-up."

"Yes. A fuck-up. A major fuck-up. But it won't happen again. The girls are good."

"They'd better be."

"You'll see, Mr Dalrymple. You'll see."

She had a name. For the first time.

Dalrymple.

30

Black drove a couple of miles outside Houston, and stopped in a layby. He needed air. He got out, took deep lungfuls. The scenery before him was flat fields, and in the distance, pockets of thin woodland. He was still in the country. It was early evening, the sky cloudless and tinged with a golden bronze hue. On any other evening, Black might have pondered its beauty. But in a quiet unassuming restaurant, he had experienced the near brush of death, and his nerves were shot. He walked to a drystone wall, leant on it, the texture of the misshapen stones feeling rough on the palms of his hands.

He closed his eyes, absorbing the sounds, the smells. The faintest breeze played on his skin. He heard the chirp of birds, the low drone of insects. He tried to clear his mind. But his mind was on replay. A gun pointed at his head. A second away from death. What had saved him? Luck. Nothing more, nothing less. He had no control. Suddenly, he felt as if he were sinking, into the ground, the world rearing up to meet him, to swallow him up and consume him. Black staggered, the wall keeping him upright.

He had seen death before, in all its forms. Once, when he

was a younger man, he had laughed at it, shrugged off its clammy touch, moved on. As he had been trained. When he'd lost his wife and daughter, his perspectives changed. Death took a different form. He sought it out, craved it, wanted above everything else to feel its cold embrace.

But now? The relationship had changed again. Now, he thought he had something to live for. Rachel Hempworth had entered his life, and he had a reason again, to keep going.

He straightened, rubbed away sweat from his eyes, ran a hand through his hair, collected his thoughts, tried to rein in his frayed nerves.

People – he didn't know who – appeared to want something from him. They would kill him to get it, so much was obvious. All he had was a name. The Blood Eagle. Now he was on a shared journey with a psychopath called Ronald Wilkinson.

The whole thing was fucked up, and Black was in an ocean of shit, being dragged to dark places by a current over which he had no control.

He got back into his car, started the engine.

Fuck them. An old familiar emotion bubbled up, one which had served him well, many times.

Fury.

31

D CI Wishart insisted on driving Rachel to wherever she wanted to go.

"Southside," she said in a toneless voice. Her mind was still grappling with the shocking events. Her neighbour – a harmless, elderly woman who she'd known for years – was probably now in a metal box somewhere in a basement, ready to be dissected and analysed as part of a post-mortem. She would have woken this morning, the bright sun in a blue sky, and would never have imagined how her day would end. Bludgeoned to death in the hall by a maniac.

They didn't talk in the car. Rachel needed silence, space. Wishart was wise enough to get that. He asked only for directions.

The first place she could think of was Black's flat. One up in a tenement block in Bolton Drive. Three hundred yards from Hampden Park, a mile from Shawlands, a short distance from Queens Park. One bedroom, living room, kitchen, toilet. He called it functional. She called it basic. Right now, it would do.

Wishart parked the car in a space in the middle of a row of cars at right angles to the pavement.

"I'll see you up," he said.

"There's no need, really."

"There's every need, really," he chided. He squinted up at the red sandstone building. "Where's this?"

"Adam's place. Adam Black."

Wishart raised an eyebrow.

"The same Adam Black? The hero of the day?"

She gave a small half smile.

"Ah," he said. "I was unaware you knew him."

"I'm not sure if anyone really knows him."

"Still, a useful man to have at your side."

"But he has to be there," she said quietly. "And he can't be there all the time." She felt tears well up. "Doreen's dead. I keep thinking any second I'm about to wake up, and none of this really happened."

"It happened, Rachel," responded Wishart in a flat voice. "Keep remembering it."

Rachel breathed in, breathed out, using every effort to dam up a flood of tears. "I hope you get the bastard."

"That we shall most certainly do."

They got out, and made the short walk to the front communal door. It was after 7, and the raw heat of the afternoon had filtered down to a pleasant, mild evening. Next to the door, on the wall, was a column of names, with metal buttons underneath each one. Flat 1/1. Adam Black. She pressed the buzzer, not knowing if he was in. If he wasn't, she had a key. A voice answered. His voice.

"Yes?"

"It's me."

The lock on the door clicked. She pushed it open. They both entered a hall with walls of cream-coloured stone, a grey stone floor. It was clean and tidy. They took the steps up to the first floor, arrived at a door of frosted glass. It was open.

"Adam?"

"Come in!"

She and Wishart entered. Black was standing at the bay window of his living room, facing them. The place was a mess. Books, papers scattered on the floor, furniture upended.

Along one wall, written in a red scrawl, were words Rachel recognised instantly.

The Book of Dreams

"What happened?" she stammered.

Black fixed his gaze on Wishart. "Looks like we've had a guest. You are?"

"DCI Wishart. A friend of Rachel's."

Black nodded. "Nice to meet you. I'm Adam Black. And I think we have a problem."

32

Dalrymple followed the minibus north from the service station in Carlisle, as he did with every new batch, acting as an escort on the final leg of the journey. To ensure the goods arrived in one piece. Intact. It was not a distrust of the Romanians, who showed a cruel efficiency in their task of kidnapping and transporting, and got well paid for their efforts. It was a healthy wariness of Police Scotland.

In the last five years, slavery and human trafficking had climbed to the top of their agenda. If the bus got stopped, then trouble. The main route was the M74, and to be avoided. Instead, a twisting roundabout route using back roads, country lanes. Heading first east, then slowly north, gradually sweeping back inland, heading to Stirling, then through places like Callander, Kingshouse, Strathyre, veering round to Tyndrum, then further north, to the expanse of land known as the Rannoch Moors.

To the Farm.

A place he hated. Barren, desolate, full of endless bogs and marsh and wild gorse, and little else. But it was remote. Invisible from the main road. Eight miles from the passing traffic, along a winding single lane dirt track, close to Black Water Reservoir.

Impassable in the winter. Bumpy and midge-ridden in the summer.

A veritable shithole, in his opinion. His opinion didn't count. He followed the minibus, pressed a speed dial on his mobile phone. He got connected to an answering machine. An automated voice answered – *please speak after the tone.*

"I'm following them now," he said. "No trouble. One of the girls, though..." he thought back to the encounter in the cafeteria. "She has spirit. And she's a beauty. I think she should do. She has my..." he smiled when he said this, "...seal of approval. I'll get her when they're ready to be shipped on." He disconnected.

He never, ever sampled the goods. Though he was tempted. But it was unprofessional to get too close. This was a business. A very lucrative one. Where these girls ended up, he didn't care. Nowhere good. The process was simple. The purpose of the Farm was to break them down. Make them comprehend the new reality of their lives. The Romanians were especially good at that. Once suitably brutalised, they were farmed out, sold on. To street pimps, brothels, slave markets, whoever. Most forced into addiction. Fucked a hundred times a day, until they were fucked dry. And then? No one really bothered.

The money never stopped flowing. Pretty young women were always in demand. One in particular paid a king's ransom, for a specific type.

His thoughts returned to the runaway at the service station. Her wild eyes, her supple body, her firm breasts, her flaming hair.

She would do, he decided.

In fact, she was perfect.

33

Black had never met DCI Wishart. Rachel had introduced him as an old friend. Black would have preferred to have kept the police out of it, whatever *it* was. Too late now.

Wishart was two inches shorter than Black, not overweight, but then not underweight. Went to the gym just enough to keep from tipping over, he thought. Hangdog features, droopy eyes. A man who doubtless had seen it all, and then some.

Wishart looked about, glancing at Rachel, then spoke.

"I'll have to call this in. What happened here, Mr Black."

Black sighed, sat heavily on a chair. "Please. Call me Adam. If you're a friend of Rachel's, you're a friend of mine. I arrived ten minutes ago. The front door was open. Opened by a jemmy, looks like. Subtle, this was not. I went in, and discovered exactly what you see. A bloody mess."

"Nothing been taken?"

Black shook his head. "Don't think so."

"And this?" Wishart gestured to the artwork on the wall.

Black responded with the merest of shrugs. "Kids, I reckon. Crazy stuff. They get an empty flat, and write shit on the wall. Who wouldn't?"

Wishart said nothing.

"It's more serious than that," said Rachel quietly.

"What do you mean?"

She's scared. Suddenly Black was scared too.

"The same words have been written on the wall of my living room. Whoever did it killed a neighbour. Used her blood as ink." Rachel swallowed, gazed at the scrawl. "This could be her blood, too." Her bottom lip quivered, as she fought back tears.

"Whatever this is, neither of you are safe," said Wishart. "Can I suggest something?"

Black looked up at him.

"Perhaps you could both stay with relatives?" he continued. "Or maybe book into a hotel? For a short time only. Until we clear this up."

"I agree," said Black quickly. He turned to Rachel. "You could stay with your sister. She lives where... York? You could take a few days off."

She gave him a fixed look. "You're kidding, right?"

Wishart looked from one to the other. If anything, his face seemed to droop even more. "I meant both of you. Let's not underestimate the situation. There's a pattern. You're both connected somehow." He appraised Rachel with those hangdog eyes. "You don't want to join Doreen in the morgue."

"Of course I don't!" she snapped. Her eyes filled up. "Sorry... this is all too sudden. Too strange."

She sat down on the only other chair in Black's living room.

"What's happening?" She stared at Black. "What does it mean?"

She was of course referring to the words on the wall. Black could give an answer, but not now. Not in the presence of Wishart. The last thing he needed was the police involved. An image flashed in his mind. A pistol pointed at his head; one bullet; the spin of the chamber; the acned face of Wilkinson watching him with eyes black as burnt pebbles.

"Who cares," he said. "Let the police sort this. You've got to go. Far away."

"Don't exclude yourself, Adam," interrupted Wishart. "You should think about alternative accommodation. In the short term."

"Of course," he said. "Wise precaution. Stupid not to."

"Stupid not to," echoed Rachel. "Sure."

She was possibly in mild shock. She had entered his life, been with him for six months. What else should he have expected? His world was one of death, outrage, savagery. Adam Black's world, he thought grimly. No place for any civilised person. No place for Rachel Hempworth.

Wishart turned his back, started speaking into his mobile phone. He finished, faced them both.

"Uniform will be here in fifteen. And forensics. You can't stay here. Once they've taken your statement, then you'll need to find a place to stay." He looked at Rachel, almost pleadingly. "Somewhere safe. If you can think of anything, or anything happens, then you phone me." He handed them both cards. "Anything at all. We'll find this guy. But until we do, keep a low profile."

"We can do that," replied Black.

"It doesn't compute," said Rachel suddenly, her voice flat, toneless.

Neither Black nor Wishart said anything.

"That sentence." Rachel looked at Black, and gave a small, sad smile. "Low profile and Adam Black. In the one sentence. It doesn't compute. What the fuck's going on?"

34

After what seemed to Danika an endless road journey, and an endless drifting landscape, the minibus turned off a main road, and headed up an almost invisible track, cutting through a vast stretch of rolling, unpopulated moorland. In the distance she saw mountains with twisted peaks. They each would have quaint names, she was sure, but she didn't know what they were, nor did she care.

She did know she was somewhere in Scotland. She saw signs for cities she recognised – Glasgow, Stirling, Edinburgh. And she knew she was heading north. North meant remote. It was maybe mid-evening. She had no way of telling the time. The landscape was wild and barren. The minibus lurched and bounced over ruts and contours, rattling as it negotiated the terrain, sometimes slowing almost to a walking pace. No one talked. Even the men had stopped their chatting. They'd run out of things to say, she surmised, though the chain smoking didn't stop. She felt nauseous. Others had already puked on their laps, the floor. The men watching didn't seem to care. The minibus stank, of puke, of tobacco, of sweat. Of fear. But the nostrils got used to the stench until the rank air seemed normal.

She saw something maybe a quarter mile in the distance. Walls. And beyond them, rooftops. They were approaching buildings.

They got to an open double gate. A man stood to one side, waving them in. She gazed down at him as they passed. He stared back. He was grotesquely obese, loose jogging trousers, stained yellow T-shirt, greasy hair tied back tight from his forehead into a long ponytail.

The minibus pulled into a courtyard of sorts. One of the men stood in the narrow aisle, addressed them, grinning when he spoke.

"Welcome to the Farm, ladies. Hope you enjoy your stay. Now fucking move it."

They got off the minibus, traipsing out one at a time, listless, exhausted. They huddled together, fourteen of them. The minibus drove off, into a large wooden barn to one side. Before them, a house built of stone the colour of wet mud. Around them, outbuildings, sheds, ramshackle structures, forming a rough square. Beyond the buildings, six-foot-high walls. Once a farm, she thought. Now used for a different purpose. From one of the buildings, she heard dogs barking.

The men also had got off the bus, and were discussing matters. The fat man waddled into the square, greeted the others with hugs, handshakes, claps on the back.

Another car entered. Danika recognised the driver. The man in the suit. He stopped, got out, approached the men. He handed one of them an envelope. More discussions, this time in English, for his benefit, she assumed. She was too tired to concentrate.

He looked away from the men, directing his gaze at the women, scanning their faces. His eyes rested on her. He smiled, nodded politely. More hand shaking, then the man in the suit got back in his car, and left.

The men filtered into the house. It was big. Three levels. The windows on the top floor were boarded up.

Two men remained. The fat one and another. One from the bus.

Jesus Christ. The fat one was rubbing the front of his jogging trousers.

He pointed to the front door. "Inside."

She shuffled in with the others. Suddenly she was thirsty. She realised she hadn't had anything to drink for hours. They emerged into a large kitchen. High ceiling, bare grey walls. Square. Basic. In the middle a wooden table with six chairs round it. The men followed them in. They stood around the table, uncertain, like cattle waiting to be herded.

The fat man pointed again. "Through. Last door on the right."

They made their way out of the kitchen, along a corridor with bare floorboards. Doors on both sides. A set of stairs. They got to the last door on the right. Danika was first. She turned the handle, opened, entered a large room. Devoid of furniture. Like the kitchen, bare grey walls, high ceiling with jagged cracks in the plaster. Same bare floorboards. In the centre was a double mattress, stained and soiled.

The two men entered the room behind them.

"Against the wall."

The girls did as they were told, lining up, backs to the wall. They each kept their head down, staring at the wood beneath their feet, including Danika. Instinct. Eye contact was to be avoided.

The room was cold, despite the balmy evening. The single window was filthy, offering no view. The fat man stared at each of the girls, little pig eyes glittering.

The other man spoke.

"Welcome. This place you're in. We call it The Farm. You'll be staying here for a little while. Maybe a week, maybe two. Maybe longer." His lips stretched into a wide smile, revealing a row of tobacco-stained teeth. "Then you're moved on. For a new life. To work hard." He glanced round at the fat man. "Thirty men a day, eh?"

The fat man nodded slowly. He had his hand down the front of his trousers.

The man who had spoken turned his attention back to them.

"But we have rules. Rules of the house. Rules which have to be followed. And there's only two, so very simple to follow. Rule one. Do as you're told. Easy, yes? Rule two. No running away. No point in trying. There's nowhere to go. And we have dogs. They can sniff you out. In the dark, in the light. You'll get caught. And when we catch you, we do terrible things. We're going to show you now what we do. This is so that you have a clear... what's the word... what's the word – *understanding*. Yes. A clear understanding of the penalty of running away. My brother here will show you all. His name is Besnik. Some know him as the *Beast*. He will explain everything, in his fashion."

Besnik stepped forward, appraised the girls. Danika tilted her head up, watched him askance, heart beating hard. Never had she known such fear. He looked at her. She dipped her head. The floorboards creaked as they carried his weight. He stood in front of her, inches away. She smelled sweat and dirt.

"Not that one," said his brother, from the other side of the room. The fat man grunted. He licked the tip of his index finger, pressed it against her forehead. Time seemed caught. The world stopped. He moved on. She flicked a glance round. He stopped at each one. No one dared look at him.

He made a low, growling sound, suddenly seized one of the girls. She screamed. Everyone jerked round.

It was Monica. He yanked her from the wall, dragged her to the mattress. She resisted, finding sudden new energy. The fat man slapped her, once, across the face, stunning her, rendering her lethargic. All the while, the other man – the fat man's brother – was giving a dialogue. Almost like a commentator at a sports event. His voice was flat, emotionless. He didn't give a shit what his brother was doing. Part of the job.

"To make you appreciate what will happen should you break the rules, that you understand, telling you won't have the... impact, yes? Visual makes you understand. Seeing, in front of you. It makes it real. Because it is real."

The fat man flung her on the mattress, and ponderously climbed on top of her. With one forearm, he pressed on her neck. With his other hand, he tugged down his jogging trousers. She tried to wriggle free, but it was useless. The fat man spread her legs with his, pulled up her dress.

"Bad things happen," continued the other. "No idle threats. Bad things like this. You run away, the dogs catch you, we bring you back to this room, and we allow my brother to do what he does."

Monica gasped, tried to cry, but he was choking her, choking her life away, all the time thrusting harder.

Danika couldn't watch. None of them could. After a minute, the fat man finished. He got to his feet, pulling up his trousers, wheezing heavily, face shiny with sweat. He stood, looking down at her. She was perfectly still.

Danika stifled back tears.

He had killed her. Before them. Casually.

His brother spoke on. This was their induction. Rape and death.

"Now you see what happens to naughty girls. They pay. And we're serious. You get that?"

He suddenly strode forward, before them. "You get that, you fucking whores?"

Danika jumped. They all did. They nodded, in unison.

"Good." He turned to his brother and pointed to Monica's lifeless body. "Burn it."

35

Victor Cromwell had arranged with the hotel that he would have exclusive use of the basement sauna for two hours every evening. He was sitting on a wooden bench, a white towel wrapped around his waist. He fed water to the coals, the air suddenly alive with a fresh wave of deep uncomfortable heat. But he liked it that way. Sometimes it made him forget, sometimes it didn't.

He would never really be allowed to forget. Perhaps, he thought grimly, he didn't want to.

He thought back to the meeting with Lyle Taylor earlier, whom he hadn't seen for years. How strange the circumstances under which they met. Taylor had sought him out. He, likewise, wished to speak to Taylor.

They had both received a handwritten letter, bearing the same message. In Cromwell's case, the letter had been left at hotel reception. They both knew exactly who had written it. Which made no sense. Cromwell had been more bemused than panicked. Lyle on the other hand, was fearful. And this man called Adam Black was introduced into the equation. Cromwell knew nothing of him. Lyle would sort it. He was good at managing things. A fixer. Which was why Cromwell had been keen to see him. To fix things. And more particularly, to provide a very special commodity.

He lay back on the bench, pulled his knees up, breathing the sharp heat. The fact was, since his arrival back in Scotland, he had received two letters. Like the first, the second was also handwritten. But much shorter. In fact, it comprised only three words. Plus, folded neatly in the envelope with the letter was an enclosure which, when he opened it out, took his breath away. An object which sparked vivid, glorious memories. He held the object in his hand, scrunched in his fist, as he lay in the heat of the sauna. Since he'd got it, he kept it close.

The words – **You owe me.**

The object – a blood-stained, silken handkerchief. Mingled blood. His blood.

And the blood of another.

36

The man called Ronald Wilkinson was unable to think of anything other than his conversation with Adam Black. The restaurant was closed, the last guests having left a half hour earlier. Wilkinson was sitting at his favourite corner table, at a window overlooking the main road. The evening was balmy and still. Since Black had left, he had consumed almost a litre of vodka. Straight. He was drunk, and knew it. But he was the type of man who got quieter as the drinking wore on. When Wilkinson grew quiet, people knew to tread warily round him.

The lights were low. He was a shadow in the corner. Another man sat at a stool by the bar. They were the only people in the room.

"Do you believe in heaven, Tommy?" Wilkinson asked suddenly.

Tommy – the other man – looked puzzled. It was clear from his expression, that he wasn't sure whether this was a question to be answered.

"There has to be," Wilkinson continued. His voice was tinged with the slightest slur. "She's there, for sure. Happy. At peace. Do you think there's peace after death?"

A silence followed.

"Never really thought about it, Mr Wilkinson," said Tommy, eventually.

"I think about it. Every day. I reckon some find heaven, some find torment. Do you want me to give you a prediction, Tommy?"

Tommy said nothing.

"People like you and me, our souls are destined for an eternity of suffering. Which makes me sad. I'll never see my daughter again."

Another silence. Wilkinson downed another shot of vodka.

"Adam Black. Adam Black. Who is Adam Black?"

Tommy dared to reply. "We should have killed him. The guy knows who we are. He's a risk."

Wilkinson released a long sigh. When he spoke, his voice was quiet, calm.

"I don't pay you to think, Tommy. I pay you to do other things." He paused. "I haven't heard that name for many years."

"What?"

"The Blood Eagle. Then, one sunny afternoon, from nowhere, a man appears into my life, and he mentions this name. A man called Adam Black. Why is this happening? Is it a sign?" Wilkinson looked round to Tommy, his eyes glazed, his mouth slack. "Is he a sign?"

"A sign?"

"From God above. That this is the moment." He turned back, to stare at the glass on the table before him. "The moment for revenge," he said softly. He shook his head slightly, took a breath.

"What did you find out about him? Does he add up?"

Tommy nodded. "He's a lawyer. Works in the Southside. It's all there, on the internet. He works on his own. But there's more..."

He waited while Wilkinson poured another neat vodka in the little shot glass, and slung it back.

"Speak," said Wilkinson.

"The guy's a fucking war hero. He's the one who found the Prime Minister's daughter. He was in the news. He served in the SAS. Won the Military Cross. These men... they're fucking bad asses. We should have killed him when we had the chance."

"I knew there was something about him," murmured Wilkinson. "Too cool, by far. We need to liven him up a bit. What do you think, Tommy?"

Tommy waited.

"You know where he lives?"

"Sure," said Tommy. "A couple of guys are keeping tabs on him."

"And?"

Tommy looked uncertain.

"His Achilles heel," explained Wilkinson.

Tommy understood. "We think he has a girlfriend. A reporter."

"Like I said, we need to liven this game up a little. Make him understand clearly what the rules are. That I am a serious man. That the act of me allowing him to leave with his life has consequences." He turned again to Tommy. His eyes seemed to dance in the soft lighting, as if they contained their own dark flames.

"What do you want me to do?" asked Tommy.

"Take her to the basement. Let's give our Mr Black extra incentive."

Tommy nodded. "Tomorrow?"

Wilkinson didn't respond, lost in thought.

Tommy took that as an affirmative. *A new dawn, a new day.*

A day Black's lady friend would never forget.

37

B lack and Rachel booked into a hotel in the city centre. For a micro second, Black toyed with the idea of booking a room at the Radisson Blu. Kill two birds with one stone – get a room for the night, and pay Victor Cromwell a visit. The latter was high on Black's agenda. Cromwell had explaining to do. It was Cromwell who had directed him to the Raven's Crown, and Black, like a fool, had blithely danced to his tune. Black was keen to rekindle their friendship, and perhaps introduce him to a style of questioning he had never encountered before. Hollywood movie star or not, Black didn't care. Cromwell would talk.

But he dismissed the notion. Cromwell could wait. For a little while. Instead, they booked into the Hilton, in the West End. DCI Wishart said they could be back in their respective homes in a day or so. Once forensics had finished.

They had dinner in the restaurant. It was Monday evening, it was late, and the place was empty. Rachel ordered wine. Black got whisky. After the day he'd had, which he could only describe as remarkable, he needed some strong liquor.

Rachel was quiet during the meal. Black didn't try to prise

any conversation from her. Her neighbour had been murdered. She would need time. He thought about his own afternoon. He'd killed two men, then almost got killed himself. Confusion and death. A day in the life of Adam Black. He took another swig of whisky, dulling his mind. He'd killed many men. His past was littered with dead bodies. It never got easier. Each death sliced away a sliver of his soul, until, eventually, he would be hollow inside. A husk.

But this afternoon... His mind travelled back, to the restaurant, to sitting at a table opposite the gangster called Ronald Wilkinson, to the chamber of a gun loaded with a single bullet, to the trigger being squeezed. Old memories reared up. Black ordered another drink. Glenfiddich. Double. Neat. The waiter returned after five minutes. Black sipped, came to a decision.

"We need to talk," he said. "Let's sit in the lounge."

She nodded. She was pale, her face pinched and tired. They took their drinks, left the restaurant, crossed a foyer into a large room with plush carpets and soft leather couches. They sat opposite each other, an ivory framed coffee table in between.

"The Book of Dreams," he said. "I know what it is."

She held her wine glass in her left hand, gazing at Black with emerald eyes. For the millionth time, he was struck by her beauty; her slender figure; her short straight nose and delicate chin; her silk-smooth skin; her hair flaming red. She wore a simple blue dress, blue sandals.

"Tell me," she said.

"But whatever I say doesn't change a thing. You do as Wishart suggested. You stay with your sister. Please."

"And you? I recall he gave us the same advice in equal measure."

"I don't want you getting hurt."

"That's what I call avoiding the question."

"But it's true."

"I'm sure. Tell me."

"Let me show you. Give me five minutes."

She said nothing. Black left the lounge area. He felt light-headed. The whisky was working. If he were attacked now, then he would be less than effective. He was happy to take the chance. He left the hotel, to the car park, unlocked his car, retrieved the item from the glove compartment. He returned, sat back down on the couch.

"The Book of Dreams."

He placed the book he had been given by the old man on the coffee table, still wrapped in string. Black, giving it little thought, had tossed it into the glove compartment without opening it.

Rachel stared at the object, eyes wide. "This is it?"

"I assume so. Unless we have the most incredible coincidence in history."

"What is it?"

Black finished his whisky. He had a tale to tell.

38

"Am I seeing this?"

The man who spoke was Detective Sergeant Paul Foster. Beside him was his boss, and long-time friend DCI Bob Wishart. They were both staring at the same thing. A thing which would undoubtedly capture most people's attention.

"I believe we're both seeing this," replied Wishart quietly. "But like you, I think it must be a mirage. And not a good one."

They were standing in a disused warehouse, in an industrial complex in the east end of Glasgow. It was midnight, and the air was still and warm. A night watchman had called it in. He'd been taken to hospital, suffering from shock. No wonder, thought Foster. The place smelled of rust and dampness and rot. Amazingly, the building still had electricity, and above them, two strip lights flickered, giving a pale-yellow sheen to the objects scattered about – open crates, metal benches, tarpaulin sheets, bits of broken equipment used for God knows what. Uniformed police were already there. A forensic team would be arriving shortly. Temporary lighting was being rigged from a portable generator. Tape was stretched across the scene, beyond which they could not pass until they'd changed into their white plastic outfits.

Before them, hands nailed into a low wooden beam above her head, hung a woman. She was dead. The doctor had checked her pulse, as he was obliged to do, but it was clear to anyone who looked at her, that life had departed. It was difficult to even guess her age. Her face had been gouged away, to an unrecognisable lump of bone and sinew. Features eradicated. No eyes, no lips, no nose, no skin.

Which was only part of the horror.

"If I close my eyes, and open them, I'm still seeing this," mumbled Foster, "which means I can't be dreaming."

Her back had been split open. Her ribs had been removed, scattered on the floor at her feet, in no particular order, like pale sticks. Her lungs had been pulled from her body, and spread behind her, like little pink wings.

"I've had this dream before," said Wishart.

Foster looked at him, askance. "What?"

"Looks like an old friend's returned." Wishart rolled his eyes up at the ceiling, turned away. "This fucking job."

"What do you mean? Who's returned?"

"This... scene is not an original piece of work. You would be too young to remember. Unfortunately, I'm not. The charming individual who did all this, has done it before. Many years ago. His enthusiasm for the macabre hasn't diminished any with the passing of time. We never caught the bastard. Maybe this is God smiling, in his own way."

"I don't see many smiles," said Foster.

"Nor me. But we get a second chance."

Foster shook his head, knowing the image before him would stay in his mind until the day he died.

"Who the fuck would do a thing like this?"

"The Blood Eagle," replied Wishart, voice quiet as a breath. "The Blood Eagle."

39

Lyle Taylor had made a point of visiting his brother at least once a week, and telephoning him as often as he could. He phoned the landline, because a mobile was too difficult. If his brother didn't pick up, he would head over, check up on him, usually finding him asleep, or sitting in his garden watching the flowers.

His brother – Martin Taylor – lived in a large house in an area of Glasgow called Whitecraigs, an area dotted with million-pound houses. Martin Taylor lived in one of the biggest. A mock Tudor-style construction, with black beams and cream walls and a Mansard roof of red tiles. Sitting on an acre of land, with a neat lawn and rectangular flower beds, and in the centre, a wooden gazebo with a blue roof. A gardener came once a week. Lyle saw to it. Lyle paid him. Lyle paid all the bills.

He'd received the letter his brother had written a week earlier. By Royal Mail, first-class stamp. He'd thought, initially, how different. Someone had written to him the old-fashioned way. Not an email, or a text, or a tweet. He'd read it, re-read it, then a third time, then burnt it. A variety of emotions rippled through his mind at the time – bemusement; shock; rage. It made no sense. Then, after reflection, he thought maybe it did. His brother was ill. Penance, perhaps? A last confession? It didn't matter what the hell it was. He'd created a storm, where none before had existed.

The mention of the book was the *piéce de rèsistance*. The real showstopper. Lyle had no idea his brother had been so careful. And stupid. This fact, and the introduction of the man called Adam Black, was a problem. Lyle Taylor didn't like problems. He was adept at removing them. Or at least, arranging their removal.

When he'd got the letter, he'd telephoned his brother. There had been no answer. He'd gone round. There was no car in the drive. He had a key. The house was empty.

His brother had gone missing before. All Lyle could do was wait. And wonder.

He'd got back from his meeting with Cromwell at just after 6pm. The landline was ringing as he opened the front door. It was the police. They had received a message from the Queen Elizabeth Hospital in Glasgow. Martin Taylor had been found. Apparently, he'd driven to Loch Lomond, dumped his car, and was then found wandering along a path skirting the water, in a distressed state, half out of his mind. Shouting, crying. Screaming. He was disorientated. He was unable to give his name or address. An ambulance had taken him back to Glasgow. His wallet contained his driver's licence and credit cards. The police, when contacted by the hospital, had discovered that he, Lyle Taylor, was his next of kin, and appointed guardian.

Lyle was given a number. He'd spoken to a young doctor, who explained that his brother was being kept in the hospital for observation. He'd been sedated, and was sleeping. He'd be able to pick him up the morning at 10am, if his condition improved. He wondered if he was on medication.

Trazodone, Lyle had replied. *For depression.*

The doctor had asked if he was aware if his brother had maybe stopped taking it. To trigger such an episode.

Lyle had remained silent for a few seconds before he answered. *The court has appointed me his guardian,* he'd replied. *But I can't check up on him every day. You know why he's been prescribed Trazodone?*

Your brother suffers from depression, the young doctor had replied, and was about to say more, when Lyle interrupted him.

Don't you fuckers read your notes, he'd snarled. *My brother has fucking brain cancer!*

Lyle played the conversation over in his mind as he sat in the warm, close evening, in his garden. It was bigger than his brothers. He'd created a pond in its centre and arching over it, a wooden Japanese moon bridge, painted red, replete with white wooden balustrades, and copper box lanterns flickering with candle flame. Pink Indian flagstone wound through sections of flowers, bushes, trees. Colours everywhere, candles on bamboo stems, and fairy lights netted through low branches. A fairy-tale scene. A million miles from the real world of Lyle Taylor.

Lyle wasn't admiring the colours, or the moon bridge. He saw none of it. An untouched glass of gin and tonic stood on the garden table before him. Beside it, an ashtray, in which burned a cigar. Beside that, his mobile phone. He was waiting for it to suddenly buzz into life. For his orders. His instructions.

He would pick his brother up tomorrow. Then what? His thoughts took him down dark paths.

The men sent to kill Black were dead. Their bodies would already be gone. Cleaned up. The trap was simple, direct. And had failed. Now Black was warned. Other men had arrived at the

Raven's Crown, their identities unknown. The whole thing was a mess. Spiralling out of control. His brother had a disease in the brain, and it had spread, affecting everything around him. Like a virus.

The past, he thought. No matter how far you run from it, it comes back. It never really leaves. It sits, in the shadows, hidden, like a beast, waiting to pounce. The irony didn't escape him. Nor the grim symmetry. First, Robin Black. Now his son. Lyle's thoughts drifted to a much earlier time. Over twenty years earlier.

He and his brother ran the Raven's Crown, and so much more. The girls, streaming in from the continent, were a constant supply. Bought, used, and then sold on. The trade from Eastern Europe was in its infancy then. Not like now.

The Raven's Crown. A very special place. Not like the other two-bedroomed brothels, where men walked in from off the street, the girls taking easy thirty or forty a day. But the Raven's Crown. That was the pinnacle. That was a thing of beauty.

He picked up the cigar, placed it to his lips, drew in the heavy rich tobacco. He was seventy-four, had smoked and drank all his life, had a clean bill of health. His brother, however, never touched alcohol. Never puffed a cigarette. Yet he was the one that got cancer. Another sad irony.

His thoughts drifted back again. The Raven's Crown. Where it all started. Where it all ended. Beautiful girls, servicing very special clients who'd money to burn. Where he'd first met Vincent Cromwell, Hollywood movie star, but then just a young kid, who spent money on women like it was going out of fashion.

But, as happens in all aspects of life, they became too successful. People talked. Scared girls blabbed to upstart social workers. Investigations started. Suddenly, The Raven's Crown bleeped on the radar of the authorities. More particularly, Robin Black, a police officer interested in Organised Crime. Interested in them.

Black had died. Years back. But the problem didn't go away. It was merely handed on, like a runner's baton. Handed to someone who was even more relentless, even more dogged.

They made that problem disappear, in dramatic fashion. Now, it was coming back to haunt him, and from all people, his own brother.

His phone suddenly vibrated. He picked up. A text. The one he was expecting. The one he was dreading.

Well?

He responded.

He's at the hospital. I'll pick him up tomorrow, and take him back to the house.

He waited, imagining the recipient thinking, plotting.

Yes. Take him there. I'll take care of it.

What will you do? he texted, knowing the question would go unanswered. To his surprise, he got a response.

We'll take him on a visit. Back to old places. Back to where it started.

Lyle sipped his gin and tonic, took a deep breath. He felt as if a cold weight had been dropped down his gullet, into his chest. But there was no other way.

Death rides a pale horse.

He thought of symmetry and irony.
Old memories. He was haunted by the past
He was haunted by the pale horse.

40

Black decided he would order another Glenfiddich before he started his story. Rachel waited, offering no complaint. He admired her patience.

The waiter arrived, placing a fresh glass and a new paper place mat on the table. Black waited until he was out of earshot.

He began to relay the bizarre events of the recent past.

"Saturday morning, I was having coffee early at Starbucks. A man approached me. He knew who I was. He knew my name. He recognised my photograph in the paper. I had no idea who he was. He claimed to have been in my office years back. With his wife. She was being stalked, apparently. They wanted legal advice."

"Did you remember them?"

Black shook his head. "Nothing. I didn't help them. So he said. I was too expensive. Which would be the truth. If I had helped them, I would probably have remembered."

"And?"

"They left my office. Then, hours later, the man's wife is murdered. So he said."

Rachel was silent for several seconds, then said one word – "Wow."

"Fair comment. While he's sipping some caffeine-free tea, he leaves this book on the table. *The Book of Dreams*. This is a diary of his life, so he said. But the bit about who may have committed the murder is blank. He wanted me to find out who did it."

"And he leaves you the book?"

"Yup. With a nice caveat – he's told other people that I have it. *They'll come looking*, were his exact words, as I recall."

"Nice."

"At the time, I didn't give it any thought. The man was elderly. I reckon maybe late seventies. Maybe older. He looked... what? Done in, I guess. He couldn't remember his name. He wasn't well. I thought the guy was just... sad, I suppose."

"But you kept the book?"

"He wasn't for taking it back. Like I said, I thought nothing of it."

"Have you seen him since?"

Black shook his head. He sensed her mind slotting into journalist mode.

"He gives you this Book of Dreams because... why? There's a connection between it and his murdered wife?"

Black shrugged. "Maybe."

"But his prediction was accurate!" she said, almost accusingly. "They'll come looking!" Her voice had risen. Wine and shock. A heady combination.

"I believe so," said Black softly. "Whoever broke in was, presumably, looking for this." He gestured to the book.

"And in the process, bludgeoned an innocent woman, and then used her blood to practise his handwriting."

"But it tells us something."

"What?"

"It's real. The book means something, to somebody. The old man knew by giving it to me, there would be consequences."

"Christ, Adam. I can't think like you." She downed a large gulp of wine. "I can't be so fucking matter of fact. Sometimes you're like a fucking machine. What's wrong with you! My neighbour was murdered. I knew her."

"Which is why I want you to stay at your sister's. Until this gets sorted."

"And who exactly is going to sort this. The police, or Adam Black?"

Black said nothing.

Rachel sat back on the leather couch, fixing him a level stare. She cast her eyes to the book.

"It's still wrapped in string," she said.

Black nodded in agreement.

"You've not opened it."

"No. Its significance didn't dawn on me until I saw the words written on my living room wall."

Rachel leaned forward. "Shall we? Should we?"

"Yes, to both. Let me."

He pulled out a Swiss army knife from his trouser pocket, opened one of the many blades, cut away the string. "Be my guest," he said.

Rachel finished off her wine, caught the waiter's eye, pointed to her empty glass, signalling she wanted another drink.

"I hope this is all worth it."

She picked up the book. It was chunky, the cover plain, the corners curling. The words "The Book of Dreams" were written in block capitals in heavy black felt pen. No thought to neatness. The writing was careless, uneven.

She opened it, from the middle. She darted a glance at Black, frowned, then leafed through the pages, back to the first page. She stared at it, looked at Black. "What does this mean?"

She handed it across to Black. He opened it.

The pages were blank.

"The first page," she said.

Black found the first page, did exactly as Rachel had done. He stared at it for several seconds.

Three lines. Twelve words.

They'll come for you, Mr Black.

Avenge my wife.

Kill them all.

"What does this mean?" Rachel asked again.

Black was silent for a spell, as he collected his thoughts. He chose not to tell her about his encounter with the men at the Raven's Crown, nor the afternoon spent in the company of Ronald Wilkinson.

"It means the old man I met on Saturday morning has gone out his way to start something."

"What?"

"A war."

41

To the chorus of barking dogs, they were led back out the front door, across the courtyard, and into an outhouse – a wooden barn, converted into basic living accommodation. They each remained silent as they shuffled along, like a troupe of ghosts, cocooned in their own bleak thoughts. What had happened to Monica's body, Danika had no idea. A spark of life, snuffed away. She'd barely known her. But their shared horror had created a bond. Now she was dead. *Perhaps she was the lucky one*, she thought. Death had to be better than this.

The barn had an open-plan mezzanine level, access by way of an almost-vertical stair and comprising a large space with twenty beds in two rows, like a dormitory, all under criss-crossing rafters under a low gable roof. Beside each bed was a plastic bucket. There were no windows, no obvious ventilation. The heat was intense. Each bed was a bare mattress on the hard wood floor, a pillow, and a single coarse brown sheet. A half dozen litre bottles of mineral water were in a box in a corner. Chairs were scattered about, in no apparent order.

The brother of the fat man had waited at the bottom of the

stairs. When the last had made the climb, he'd shouted up at them.

"You fucking bitches stay there. You piss and shit in the buckets. Breakfast in the morning. If you try to escape, I'll set the dogs on you, and they'll rip your fucking guts out."

He'd left them with these parting words, locking the barn door behind him.

It was late evening. Pale moonlight glinted through cracks and spaces in the roof. Danika was sitting on the mattress. She was exhausted, but sleep evaded her. No one slept. Around her, she sensed shapes and outlines. Ghostly silhouettes of other young women, all lost and terrified. Their lives changed forever.

"What will they do?" whispered one, in English.

"We must be quiet," said another. "Hush, or they'll come back."

A silence fell, punctuated by coughs and sniffs and sobs.

"We're going to die," said Danika, her voice lifeless, flat. "Maybe not here. Somewhere else. We'll be used, and used. And when we've been used and our bodies can't take it anymore, then we'll either die in a corner somewhere, or they'll kill us."

The silence was complete. She spoke her mind. She spoke the truth. And they all knew it.

"Unless we escape," she said.

Someone began to cry.

"There's no escape. You heard him. They have dogs."

"They won't know until the morning," said Danika. "We'll be long gone."

"Gone?" said another. "Where to? There's nothing out there."

"Then you stay and fucking die!" said Danika.

She got up, made her way to the edge of the mezzanine, groped with her hands until she found the top of the stairs. She twisted round, made her way down carefully. Nothing was said. She could feel their fear. It mirrored her own. She reached the bottom, placed one foot on hard concrete. She looked about. There was nothing to see, the place shrouded in gloom. Vague outlines of indeterminate objects. She had an idea where the door was. Slowly, placing one faltering foot in front of the other, she made her way to the side of the barn. Using her hands, she felt the rough wood. There! The frame of the door. She found the handle, turned it. The door was locked. She pressed her shoulder against it. It was solid.

Voices, outside, only feet away. Laughter. She gasped. She scampered back, finding the foot of the stairs, climbed back up, so scared she could hardly breathe.

She got to the top. She could feel their eyes, staring, piercing the gloom.

"The door was locked," she said.

"You'll get us all killed," someone said.

"We're already dead."

She sat back on the mattress. The noise continued outside. Men were talking loudly. She knew the language well. Romanian. Talking and laughing without a care, knowing that they were untouchable, that they would never be caught here, in the wilderness. In the Farm.

She looked up, shards of moonlight falling on her face through cracks and spaces in the timbers, and wondered what the fuck God was doing about all this.

She lay down, and closed her eyes. Sleep came eventually, amid the sounds of tears and the smell of fear.

42

Rachel slept, assisted by a bottle and a half of Pinot Grigio. Black sat on a chair by a table. Sleep evaded him. On a table was a glass of Glenfiddich. In his holdall was a bag with another full bottle, which he knew he would open and consume.

He watched Rachel as she slept, listened to the sounds of her gentle breathing, inhaling, exhaling. Black wondered, with some dread, how this would end. Rachel had never asked for any of this. But here she was, immersed in Black's world. Someone had broken into her flat. If she'd maybe come home a little earlier from work, then it might have been her blood decorating her living room wall.

He took a deep breath. The alcohol helped. It helped to dampen... what? Everything. His life. Which was a wreck.

It was all about the book. The Book of fucking Dreams. The old man knew that by giving it to Black, trouble would follow. He'd also assumed that Adam Black was capable of dealing with it. Presumably he'd made his decision based on the story in the papers. The story of Black rescuing the daughter of the Prime Minister, months earlier. How Black had served in the British army, had won the Military Cross.

How he was a hero.

He was no hero. Bitter thoughts ran through his mind, the whisky failing to prevent them intruding.

He was a killer. He killed. He was extremely good at it. He was good at it because he felt no remorse. He lacked the one emotion which most other human beings possessed. Empathy. Which was why he'd been a superb candidate for the SAS.

And everyone around him suffered. Everything he touched, he destroyed. His wife and daughter, murdered in his own home. His friend, the colonel, run down in the streets and left for dead. Who next?

The Military Cross. Won for bravery. The events of earlier this afternoon had reminded him. Shaken him. Playing with a loaded revolver in Wilkinson's restaurant. His thoughts drifted back, to another time, another world...

The cell was hollowed out from black stone. No windows. It was deep down. Deep under Saddam Hussein's Golden Palace. The only illumination was a solitary light bulb in a corner, high up. The bed was a sheet on the rock floor. A single iron door. He and his men had been captured – betrayed – and taken here, weeks ago. Months ago. He'd lost track of time. Every while, the door opened. He was taken out. To different rooms. Questions. The questions stopped. Just torture, for its own sake. Beatings with sticks. Water boarding for fun. The tip of a white-hot knife scoring the length of his torso. Two men holding him secure on a heavy block of wood, his neck on a grove, another standing still to one side, in both hands a double-headed axe. Shouting in a language Black didn't understand. Holding him down, as he squirmed and shouted and screamed. To be met by laughter. The man loomed over him, swung the axe high, let it fall. To imbed the blade an inch from his head. More laughter. Dragged back to his cell. Hung up by his wrists, as he watched one of his men being beaten, then having his throat slit. "You're next," said the guard who'd done it.

Then it changed. The games started. Sitting on a chair at a table.

On the table was a handgun. A Smith and Wesson, with a revolving chamber. Rifles pointed at his face. Cash changing hands. One of them picking up the gun, popping the chamber out, installing a single bullet, clicking the chamber back in, spinning it. Smiling. "You know what to do," the guard said, placing the gun back on the table. In front of him.

Black took another slug of whisky. He reached round, pulled out the bottle from his holdall, twisted off the top, drank it straight.

Placed in front of him. Laughter, talking, shouting. Light glaring. He hadn't eaten properly for a hundred years. He was thirsty, starving, body beaten. But he could still smile.

"Fuck you."

"Pick it up!" Prodded in the face by the muzzle of a semi-automatic rifle. "Pick it up!"

He shook his head. Slapped in the face. Punched in the back of his head.

"Pick it up!"

"Fuck you."

More slapping. The butt of a rifle slammed down on his neck, knocking him from the chair. Being hauled back up again, propped back on.

"Pick it up!"

"Fuck you."

"Okay."

One of them picked up the gun. The laughter subsided. A hush. The tip of the barrel placed on his temple. The metal felt cool on his skin. He was going to die. He'd died already, a million times. This was no different. Fuck them all. He braced himself, for the explosion in his brain, the instant darkness.

The trigger clicked. Nothing. Shouting. Money being counted, given out to eager hands.

"Again! Again!"

The process was repeated. He closed his eyes, let time drift. What will be, will be. Three times. Three clicks of the gun. Three empty chambers.

Being taken back to his stone tomb.

"Tomorrow," said the guard gleefully. The guard who had slit his friend's throat. "You're lucky."

Black took another long gulp. The whisky tasted good. But it couldn't make him forget. Nothing could.

He wouldn't last another day. He slept. The door opened. He was tossed a plastic bottle of water. He drank. Two guards. He was lifted up, taken back to the room, to the chair, to the table. To the gun.

He was told to sit. He said no. No more. He was forced down. More guns, pointing at him.

This time, they dispensed with the prelude. They didn't tell him to pick it up. One of them did it for him. With a flourish, the chamber was flicked open. This time, two bullets. The spin of the barrel, like a roulette wheel.

Money flashed. Money, money, money. The gun against his head. He shut his eyes. Hurry the fuck up. The gun clicked. Nothing. Whoops of delight. People were winning big, on Black's life.

Then the sound, deep, booming. Like the sound of his heartbeat. Thump! Thump! Thump! The world shook. Rock dust drizzled down from above. A fucking earthquake? Not an earthquake. Bombs. Maybe Tomahawk Cruise Missiles. Maybe F-16s. Chaos. Suddenly, he was no longer the focus of attention. Guns shifted away, as they all looked up. Panic. He took his chance. He stood. One of them pointed his rifle.

Black swiped away the barrel. The gun fired, punching a hole in another's chest. He pulled the rifle in, the man jerking forward, rammed his fist into his windpipe. Nerveless fingers loosened their grip. He grabbed the gun. Fired all around. Killing everything in sight. Four dead men. One running. Keys jangling from his belt. Black chased, fired, the man down, shot in the shoulder. Black strode towards him. The man dragged himself across the ground, glancing back.

Thump! Thump! Thump! They come in threes. The place moved, as if a shiver had passed through the world.

Black knelt, flipped the man round. The guard. The guard who'd sliced his friend's throat.

Shouts all about. Running feet. Black stared at the man. The man stared back.

"You're next," said Black.

The man squirmed. Black placed a knee on his neck. A leather sheath attached to the man's belt. Black unclipped it, pulled out the knife.

"You're fucking next," he hissed. The knife was a big fixed-blade fucker with a razor edge. The man cried out. Black pushed the knife up through his chin, through his mouth, up into his brain.

He took the keys. More guards, coming from nowhere, running past him. Running to get out. Swivelling round, resting on one knee, he shot them in the back while they fled. Six shots. Six down. Easy. He half ran, half staggered. Unlocking doors. His men, pale, emaciated, embracing him. Other prisoners. American. French. He led them, out that fucking hellhole. Killing as he went. Killing. Killing.

Black snapped himself to the present. He gazed at Rachel's sleeping form. She could never be a part of his life. He couldn't allow it. It was a virtual death warrant.

People wanted The Book of Dreams. The two men he'd

killed at the Raven's Crown, and whoever had broken into their flats. He had no idea why. But he sensed they wouldn't stop.

Fair enough. Let them come.

Bring it on.

Bring it fucking on.

43

With the morning came another day, thought DS Paul Foster, but it didn't feel like it. He hadn't gone home, so it seemed both days had morphed into one. He doubted any morning would now be quite the same for him. The image of the dead girl, strung up and dismembered, would play in his mind for a long time to come. Until his dying day.

The Blood Eagle, Bob Wishart had said. He was discussing it now, in a hastily prepared Incident Room, deep in the interior of Aitkenhead Police Station, in the south side of Glasgow. A large, ugly red concrete building ten yards from a main road, close to nothing much, except a superstore, MOT garages and tyre repair stations.

Wishart was team leader. Like Foster, he'd worked right through. On a large whiteboard, were various photographs. Photographs of the dead girl, taken from various angles. But they all looked the same. All abhorrent. All barbaric. Scenes from a nightmare.

The post-mortem was being carried out later that morning. The girl was dead, her face removed, her body ripped open, the innards pulled out. These were the bald facts, and Foster had never seen anything like it.

Below the photos were others, smaller, of a similar vein. Three women, suspended, spread. Under each picture was a name, a date of birth, a date of death, location.

Wishart was talking to the group – eighteen men and women. They each had been given copies of old case notes.

"Read the files," said Wishart. "You've all got a copy. Twenty years ago, three women were killed. Killed in the same... exotic fashion as this poor unfortunate." He pointed to the picture on the board. "They were found in different parts of Glasgow. In different environments." He took a deep breath.

"The first was Molly Deacon. Eighteen. Worked in a department store in the city centre. Went out clubbing one Saturday evening with a group of friends. They got separated. Molly never came home. Found two days later on the flat roof of a high-rise tower block by workmen, sent to fix a leak. She was strung up on a television mast.

"The second, Norma Stark. Twenty-three. Worked as a lawyer for a firm in Cambuslang. That night she worked late. She didn't drive. Her husband couldn't collect her. She took the bus. Problem was she didn't take it. She never got on it. She never came home. Her body was found the next day. In a derelict carpet warehouse, by a group of kids bunking off from school. She was attached to a weaving machine.

"The third, Evelyn Wilkinson. Twenty. Student at Glasgow University. Studying Veterinary Science. Left the family home early one morning to go out jogging. Never returned."

Wishart lowered his head, paused, as if summoning up the courage to continue. "Evelyn was found two days later. In a kids' play park in a village eight miles from Glasgow. Hanging, suspended from climbing bars. Tied by piano wire, I might add.

It's not relevant, but her father is Ronald Wilkinson. Some, if not all of you, will have heard of him."

Foster sighed. Christ, Bob Wishart looked bone weary.

Wishart continued. "There was nothing to connect each of the victims. They came from different parts of the city, different backgrounds, they bore no physical resemblance, other than their youth. They had never met each other, nor associated in the same social circles. No connections whatsoever. The conclusion reached at the time was that they were randomly chosen. Everything else, however, was calculated, planned. Thought through. The perpetrator was meticulous and clever. The other conclusion reached, was that we were dealing with a serial killer. Someone who was killing for the sheer enjoyment of it. The thrill."

He cleared his throat. He met their stares.

"The only consistent thing was the manner in which they died. Their backs opened, ribs cut away, the lungs pulled out. A ritualistic killing performed by the Vikings, back in the day. Known as The Blood Eagle, so we were reliably informed. These young women died in an agony we cannot comprehend.

"We never caught him. Or her. We had nothing to go on. No fingerprints, no CCTV. No witnesses. We drew a blank. Everybody was questioned. Friends, family, work colleagues. We spoke to every sadomasochist, every fetishist, every pervert, every piece of sewer-life we could think of. We came up with nothing.

"Three women dead. And then, suddenly, the killing stops. Why, we have no idea. Did he get bored? Did he die? Did he get scared? Prison? Nothing. Until now. The fourth victim. Other than her face having been removed, the similarities are there to be seen."

Wishart drew a deep breath in, exhaled a long sigh, rubbed his eyes, making them red and bleary.

"It appears our pilgrim has returned. Or a copycat, which I doubt. So we start again, ladies and gentlemen. We trawl through the case notes. We check the cameras in the area. We speak to the owners of the warehouse. We speak to the night watch who found her, and everybody connected to him. We speak to every fucking person we can think of. And every fucking person we can't think of."

He paused. "We haven't established her identity yet. But we will." He pointed to another photograph on the board. It was an enlarged picture of the woman's wrist.

"She has a tattoo. A number. Unusual, I would think. I seem to remember the Nazi's used the same tactic."

"Like a serial number?" ventured a DC.

Wishart nodded. "Like a brand."

44

The following morning, they had reached an agreement. Black would drive Rachel to work, where she would explain to her boss the situation, then he would drive her to Glasgow Central Station, where she would get a train to York, to stay with her sister. Until the thing had blown over.

"And you?" she had asked.

"I'll stay low," he had replied.

"Sure you will."

The train left at 11.15am. The journey was three and a half hours, approximately. They had bought some coffee, and sat in one of a row of trendy coffee shops. Glasgow Central was busy. People milled about, waited, waved hello, waved goodbye, sat on metal benches with stacks of luggage. The air droned with a thousand conversations, like the buzz of insects. The day was hot and sticky. There was no air con in the massive metal and glass structure. The loudspeaker system chimed every few minutes, a woman's voice crackled, announcing arrivals, departures, delays.

The train to York was on time.

Rachel sipped a flat white.

"You realise there's no such a thing as a free lunch."

"That would be the general rule," said Black. "What is it exactly you're referring to?"

"I go down to York to stay with my dear sister. There's a price to pay."

"Which is?"

"Dog walking duties. Four chihuahuas. Incessant noise. Staying in Glasgow would be the preferable option."

Black could only nod, sharing some sympathy.

"Plus," she continued. "I really will be missing on a free lunch."

Black raised one eyebrow. "How so?"

"I didn't tell you. Why would I? A lot's been happening. Your brand-new friend telephoned me. Yesterday. Invited me out. One o'clock. At the Princess Hotel, no less. For lunch."

Black was intrigued. "My brand-new friend?"

She leaned across the table on both elbows. "And I know you set it up. Come clean." She looked tired, wan. Still, a mischievous smile played on her lips.

"I would, if you could narrow it down a bit." Black didn't return the smile. A wisp of dread brushed the edge of his mind.

Rachel rolled her eyes. "I'll give you a clue. His second name is Cromwell – and not *Oliver* – and his occupation is *Hollywood Movie Star*. I hope that narrows it down enough."

Black sipped the hot coffee, mind racing. "Of course. I forgot all about it. I'll pass on your apologies."

"You forgot? How could you forget about something like that?"

Black shook his head, shrugged. "A lot's happened." He attempted a smile. "Let's concentrate on getting you down to York, and doing some serious dog walking."

"Funny man."

The voice on the speakers crackled. Her train had arrived. They got up. She had changed into blue jeans, running shoes, a simple white cotton T-shirt. She carried hand luggage only, the intention clear – the stay with her sister was temporary. She reached up, kissed Black gently on the lips. Black held her, savouring the soft fragrance of her hair, her skin.

"Be good," she said. She left him, heading for the platform. She turned her head, fleetingly, blew him a kiss. She joined a throng of people filing through the entry gate. She disappeared from sight.

Black felt considerable relief. With Rachel gone, his vulnerability had lessened. Considerably. He sat back at the coffee table.

Cromwell had directed him to the Raven's Crown, where two men had been waiting. Two men looking for something. *The Book of Dreams*, probably. Black had killed these men. Cromwell had arranged to meet Rachel. *Cromwell and the Book of Dreams.* Connected. Tangled together, like snakes in the shade. Black looked at the digital clock on a large display running the length of the station. Seconds were ticking. A man called Ronald Wilkinson would also be looking at the time. Black had been given forty-eight hours to find *The Blood Eagle*, whatever the hell that was. Black allowed himself a cold smile. Wilkinson was an irritation, no more. If he wanted trouble, Black was his man.

Be good. Rachel's words.

Black felt no such inclination.

Next stop, Hollywood movie star, Victor Cromwell.

One p.m. for lunch at the Princess Hotel.

Black wouldn't let him down.

45

The train was Virgin Express. Three hours to York, with no changeovers. Rachel got a window seat, by a table. She pulled out a Kindle from the front pouch of her holdall, placed it on the table, and put the holdall on the chair next to her. The train was due to leave in about ten minutes.

She stared out the window, but nothing registered. The thought of her neighbour was never far from her mind. Her blood on the floor, spattered on the walls and ceiling. Used as a means of conveying a message.

The Book of Dreams. More like The Book of Death.

What had she gone through, Rachel wondered for the millionth time, when the moment came, when the blade pierced her heart, her lungs, her stomach? When her skull was crushed. What had Wishart said? She'd been stabbed multiple times. Who could do such a thing? Rachel took a deep breath. The man she loved was no stranger to such things. She only knew part of Adam Black's story. He'd saved the Prime Minister's daughter. She had been allowed to write the story. Her newspaper had been granted exclusivity, thanks to Black, who had insisted that she, and only she, should tell the tale.

But it came at a cost. The story had been edited. Not by their in-house editor, but by nameless strangers at a branch of the Government shrouded in secrecy. British Intelligence. Edited, revised, abridged. Butchered. Only a thin veneer of the truth was publicised.

She knew only wisps and fragments of the man called Adam Black. He divulged little. But certain facts were self-evident. Violence followed him, like a shadow. Clung to him. If she were honest with herself, she would admit he was the personification of violence. He gave out as easily as he got. More so. Because...? She didn't want to finish the thought, didn't want to face a reality. But she knew it was the truth – Adam Black was a man who enjoyed the thrill of the feud.

She thought of her neighbour. Wrong place, wrong time. Collateral damage, in Black's world. Now her world.

She picked up her Kindle, switched it on. A man sat down opposite her. She glanced up. Regular features, hair shaved close. He smiled. She returned the smile. She settled back to the Kindle. A tinny voice relayed information from a loud speaker in the carriage – the train was leaving in five minutes.

"That makes a change."

A voice. Belonging to the man opposite. She looked at him.

"Sorry?"

"That makes a change."

She frowned.

"What does?"

"The train leaving on time. Wonders will never cease."

She nodded, her smile resuming. "Sure."

She pointedly returned to her Kindle. She was in no mood for a conversation with a stranger. If he kept going, she would move.

"That doesn't leave us much time."

She lifted her head again. "I beg your pardon?"

The man had placed a newspaper on the table in front of him. He lifted one side. Underneath rested a handgun.

She froze, eyes fixed on it, then him. Not once did he lose his smile.

He dropped his voice to barely above a whisper.

"The pistol is called a Glock 17. It's semi-automatic. That means I can keep pulling the trigger, and bullets keep firing. I could load three bullets into your face in less than three seconds. It's very powerful. Your lover Adam Black would find it difficult to identify you when they slide your body out a cabinet drawer at the morgue."

She swallowed, found her mouth was suddenly dry. She worked her lips, tried to form words, but nothing came.

"Don't try," he said. "If you scream or shout, or do anything you know you shouldn't do, then I will pick up this gun, and shoot you in the head. It's really not worth it, Rachel. Do you understand what I'm saying?"

She nodded again. A sound drummed in her ears – her heart.

"We're going to leave. Together. Nice and calm. I'll be behind you, pointing the gun into the small of your back. Let's go."

She got up, and manoeuvred past the table, into the corridor.

"You forgot something." He gestured to the Kindle. She picked it up. "And your bag."

She got her holdall. He followed her, close behind, holding the newspaper around the Glock, pressing it up to the base of her spine.

"Nice and cool," he whispered in her ear. "Anything silly, then I'll kill you."

They got off the train. Another two men were waiting. Casually dressed. Jeans, shirts. Normal. They approached, instantly surrounding her, one on each side, the first man still behind.

"Not too quickly," said the man to her right, placing an arm through hers, pulling it in close. They walked back along the platform, passing people, station guards. Two transport policemen stood at the exit gate, chatting to a woman with a cart of luggage. Rachel tried to catch their eyes, convey her jeopardy by sheer force of will.

The man to her left leaned in, whispered. "Don't fucking try it."

They passed, the policemen oblivious. They made their way through the station. There! The coffee shop where she and Black had sat, sipping coffee. Someone else was at their table. Her eyes frantically roved the people there. No sign of Black. He was gone.

"He's deserted you," said the man behind her. "Keep moving."

They made their way out, through the main entrance, into daylight, to Gordon Street.

"Where are we going?" Her voice was strained, her throat tight.

"Nowhere good."

46

Remember – there are many other capable men. Be cautious. Be aware.

In short, do not make an overvirtue of courage or heroism. Trepidation – call it fear, if you will — is a highly desirable adjunct for men like yourselves, whose one fault might be said to be an almost mystical faith in the success of your destiny.

Do not be fooled.

We are each mortal.

Especially heroes.

Address given to new recruits of the 22nd Regiment of The Special Air Service.

L unch at the Princess Hotel. 1pm. An impressive building, fronting George Square, the centre of Glasgow. Walls of smooth sandstone, Gothic curves and slants, sculpted architraves. An age when architects designed buildings to look good. Black admired it from the street outside.

It was hot, the streets were busy at this time. Office workers jostling towards coffees shops and bakeries, shoppers, sightseeing tourists. Black was a half hour early.

He made his way into the front bar, sat at a corner table with a view of the entrance, got a tall glass of lemonade and ice. The place was half full. He opened a courtesy newspaper, pretended to read, one eye on the doorway. Around, the low hum of polite conversation. Waiters milled about, attentive. Black glanced at the menu. Movie star prices.

He sipped his lemonade. Events were moving quickly, over which he had little control, and which he didn't understand. What he did understand, was that Victor Cromwell, somehow, was the answer.

Black looked up. The man himself had entered. Wearing sunglasses, a hoodie, the hood pulled over his head, blue jeans, white training shoes. Black recognised him immediately, his gait, his confidence.

Black watched, as he approached a head waiter standing at the entrance to the restaurant, at a booking table. A quiet word. The head waiter gave an effusive smile, showed Cromwell into the room, beyond Black's scope of vision.

Black finished the lemonade, returned the newspaper to the rack, and entered the restaurant.

There, by a window, was Cromwell. He was on his mobile phone, oblivious to Black's entrance.

Black approached the table. Cromwell looked up. His lips drooped; behind his sunglasses, his eyebrows arched up. He switched off his mobile. He took off his glasses.

"Do you mind?" Black nodded at the chair opposite.

Before Cromwell had a chance to answer, Black sat down.

"Thank you." Black gestured at a menu on the table. "Recommend anything?"

Cromwell spoke in a voice like soft silk. "Lobster. You can

never go far wrong with Lobster Thermidor. It's the hotel's signature dish."

"You know, it's something I've never tried. This is your treat?"

Cromwell gave the merest of shrugs. "Of course."

"Excellent. Lobster it is. Rachel passes on her apologies, by the way. She would love to have come, but her flat was broken into, and her neighbour murdered in the process. You can see why she's a little distracted."

Cromwell frowned, shook his head. "That's awful news. Poor girl. I hope she's well?"

"As well as one would expect, given the circumstances. And the circumstances have been a little odd recently. Wouldn't you say?"

A waiter appeared, notepad and pen at the ready. Cromwell smiled up at him.

"Two Lobster Thermidors. And to drink?" He looked at Black.

"Glenfiddich goes down well. Neat, preferably."

"I agree. I'll have one too. Neat. Make them both doubles. Thank you."

The waiter acquiesced with the slightest twitch of his head, picked up the menus, swished away.

"What circumstances are you referring to?" continued Cromwell. "Our meeting? A trifle sudden, I agree. Did you manage to sort out the hotel acquisition?"

Black rested both his elbows on the table. "I encountered some issues in that regard."

Cromwell raised an eyebrow. "That sounds ominous." Another waiter appeared, placing a bottle of sparkling mineral water on the table, and two wine glasses. He opened the bottle, poured, left.

"The owner, I assume, is unwilling to sell," said Cromwell.

"Though if I recall, there was a bit of a mystery there. Your father, so we were told, was the owner."

"And if *you* recall, I mentioned my father had died some time ago. I visited the hotel in question. The Raven's Crown. As you thought I might."

"It would have been the reasonable thing to do."

Black sipped the water. It was ice-cold. "Reasonable. Yes. But the reception was a little... how can I put it? Frosty."

The first waiter appeared, carrying a tray, upon which were two stubby glasses of whisky, which he placed before each man.

Cromwell lifted the glass, hovered it under his nose, smiled, showing his stunning white teeth.

"When you've been away for as long as I have, you forget the real luxuries in life." He took a drink. Black did the same.

"Frosty?" continued Cromwell.

"Maybe 'frosty' is the wrong adjective. Maybe you can do better. Two men were waiting for me, armed with guns. Their objective was to kill me. How would you describe that, Victor?"

Cromwell's forehead wrinkled. "You're not being serious, surely?"

"As serious as it gets. But it's okay – do you mind me calling you Victor? We hardly know each other, and I'm calling you by your first name. It's okay. We met, we had a chat. And it got resolved."

"Resolved?"

"I killed them both."

Cromwell fixed Black a stony stare.

"I threw a knife into the throat of one, and shot the other through the head. All's well that ends well, yes?"

Cromwell remained silent.

"A neat conclusion." Black took another sip of the whisky. "But still, questions."

Black rested his gaze on Cromwell. "This is like a child's

puzzle. The answer is simple. One person directed me towards the hotel where two assassins were waiting. The bait? Mention of my dead father. It was bound to pique my interest. And who is behind this conspiracy?"

Black finished off the whisky, continued. "A man who likes expensive cigars. A man who is, arguably, the hottest movie star on the planet. So, Victor. In a nutshell – what the fuck is going on?"

Cromwell stirred, suddenly raising both hands in placation. "My God, Adam. You killed two men? Seriously? And the police? Did you call them? Honestly, I have no idea what you're talking about. This is insane! I need the hotel for a movie. The man who claimed he owned it, said he was your father, that he would only deal with you. What more can I say? Wow – two men? I don't know what I can say, Adam."

The sarcasm in his voice was not lost on Black. He responded in a quiet voice.

"Why don't you start with the truth. The Book of Dreams. Start with that."

"Now you're talking in riddles, old chum. But perhaps I can help. May I?"

He shot another of his winning smiles, and gestured to his mobile phone on the table.

"Let me text my good friend and general aide-de-campe, Mr Dalrymple. He organised the whole thing." He dropped his voice to an intimate whisper. "The truth is, he's been organising all sorts of things while I've been in Scotland. Don't know what I'd do without him. You don't mind? I don't want to appear rude."

Black acquiesced. "Of course not."

Cromwell pressed the buttons on his phone. "I've texted him. He'll be here in about one minute."

"He's here? In the hotel?"

"Oh yes, Mr Black. Right outside. Dalrymple is not only my assistant. He's my bodyguard. He's my... everything. He has special talents. Picked up in the not inconsiderable time he spent in the Special Forces, when he was a Marine, in the army."

He raised a hand to the side of his mouth, as if he were imparting a sensitive message. "He's useful when I feel threatened."

"Of course," said Black in a neutral tone. "One can never be too careful."

He waited, senses increased to a higher competence.

A man appeared at the table. Stocky, solid, blond hair cropped short, flat, hard features. Dressed in a fashionably cut dark suit, white shirt, dark tie. Black looked up at him, nodded. Dalrymple nodded back.

"Mr Black."

"Mr Dalrymple."

Cromwell sat back, assumed an easy posture.

"Thanks for coming so swiftly. To be blunt, Mr Black is becoming an irritation. Perhaps you would be so kind as to ask him to leave."

Cromwell stared at Black with eyes like flints. Dalrymple reacted with an almost-imperceptible shrug.

"Time to go, Mr Black."

Black's face changed to sudden consternation. "But the Lobster Thermidor!"

"Another time, perhaps," said Dalrymple.

Black stood. "That's a shame," he said, addressing Cromwell. "I was beginning to enjoy your company. Doubtless, we'll meet again."

"Who can say?" replied Cromwell.

Black turned to Dalrymple, facing him. They were a foot apart.

Black's tone was almost conversational. "Touch me, and I'll break your arm. That's a promise."

Dalrymple opened his eyes wide in mock horror. "Wouldn't dream of it, old boy. Now let's move along, shall we? Mr Cromwell has made his position clear. I believe he said you were an *irritation*. Let's keep this amicable."

"Let's."

Black nodded at Cromwell. Cromwell's lips curled into a sardonic smile, nodded back.

"Goodbye, Mr Black."

"Goodbye, Mr Cromwell."

47

B lack left the hotel, Dalrymple close behind him. Dalrymple waited back at the hotel entrance, as Black emerged onto the busy street. Black turned. "It was a pleasure. I hope we run into each other soon."

"Honestly," replied Dalrymple. "I don't think we'll be meeting again. Victor has a busy schedule. But I wish you the very best, old boy. In all your endeavours."

Black didn't respond. There was nothing he could do. The place was too public to try anything remotely physical. The encounter had been fruitless. He walked away, seething, with no clear plan. But then, what did he expect? To strongarm Cromwell into talking in the middle of a busy restaurant, as they sipped whisky, and waited for Lobster Thermidor? Even then, Black couldn't be sure Cromwell knew anything. But the arrows pointed in his direction. Plus, he had arranged lunch with Rachel. Presumably to illicit information. Black cursed his ineffectiveness. He was wandering in a fog, not knowing what was happening around him, lacking any control. What was the expression? *A hostage to fortune.*

He glanced behind him. Dalrymple was still there, ensuring his departure. Black had been shown the door with ridiculous ease. Perhaps he was losing his hard edge. He took a deep calming breath.

Wilkinson had given him forty-eight hours to find the Blood Eagle. He'd been told. Ordered. And if he didn't comply, Wilkinson had made it clear he had it in his power to hurt Black. Black hoped he'd minimised the risk, Rachel having gone to York. Still, Wilkinson was undoubtedly a resourceful man. Then again, so was Black. It seemed, however, at this moment, he was dancing to other people's tunes. He had to turn the tables. He had skills few others possessed. Now was the time to put these attributes to the test.

Cromwell was still the key. He knew where he was staying. The Raddison Blu. He would wait until later, and pay him a more intimate visit. He would take his chance with Dalrymple, and anyone else Cromwell brought in. Still, indecision rippled through his mind – Cromwell would undoubtedly be expecting him. He might change hotels. He might leave the country. A range of possibilities helped to muddy Black's plan. He turned a corner, into Ingram Street, just off George Square, and entered a small coffee shop. He ordered a flat white, and sat, disconsolate.

Everything emanated from the book he had been given by a stranger only days ago. The Book of Dreams. Or rather The Book of Nothing. It had been a ruse, a device, to persuade others that Black had been given something important, something which might jeopardise those people. The reason? Black could only guess – by attacking Black, Black would retaliate, and in the process, discover who had killed the old man's wife.

Black sighed. He was in the dark.

A man entered. A muscular, long-legged man with wide shoulders, dressed casually in narrow jeans, grey leather jacket.

Black recognised him instantly. Wilkinson's minder. Black recalled his name. Tommy.

Tommy waved, and sauntered over to Black's table, and sat opposite.

"Mr Wilkinson says hi."

Black sipped his coffee.

"He wonders how things are doing? How you're progressing?"

Black pursed his lips, as if considering a weighty response, then said, "Why don't you tell Ronnie to fuck right off."

Tommy narrowed his eyes. Black scrutinised the face before him. Lean, hard features, high cheekbones, robust jaw. A man who undoubtedly excelled at physical fitness. A man who exuded danger and lethal competence.

"That's just rude, Adam. And careless, for a man in your..." his brow creased as he searched for the right word, "...predicament."

Black made to leave.

"Don't you want to see Rachel?"

Black tensed, became still.

"Aha. Thought that might get your attention. Here, let me show you."

He pulled out his mobile phone from the inside pocket of his leather jacket. He swiped the screen, pressed some icons, stretched it across to Black, holding the screen towards him.

Black watched a video play. It was Rachel. She was sitting on a chair. She was bound and gagged, eyes wide, terrified, staring at the camera. A man he didn't recognise was standing behind her. In his left hand he held a revolver. Likely the same one used in the little game of Russian roulette played not so long ago.

The man at her side spoke, his voice clear. "Clock's ticking, Adam. And when the time comes, we start having our fun." He spun the chamber. "We'll see if she's as lucky as you." The video stopped.

Tommy tucked the phone back in his jacket pocket.

"So you see. You have a predicament. Or more accurately, Rachel does." He leaned forward. "Cute tits, by the way." He appraised Black with a broad grin. "Seems you need to come up with the goods. Mr Wilkinson is not a man who likes to be let down."

Black regarded him with a wintry gaze. "Whatever happens, I can guarantee the outcome remains the same."

Tommy's grin widened. "And what outcome is that?"

"Me killing you. By ripping off your head, if I'm lucky."

Tommy's face drooped in exaggerated disappointment.

"Strong words. Now you're being irrational. That will never happen. Plus, you have other much bigger things to think about. Take care, Adam."

Tommy nodded in a gesture of farewell, about to take his leave. Black darted forward, grabbed the back of Tommy's head, slammed his face down onto the tabletop. The movement was swift and unexpected. People jerked round at the sudden clatter. Tommy rebounded back, eyes glazed. Black patted him on the shoulder, as he made a hasty exit.

"Enjoy the coffee, Tommy."

Black left the building, walking quickly towards his car, parked a short distance away.

Now, circumstances had changed. He felt hollow inside, life sucked out of him. Matters had moved yet further from his control. He stopped, took deep breaths. Now was not the time to panic. Panic destroyed clear thinking.

If he failed to deliver the Blood Eagle, then Rachel would die. He had no doubts on that score.

Black straightened, kept his emotions in check. He had to

think. He had to act. He got to his car, got in. It was another hot, sunny day. He pressed a button. The driver's window slid down. He decided his course of action. He had it all the wrong way round. To act was counterproductive.

He had to do the precise opposite.

48

D S Paul Foster, and eighteen others, were dealing exclusively with the murder of the young woman. Thirty boxes of files and four cart loads of bagged evidence had been brought up from archives, and were placed across a group of tables pushed together – the previous victims clothing, shoes, jewellery, personal items, keys, tissues, make-up, everything found at the scene of each death. At the time of their murder, the perpetrator had stripped them, laying in neat order at their feet their personal effects and clothing. This time, however, the clothing and effects were missing. Plus, the new victim's face had been removed, which was a break in the pattern.

It was suggested that perhaps there was a copycat killer.

"How the hell do you copycat something like that?" said Wishart, addressing the room, pointing at one of the photos. "It's the same fucker. He's just got older, and less... fastidious." Foster glared around at his officers. "We'll get him this time. We've got to. This nutjob enjoys what he does."

Foster, and indeed all the others, had a profile of each of the victims. The only similarity, as far as he could tell, was that they were all women. Different backgrounds, different ages, different interests. The only other common feature was that they all lived in or around Glasgow. Which was a start, he mused. But not much of one. The identity of the dead girl was still unknown. The only feature was the tattoo on her arm. It was a number, in blue dye, performed in an almost cursory manner. Like a brand. Certainly not a fashion accessory. The police were aware of such markings on trafficked women. But it was a common feature. Like hunting for the metaphorical needle.

"We dig, and we dig," said Wishart, his bloodhound eyes roaming the room. "We look for connections. We go over all the stuff already done. Every detail. We double check. We cross reference. Mistakes may have been made. We may have missed something. We retrace our steps. Then retrace them again."

Dig, dig, dig. Foster looked forlornly at the column of files by his desk. It was difficult to know where to start. They had been granted overtime – which meant working round the clock. Foster had no family to go back to, and could handle it. The image of the dead woman reared up in his mind, unbidden. Until now, he thought he had witnessed every gruesome deed man could inflict on his brother. But the dead woman had shaken him. It seemed evil had set a new boundary.

At the desk opposite, sat his friend and colleague, DS Stephen Blair. Older, looking at retirement in three or four years. Attractive – blond hair, straight nose, candid blue eyes, strong, stern chin – one of the fittest men in the team. Squash player, runner. But in the same vein, a buddy who could sink pints with the best of them.

Blair had at his side a similar pile of files. He was staring at his computer screen.

"Where the hell do you start?" Foster said.

Blair glanced round, gave a sour grin. "Christ only knows. There's nothing worse than going over old case notes."

"Yes there is!" barked Wishart, from the other side of his room. "Like my fucking boot up your arse!"

Point taken, thought Foster. Also a reminder – his boss's hearing appeared not to have diminished with his age.

With a sigh, he picked up the first file which came to hand. Evelyn Wilkinson. The third girl to die. He studied the notes. Evelyn Wilkinson. Daughter of Ronald Wilkinson. A known felon, extortionist, gangster.

A good place to start.

49

The morning started with the fat man bellowing like an animal. He stood at the bottom of the ladder, and waited for them to clamber down, one at a time.

He pointed to the door of the barn. "Kitchen."

Danika walked by him. She tried not to look at his face, but couldn't help herself. Rough-shaven, swarthy skin, almost doll-like features. A tiny chin, lost in a welter of fat. Hair greasy and scraped from his forehead, behind his ears, tied at the back into a ponytail. He smelled of sweat and shit. They filed out, into the daylight. She guessed it was early morning. She blinked in the strong sunlight. She was met with a cacophony of sound – the howling and barking of dogs.

Another man was standing in the courtyard. He repeated what the fat man said, pointing to the door of the main house. *Kitchen.* He was the other individual who had been in the room when Monica had been murdered. The fat man's brother. Danika studied him more closely – hooked nose, sharp jaw. Darting eyes. Skinny. Silver rings glittered from his ears. He smelled too – of sweat and stale wine.

They trouped through the door as instructed, a sad, listless line, into the kitchen. In the centre, a large table, and on it, boxes of cereal, and bowls and spoons and several cartons of milk.

They circled the table. The skinny man came in – *eat!*

Danika suddenly realised she was hungry. She filled her bowl, and began to eat where she stood.

"Good, yes?" said the skinny one.

They all nodded, pale pinched faces, etched in exhaustion and fear.

Suddenly he leaned over, banged his fist on the table. "I said good, yes? Fucking smile!"

They all jumped, jerked their heads towards him.

He slapped the girl closest to him, hard and fast. She screamed, her breakfast bowl flipping from her hands.

"Fucking smile!"

Danika did as commanded, performing a tight, frightened smile.

"Better," said the man. "You've got to smile at the men. So they know you want to be fucked. Understand? You've got to show you want it. All the time." He regarded the girl he had slapped. "Clean that fucking mess up."

They ate, silently. Nothing was said. Ten minutes passed, the man standing in a corner of the room watching them all with small piercing eyes. Danika tried not to look at him. He picked up a pile of towels on the kitchen counter.

"Out."

They went back out into the courtyard, where the fat man was waiting. He was holding a hose, connected to an outside water tap fixed on a wall.

The skinny one joined him.

"Line up," he said. "Strip."

Danika took a deep breath, glanced at the others. They wavered, uncertain.

"Okay," said the skinny one. From his trouser belt hung a

leather sheath, a foot long. He unclipped the top, and pulled out a metal-handled butcher's knife. He raised it before him.

"See this!" he shouted. "I'll use this to cut off your fucking tits. You understand? Strip!"

They did, without further hesitation. Danika stood, under the morning sunshine, naked, along with the other young women, garments at their feet. She shivered. It was not cold. It was fear which made her teeth chatter.

The fat man went over to the tap, turned it. Water spurted from the pipe, then flowed faster. He kept turning, the water surging.

He walked back, to stand ten feet from the line of girls.

"Water sports!" The skinny man laughed. The fat one aimed, drenched the first in line, then moved to the second, then the third. The water was freezing and powerful. It stung Danika's skin. She hunched against it, half turning.

He went down the line, drenching each one in turn. He finished, waddled back to the tap, turned the water off.

The skinny one spoke. "Come and get towels. Dry yourself off." Danika made her way over, dripping on the grey flagstones of the courtyard, took a towel, aware that both men were gazing at her body. She felt scared, humiliated, violated.

They each got a towel, dried themselves off.

The skinny one snapped his fingers. "Hurry! Hurry!"

Danika darted a glance at them – to her horror, she noticed the fat one rubbing the crotch of his jogging trousers.

"Your clothes, we burn," said the skinny one. "My brother will give you new clothes later. For now, you stay naked." His lips curled up into a leering smile. "Back to the barn. Any trouble, you get a taste of this." He waved the knife.

The fat one made his way back to the barn door. He waited there, each passing through and, as they did so, he cupped his hand between their legs.

Danika almost retched when she felt the touch of his rough fingers.

They climbed the ladder to the upper level of the barn, and lay huddled on their mattresses, sobbing.

Outside, mingled with the barking of the dogs, she heard the men's laughter, then more chat. Danika squinted in the sunlight slanting through the spaces in the roof timbers, and a new certainty formed in her mind. If she didn't escape, then she would rather die.

50

Rachel had been ushered into the back of a Land Rover, parked a short distance from the train station – a man sitting on each side, the third man in the front passenger seat. A fourth man, the driver, had been waiting for them.

They had driven for a half hour. Rachel had no idea where they were, where they were going. Her mind was blank. The outside passed by, but she was oblivious, blinded by terror.

The man in the passenger seat had been talkative. He'd introduced himself as Tommy.

"What do you want?" she had asked, not recognising the sound of her own voice. A voice frail, husky.

"You need to speak to Adam about that," Tommy had replied, conversationally. "When you see him again. *If* you see him again. Play it cool, Rachel. Don't try anything stupid. It'll all work out, I'm sure."

"I haven't done anything," she'd whispered.

Tommy had sighed, as if he'd heard such a statement a million times. "That's got nothing to do with it. It's not what you've done, or not done. It's *you* that's important. And while we've got you, we can influence what other people do. Like

Adam Black. You know, I think he's the type of man who would burn the entire earth down to keep you out of harm's way. That's what we're counting on. You like music?"

They had arrived at their destination to the tune of Led Zeppelin.

She had been led through the front door of a big house, set back from the road, enclosed by high copper coloured iron railings. Smooth white stucco walls, a pillared entrance, balconied windows above. She'd entered a wide hallway of dark wood panelling and vaulted ceilings, of candelabra lights and impressive paintings. They'd got to a door, which Tommy had unlocked, using a key from a batch of keys on a ring. She'd been taken down steps, to a basement – a long, wide room, with a carpeted floor, recessed ceiling illumination giving a warm, amber cast. A pool table, chairs, a dining room table. A sideboard cabinet, upon which were bottles of liquor, and an assorted selection of bottled beer.

She'd been told to sit on a chair. She'd been gagged, a strip of cloth wrapped over her mouth, tied behind her head, her wrists secured to the armrests.

"Look nice for the camera," Tommy had said. He'd pointed his phone, taken a picture.

He'd tapped a button on his phone, spoke. "Where is he?"

Tommy had raised an eyebrow when he heard the response, nodded. "I'll be there in half an hour."

He'd turned his attention back to Rachel.

"Adam likes to live it up a little. We've had him followed. Both of you for that matter. As you languish here, all tied up and scared shitless, Mr Black is having dinner in one of Glasgow's finest hotels. The Princess, no less. Lucky him." He'd given a stupid grin. "When the cat's away. I'm leaving you now, Rachel, in the company of these three fine men, who will look after you. I have to pay your lover a visit, and show him my photographic skills. I won't be long." He'd turned to the three others, who were setting up the pool table.

"If she tries anything funny," he'd said casually, "then you have my permission to knock her about a bit."

He'd winked at Rachel, and then he'd left.

Rachel sat, wrists still tied to the arms of the chair by plastic cord.

"I'm thirsty," she croaked.

One of the men came lumbering over, went to the cabinet, opened a cupboard door, revealing a small fridge. He pulled out a bottle of still water. With a penknife he cut the cord to one of the wrists, and handed her the bottle.

She drank. "Thank you."

The man, dressed in a loose, lime-green tracksuit, muscular and easy of movement, grunted in response, and headed back to the pool table.

Rachel tried to see things rationally, calm her mind, her pounding heart. But it was difficult. She was in a world strange and terrifying, for reasons beyond her comprehension. The thought which had lurked in the shadows came to the fore, suddenly. She stifled back a low sob. She had seen their faces. They didn't care. Which meant what? She sipped the cold water, her hand shaking.

It could mean anything, she reasoned. They thought she was no threat, perhaps. Too scared to testify. She rested the bottle on the side of her face. Or maybe something else... She was disposable. She was collateral damage, and her seeing their faces made no difference, in the end.

Her mind raced. There was no way out. Her life had come to this moment. And the moment was in the balance. They wanted

Adam in their power, and was using her to achieve it. The tears came, softly. The three men played their game, ignoring her, talking, laughing.

She cried, and prayed.

Time passed. Several hours, possibly. It was difficult to keep track. There were no windows, no daylight. The men played pool, ignoring her for the most part. She asked if she could use the toilet. She still had one wrist tied to the chair. One of the men cut away the cord, and gestured towards a door in the corner. She locked the door behind her, gazed at the small square mirror on the wall. The face which looked back, she did not recognise. This was someone else. Sunken eyes, deathly pale skin – a face riven with fear.

She returned to the chair. One of the men tied a fresh cord around her wrist, allowing her other arm to remain free. Unprompted, he handed her another bottle of water.

"Hot afternoon," he said.

She gave a wan, cheerless smile.

He went back to the pool table, and racked up more balls.

The door at the top of the stairs opened. She jumped.

At the top, glaring at her, was Tommy. He made his way slowly down, purposefully, to stand directly in front of her. The others stopped their game, stood silent.

She raised her eyes. He had a cut above his nose, his left eye was purpling. His lips twitched into an ugly grin.

"Blame Adam Black," he said.

Her breath caught in her chest. She stared at him. The world stopped.

Tommy was in a mad-dog rage. He'd been insulted, humiliated by Black in broad daylight, in front of strangers. Black had struck, Tommy had cracked his head on the table in the coffee shop, had momentarily lost consciousness. He'd come to his senses, to find people round him, trying to help. He'd pushed them off, left the place with a blinding headache, and sensing his eye beginning to swell.

He'd driven the fifteen miles back to the house in anger beyond words. With Tommy, once a line was crossed, the red mist descended, blocking all reason. When Tommy had parked the Range Rover in the driveway, he was far from rational. He was in a murderous frame of mind.

He regarded his captive, Rachel Hempworth, sitting before him. A guest of his boss, Ronnie Wilkinson. To create an extra element of persuasion in Black's quest to find The Blood Eagle. At that precise moment, Tommy couldn't give a shit about his boss, or the fucking Blood Eagle. What he did care about was getting even.

He could tell she was scared. It was etched in the lines in her face, it beamed from her eyes. He could smell her fear.

He turned his attention to the three men at the pool table. He sauntered over to them. "Give me that."

"What?"

He pointed. The man gave him his pool cue. He sauntered back to Rachel. He held the cue in one hand, resting against his shoulder.

"Do you love him?"

She swallowed, too scared to respond.

"I'm sure you do. Do you think he loves you?"

She blinked. She opened her mouth, didn't know what to say, eyes wide.

"Do you think he loves you because of your looks. Because you're a fine-looking woman, Rachel. A real fucking stunner. No doubt about that." He glanced round to the others. "Don't you agree, guys?" he said. "This one's a beauty."

The three men watched him, hovering over the pool table, uncertain as to what to do next. They had stopped playing. The silence was something solid, palpable.

"Or perhaps he's not as shallow as that," continued Tommy, his voice low and flat. "I hope so."

He manoeuvred the cue from his shoulder, letting it rest gently on Rachel's shoulder. She jerked away at its touch.

"Don't be scared," he whispered. He bent forward, looking at her.

"Do you think he'd love you if you were blind?"

She gave a small whimper.

"He might think differently, yes? What if you were scarred and blind? I mean badly scarred. Like, obscene. How would Adam feel about that? The type of scarring that might make him embarrassed to walk with you down the street. What do you think?"

He straightened, pool cue still placed on her shoulder.

"Here's the thing, Rachel. My boss, Ronnie Wilkinson, has given me – us – specific instructions. We mustn't kill you. At least not until Adam has fulfilled his task. But you understand, those instructions allow me scope. Scope to do other things, short of killing you. I would say I have pretty much a free rein. You beginning to see where this is going?"

She gasped, said, "Please. I have nothing to do with this."

He nodded solemnly. "I know. Which makes it a little more satisfying."

He lifted the cue, turned his back to her, facing the stairs.

He spun round, struck her on the side of the head. The cue stick snapped with the impact. The blow was enough to knock her and the chair over onto the floor. Tommy loomed over her, in his hand the broken shaft, sharp at one end, like a spear. She moaned, semi-conscious, blood welling in from her ear.

He got down on one knee, leaned his face close to hers. He spoke, his tone soft.

"You understand why I'm doing this, yes?"

He raised his arm, brought the sharp end down, through her cheek, penetrating gums, teeth, mouth. Blood spurted. He lifted, brought it down, stabbed her face – cheeks, nose, eyes. Her neck, clipping an artery. Not stopping. Six, seven, eight times. Her body convulsed. Her eyes lost focus, became glassy. All over in less than twelve seconds. Blood gushed in a rainbow arc from the gash in her neck.

The other men rushed over, hauled him back.

"What the fuck have you done?" one of them shouted.

"What I had to do," said Tommy, face creased into a ghastly smile. He dropped the shaft, hand wet and sticky.

Another crouched over her, placed his hand over the wound, in an effort to staunch the flow.

Another ran to the bathroom, came back with a towel, which was used to wrap round her neck. She convulsed again, then went into a series of spasms. Then lay still.

The carpet, the men over her, her face and the clothes she wore, the chair she was still tied to, were saturated in her blood.

Her pulse was checked. The men stood.

The man in the lime green tracksuit shook his head. He turned to Tommy. There was obviously only one thing on his mind. "You can tell the boss. No way are we taking the blame."

Tommy shrugged. "I'll tell him. Christ, that felt so fucking good."

51

Black drove back to his flat. He parked in a space in the street, directly outside. He opened the main communal door, went upstairs. The police had stuck some crime scene tape across the door frame. The lock was still broken. Black pushed the door open. It hadn't been touched since Wishart had suggested he leave. Shelves out, contents scattered, things discarded on the floor, cushions torn open, foam strewn – scrawled on the wall: *The Book of Dreams*. Black considered the words. It had all started from this.

A stranger had given him a message. The message was disguised as a book. The reason? To provoke a reaction in dangerous people, and so to establish the identity of the person who killed his wife. And why him? Black could only speculate. The old man said he had read about him in the news, which had triggered a memory from years back. Black righted one of the chairs, and sat. He pondered. The old man thought Black was a resourceful and capable man. This, coupled with Black possibly having met the old man's wife, had led him to believe Black was the perfect candidate for the job. Illogical, but then the old man was clearly unwell, displaying signs of dementia.

Matters had become vastly more complicated. Rachel was now in the equation. The people looking for the book were taking orders from someone referred to as The Blood Eagle. Wilkinson's daughter had been killed by someone with the same epithet. Wilkinson had set him a task. Rachel had been taken hostage, to ensure Black delivered.

He stood, restless. Every second was crucial. He began the job of tidying up, performing on autopilot. His senses were heightened, his nerves tingled. His plan might be foolish. He could be wasting valuable time. But what else could he do? His mind jumped from different scenarios. His only one tangible point of reference was Victor Cromwell, who presently was unreachable. Black knew if he could get to him – alone – and use appropriate measures, Cromwell would talk. It was Cromwell who introduced the Raven's Crown. It was Cromwell who wanted to talk to Rachel, presumably to get information? Black could only surmise. He swallowed down a sudden rise of panic – maybe Cromwell was a complete innocent? Maybe Black was going to fritter away the seconds, and maybe Wilkinson would follow through on his threat.

Black's plan was as simple as it was frustrating. He went through to the kitchen. Whoever had broken in was thorough. Every cupboard and drawer emptied, glasses, cutlery, plates swept out and left broken on the floor. He picked stuff up.

A noise. The creak of footfall. Black straightened. There, again! Movement in his hallway. Black resumed his tidying, his back to the open kitchen door, the nape of his neck prickling. He felt a sudden range of emotion – anxiety, excitement, dread.

He sensed a figure behind him. He turned. A man stood, framed in the doorway, holding a pistol, aimed at Black's chest. A Beretta. Two men behind him.

Black raised his hands. "I don't want any trouble."

The man before him was small, squat, wearing white jeans, a

plain yellow T-shirt. Heavy arms, broad chest. Swarthy skinned, unshaven, pinhole eyes set in a round, flat face, black hair combed up into a topknot. Beneath his right eye, a small tattoo. Lettering of some sort. Too small for Black to make out.

The man spoke, a heavy accent. Eastern European. "Where is the book?"

"It's not here."

The man's features remained indifferent. He twitched his head to the side, to the men behind him.

"Search," he said.

The two men rifled through stuff in the living room Black had only moments cleared away.

"Twice in two days," said Black. "Lucky me."

The man grunted, prodded the pistol. "Shut the fuck up."

Black shrugged. No words were spoken. The only sound was the scrape and thud of furniture being upended; items being discarded on the floor.

"Nothing," said one of the men. He was much taller than his friend, thin, spindle-shanked. Same swarthy skin, dark lank hair hanging past his ears. The other beside him was about the same height as the man with the pistol, but instead of muscle, rolls of fat. Puffy face, dark eyes, no discernible chin.

"Bedroom."

The two left, heading for Black's bedroom, while the squat man remained, pistol aimed at Black's chest.

"I promise you, you won't find it here."

The man regarded Black impassively.

Five minutes passed. The two men returned.

"Nothing."

"I told you," said Black.

"Step out of the kitchen."

The man with the pistol backed out. Black followed, slowly, showing he was no threat.

The man spoke out the corner of his mouth. "Check."

Black was gestured into the centre of the living room, while his kitchen was ransacked.

After a brief period, the two men came back into the living room. The three stood in a line, facing Black.

"Where is it?" said the man with the Beretta. "Tell me now, or I'll shoot you. Understand this?"

"That's clever," replied Black. "Then you'll never find the book. What would your boss say, I wonder? What would the *Blood Eagle* say, when he realises you killed the only person in the world who knows where the book is? Understand?"

Reading the man's face was like understanding a slab of wood.

"Come with us."

"Where are we going?"

"Wait and see."

52

Victor Cromwell had no appetite for lunch. The impromptu meeting with Black had soured his mood. He hadn't been prepared for it. It would never have happened if Lyle Taylor had fulfilled what he had promised to do. He felt exposed, vulnerable. Scared. As soon as Black had left the building, he'd asked Dalrymple to arrange another suite, in another hotel. Preferably not in Glasgow. Dalrymple arranged a suite of rooms in the Plaza, in Edinburgh city centre. Expensive, but money was no problem to Victor Cromwell. Cromwell left the restaurant, to sit in the bar area. It was busy. The décor was elegant and subtle. Sandalwood flooring, black and ivory panelled walls, slender columns. The ceiling was high, the room bathed in a soft warm glow from hidden downlighters. He sat in a booth. He felt secure in a crowd. He asked Dalrymple to join him. He ordered a Bloody Mary. For Dalrymple, it was a soda water and lime, with a slice of lemon.

Dalrymple sat, said nothing, waiting for Cromwell to initiate conversation.

"Your boss should have taken care of him," said Cromwell. "This is not funny. The man is dangerous."

"Black?"

"Who the fuck do you think I'm talking about. Fucking Santa Claus?"

"Don't get stressed over this, Victor. If Mr Taylor says he'll sort it, then he will."

Cromwell gave a sarcastic smile. "Easy for you to say. You're over there. It's me that's in the hot seat. And Lyle Taylor. He failed the first time. Maybe this guy Black is tougher than anticipated. You know his background?"

"Mr Taylor told me. Ex-SAS, I believe."

"Too fucking right."

A waiter appeared, placed the drinks on the table, each with its own little paper mat, with the hotel insignia printed on a corner. Before the waiter had left, Cromwell fired back his drink in one, placed the glass back on the table, and ordered another two. "Quick as you can," he snapped.

The waiter nodded, took the glass, swept away.

Cromwell leaned forward on his elbows, dropped his voice low.

"These SAS guys. They're fucking crazy. They're real hard asses. Maybe 'Mr Taylor' has underestimated the situation. Maybe 'Mr Taylor' has fucked up."

Dalrymple responded with a small lift of his shoulders. "I'm sure he's come across a lot worse than Adam Black. He's only one man. And anyway, I dare say if I'm asked, I'll be able to handle him."

Cromwell sat back. "Which begs the question, why didn't he ask you?"

"My job is to look after you. Not to waste my energies elsewhere. And of course, to find you suitable female companionship."

"Talking of which, have you selected one?"

Dalrymple nodded. "A batch has just come in. One girl in

particular. Feisty. Flaming red hair. Strong features. Clean limbed. I think you'll like her."

"Good." Cromwell licked his lips. "And not someone who'll... be missed?"

Dalrymple's lips curled into something approaching a smile. "They're bought and paid for. Goods, to be used as you deem fit. Owned by you. No one will ever miss these girls."

A silence fell between them. The place was alive with the constant hum of conversation, chat, punctuated by occasional laughter.

The waiter returned, with two Bloody Marys, on a silver tray, which he placed on the table before Cromwell.

"Stay," he ordered. The waiter remained, expressionless. Cromwell sank both, each in one go.

"More," he said. "Another two."

"He really shook you," remarked Dalrymple.

"No fucking wonder, Einstein." Cromwell's speech was tainted by a slight slur. "It's quite easy, really. At the behest of Lyle Taylor, I was to persuade him to take a trip to sunny Loch Lomond, to that shithole, The Raven's Crown. The idea being, because it's me, and by mentioning his father, it would be enough to arouse Black's curiosity. Let's be honest – if you were asked to help out a movie star, you wouldn't say no. To quote a cliché, Black's father was to be the icing on the cake. And it worked! But then it fucking burst apart. Black was supposed to have been... taken care of. Black didn't follow the script. Turned the tables, so to speak. You can see where I'm going with this, yes?"

Dalrymple nodded, spoke in a quiet, sober voice. "To Black, you're the key. You're the only link he has to find out what's going on. Don't fret. He'll be taken care of. I repeat. He's only one man."

"All because of some fucking book," muttered Cromwell. "All because of *him*."

"Him? You mean Black?"

Cromwell shook his head. "Someone else. It doesn't matter."

The waiter returned, again with two further drinks. He placed them on the table, hesitated, waiting for a fresh order.

"That's all," said Cromwell. "For now." He downed one glass. He sipped the other. "I have to pace myself," he said.

There was movement, over at the bar. Three females, who had been sitting on high stools, all simultaneously shuffled off their seats, and tentatively made their way over to Cromwell's booth. Cromwell had seen such behaviour a million times. They were giggling, looking sheepish.

"Excuse me, but we couldn't help wondering – are you Victor Cromwell?"

Cromwell assumed a well-practised smile. "In one."

"We're so sorry to intrude, but can we...?" She raised her mobile phone.

Cromwell clicked into autopilot, assuming a beaming smile. "It's picture time. And your name is...?"

He dialogued, played the movie star, but his thoughts churned, his mind was elsewhere.

This man Adam Black frightened him. And he had a bad feeling.

53

It occurred to Black that if this were a game of chess, he would be playing the role of pawn. A piece with little or no power or influence. Dispensable. Thrust into the action, blind and helpless, to be used and then discarded. This was the second time in two days he had been ordered to sit in the back of a car, flanked by those who would seek him harm. He didn't like it. But he had little option. His feelings on the matter were secondary to the tide of events sweeping round him.

He was in the back of an SUV. Not as upmarket as the BMW driven by Wilkinson's men. It was grey and battered. But the intentions were the same. Black was a prisoner, to be taken somewhere unpleasant. At least on this occasion he had been expecting it. The short, stocky man drove. Nothing was said.

"Where are we going?" ventured Black. No response.

Black took care to watch the passing landscape. They were heading out of Glasgow, to a place familiar. North, in the direction of Loch Lomond. They turned at Tarbet, the Tarbet Hotel on their left, trees sloping down to the waterside on their right. Funny how a day can make such a difference. The previous morning, he had passed these places, the foremost feeling one of curiosity. Now the world was upside down, inside out. Now, he was driving by these places, wondering if he would live or die. Wondering if Rachel would live or die.

They drove past the lochside, the road winding, at some points the car only feet away from the loch. The water was flat, calm. It was late afternoon. The sun was still high, casting a melancholy sheen to the surface. They passed the turn off for the Raven's Crown. Black was fully expecting them to pull in. They sped by.

They reached the village of Crianlarich, eight miles beyond the northern most tip of the loch. They continued north, through Tyndrum, then still north, the land changing. Now, both left and right, the expanse of the Rannoch Moors. Sweeping plains of boggy marsh and wild grass, speckled with the occasional moss-coated boulder, the landscape rising and falling like the swell of an ocean. In the distance, brooding silhouettes of Scottish mountains. Black had once trained here, a lifetime ago. Hefting a forty-pound Bergen rucksack, trudging through ice pools and snow plains in the heart of winter. Freezing hands and freezing feet. Not a place he had fond memories of. Now he was back again, in circumstances considerably more dangerous.

They drove on, twenty miles or so, then slowed at a narrow turn off, easily missed. A single-track road, snaking up and through into the heart of the moorland.

"I had no idea we were sightseeing," said Black. The men didn't respond.

The car journeyed for some distance, possibly ten miles or so, the main road lost from sight behind them. Nothing but wilderness all around. It was early evening. The sun was dipping. Black squinted through the windscreen. In the distance, structures, buildings, partially hidden by the curves and slopes of the land. They drew nearer. Black saw walls, a wide double gate, and behind, farm buildings and outhouses of stone and wood.

The car stopped at the gate. A man waved, rattled loose some chains, pulled the gate open, one at a time. Black noted he wore a shoulder holster over his shirt, and tucked in it, a pistol.

"Subtle," he remarked.

The SUV drove through, stopping in a courtyard of grey concrete slabs.

One of the men next to him opened the car door, got out. Gesturing with a 9mm Glock, he directed Black to do the same.

Black got out, as did the other man sitting next to him. The SUV pulled away, and drove through the open doors of an adjacent barn.

Black took stock of his surroundings. The courtyard formed a rough square, maybe a quarter acre in size, enclosed by various sizes and types of buildings. On one side, the main house, he surmised. A large three-storey structure, in need of repair. Heavy, dull grey stone; cracked windows; vegetation trailing from leaning gutters. Around, outbuildings. Three barns, one in which the SUV had gone. Several flat-roofed sheds. Plus, a compound of concrete blocks with no windows, from which came the sound of maybe a half dozen barking dogs.

The man at the gate joined them. Black faced three men, each sporting different types of handgun, each as deadly as the next. The driver of the SUV came sauntering over from the barn, rope curled round his arm. Four men.

The door of the main house opened. An obese man stepped out. He was drinking from a bottle of cola. They spoke in a language Black recognised as Romanian.

The driver eventually fixed his attention to Black.

"Turn round." Black did as instructed, his back to the house. He sensed the men approaching. One of them pressed the tip of his pistol to the side of his head. Another pulled back his hands, bound them with the rope.

"Inside."

Black turned, made his way into the main building, followed by four armed men. The fat man moved to one side.

"Welcome to the Farm."

54

Danika watched, one eye up close to a small gap in the wooden planks of the barn. She saw the big man get out of the car. The others had their guns on him. She saw them tying his hands. She saw him enter the house. The men followed him in. The door closed.

"What are you seeing?" asked the girl next to her, her voice a soft hush, a French lilt to her accent. Danika didn't know her name.

"They've kidnapped someone," replied Danika. "They've taken him into the big house."

"Will they kill him?"

"I don't know." She turned to the girl. "You know the expression?"

The girl looked at Danika, eyebrows furrowed in confusion. "I don't understand."

"The enemy of my enemy?"

The girl stared at her blankly.

"It doesn't matter," said Danika.

She thought, maybe God was listening after all. If her captors were distracted, she might have a chance. She pressed against the wood. It was loose. All the timbers were rotten and fragile. A little pressure, her hands covered with the blanket to muffle the sound, and she would be out. She could creep down the side of the roof, like a cat burglar. Provided it could take her weight. What then? She had no idea. The sound of the dogs never stopped. They would hunt her down, and if she wasn't torn to pieces, then the men would kill her.

Again, for the hundredth time, tears welled up, which she forced down. She made a decision. She would rather die than live like this. The image of the man held at gunpoint flashed into her mind. He walked into the house like a man who had a belief. Like a man who wasn't scared. Perhaps escape wasn't so important, she thought. Maybe *he was* the answer.

Maybe *he* was the miracle.

55

D S Foster started with the file on the third girl. Evelyn Wilkinson. The murders were over twenty years old. All the facts were on A4 paper, either handwritten or typewritten, treasury tagged in robust manila files. Before things were automatically committed to computer, which was the way Foster preferred.

He was quite young for Detective Sergeant. The reason was down to fast-track promotion. Foster joined the police force after getting a first-class honours degree in English and Politics at St Andrews University. He had a flair for remembering things. Some may have described it as a *photographic memory*, which in Foster's opinion, was a perfect cliché. Nevertheless, he had a sharp mind. Plus, another ability. He had, what his tutors described with some envy as, the knack of thinking out the box. Foster didn't hold to any of that. His view was simple. That once he got his teeth into something, he didn't let go, and looked at things from every angle.

Which was what he did with the file of Evelyn Wilkinson. He pored over the contents. He studied the photographs. She was a pretty girl. She was bright, and doing well. A student, her whole life before her. Her mutilated corpse bore no relation to the young woman in her earlier pictures. The file, two inches thick, was all about her, and rightly so. Every thread of her existence explored. Everything followed up, looked at, dismissed. Members of her gym club; fellow students, lecturers; she was part of the university drama club – every fellow actor was interviewed. Her dentist, her doctor, her hairdresser, her neighbours, her friends, boyfriends past and present, her school teachers. Her family.

Foster latched on to Wishart's words. He'd referred to her father, Ronnie Wilkinson. Foster had never met the man, but was aware of his reputation. A gang leader. A career criminal, who'd risen to the top by way of shocking violence. But clever. Devious. He had been questioned about his daughter's murder. It was clear he had no involvement in the matter, and indeed, why would he? But Foster chose to look from a different perspective.

He closed the file on Evelyn Wilkinson, and called up information on her father. The list of his criminal activities was impressive. Foster scrolled down. Theft, extortion, blackmail, serious assault. Suspected of murder, attempted murder. He'd been in and out of prison from a teenager, up until he was in his late thirties. Then the trouble stopped. Presumably, he'd reached a level where others performed duties on his behalf. Foster printed off a recent photograph of Ronnie Wilkinson, and placed it to one side.

Foster considered. He switched the computer off, got the files on the other two victims. Molly Deacon and Norma Stark. Again, photographs, notes, statements. Molly had three brothers. One an accountant, one owned an MOT station, one a social worker. He punched their names in the computer, expecting nothing. To his surprise, something came up. Barry Deacon. Same address. Owner of 'No. 1 MOT Garage', which then was based in Croftfoot, Glasgow South. Prior to the murder of his sister, he had been charged and convicted. Assault.

He downloaded the man's photograph, placed it beside Ronnie Wilkinson.

He sat back, rested his hands round the back of his head, pondered. It was probably nothing. But on the other hand...

He opened the file on Norma Stark, and studied its contents.

56

Black entered the kitchen, and was told to sit on one of the chairs. Three of the men had pistols, the fat man had a shotgun, all pointed in Black's direction. The fifth man untied the rope round his wrists, pulled his arms round the back of the chair, retied his wrists. He stood back.

Black regarded the men standing round him. "Which one of you is the Blood Eagle?"

He was ignored. One of them spoke into a mobile phone. His English was perfect, his voice betraying only the slightest of accents.

"He's here. He's at the Farm." He nodded, disconnected. He scrutinised Black with burning intensity. He was thin, narrow head, sloe-eyed.

"Let me introduce you. My name is Marco. These men beside me are Cristian, Stefan and Darius. And this is my brother." He pointed to the fat man. "You can call him Beast. That's his nickname, and for good reason. We're pleased to have your company. I would have introduced you to Luca and Andreas, but you met them already. Maybe you remember?"

Black met the man's gaze.

"I do. Charming men. Killing them was..." Black pursed his lips, "...most enjoyable. Where is the Blood Eagle?"

"Why so impatient? We have all evening to spend together. Are you comfortable? Would you care for something to drink?"

"Glenfiddich, if you have any. Neat. No? Fair enough. Where are you from? Moldavia? I recognise the accent. Though you hide it well."

The man shrugged. "Where I'm from has little consequence. You should have other things on your mind, Mr Black."

"I'll only talk to your boss. The Blood Eagle."

The man's heavy eyebrows curled inwards, in a gesture of puzzlement.

"How do you know I'm not the Blood Eagle? Or my brother, for that matter?"

Black's face broke into a wolfish grin. "You're far too stupid. And your brother? Not only stupid, but fat and ugly. And he stinks. Please. I hardly think so."

The sides of the man's mouth drooped. The fat man strode forward, slapped Black across the face with the back of his hand. He was pulled back by the others. His brother clicked his tongue, indicating mild irritation.

"I sense it's going to be a long night, my friend."

Black's head spun. The blow was stinging. His cheek felt numb.

"Not if you let me speak to the Blood Eagle. I know what you want. What he wants. Face to face. I'll tell him where it is."

The man sniffed. "Tell you what, spend some time with us first. See how that works out. You might find, after a little persuasion, that there is no need to speak to anyone else. That sounds like a good plan, yes?"

Black moved his jaw up and down, trying to shake off the gathering pain.

"Lovely establishment you have here, though I would sack

the interior decorator. What is this? Let me guess. Women. Children. Trafficked. You bring them to this shithole, and then what? Move them on? Ship them out to the highest bidder?"

"What difference is it to you? Tell us where the book is."

Black continued as if he hadn't heard.

"But then abduction and enslavement are your speciality. It's what you do. But really, what's with the wallpaper. And the smell. Maybe your fat brother should consider a bath. For the sake of humanity."

The fat man tried to burst forward a second time, but was restrained by hands gripping his arms and shoulders.

"You're making this very difficult. But if that's what you want."

He turned to the other four men.

"Lift the chair. Take him to the Big Room."

57

Tommy left his men in the basement with the dead body of Rachel Hempworth, instructing them to clean the blood off the carpet, and wait until he returned. This was something he would need to report to Ronnie Wilkinson about personally. As soon as he had calmed down, the enormity of his actions permeated. He'd gone too far. The orders from Wilkinson were simple. Get her. Hold her. The chances were she was to die anyway. That was not a decision for Tommy to make. But he had made it nevertheless. Still, to Tommy, it was not his fault. Black had brought this on. It was down to him.

Wilkinson was at his restaurant. It was early evening. The place would be getting busy. Tommy decided he would drive out to Houston. Twice a week, Wilkinson liked to dine at a small discreet table while customers ate around him.

Tommy arrived at the Thirsty Fox, parked the car, made his way through the pub, then upstairs to the restaurant. He spied Wilkinson immediately, sitting unobtrusively in a corner.

The place was full. Also, several people sat at the bar, waiting for a vacant table. The room was alive with the sound of conversation. Three waiters and two waitresses scurried about, scribbling down orders, bringing food, lifting plates. Tommy went immediately over to Wilkinson's table. He was eating lasagne. On the table was the customary bottle of wine and a full glass, from which he was drinking. He claimed he hated the stuff, but consumed copious amounts.

"Can I?" Tommy nodded to the single chair opposite.

Wilkinson stared at him for an uncomfortably long time before he answered. "This had better be good."

Tommy sat.

Wilkinson shovelled a forkful of food in his mouth, swallowed, took a sip of wine. Tommy waited.

"Well?" said Wilkinson.

Tommy scratched his head. He was careful to keep his voice low. "We've hit a problem."

"We?"

Tommy licked his lips, which suddenly felt very dry. "The girl. Something happened."

Another mouthful of food. Another drink of wine.

"Tell me, Tommy – what happened. I'm interested. Because the instructions were very simple. You grab her, and you take her to the house, you show Black a nice picture, and you keep her there. A child would understand, yes? So, what happened, Tommy?"

Tommy leaned forward. "It was that bastard Black. He did it."

"Did what?"

"Look at my face, Mr Wilkinson."

"Looks like someone's given you a battering. But I fail to see where this is going."

Tommy ran a fretful hand across the top of his shaved head. "We got the girl. No problem. We took her to the house. We followed Black to a coffee shop in town. I showed him the picture." Tommy fell silent.

Wilkinson finished off his glass. "Let me guess. Black didn't take too kindly to seeing his girlfriend kidnapped and all trussed up. Hence the bruising on your face, I imagine. What did you expect? But that's not the problem, is it Tommy?"

Tommy bowed his head. "No, sir."

"No, sir. It's nice when you're respectful to me. But it also tells me you're about to impart something I don't want to hear."

Tommy leaned forward, his voice cracking when he spoke. "He did this to me in front of strangers. I was..."

"You were offended. What did you do?"

Tommy took a deep breath. This was it. "I went back to the house. I was in a rage. Saw red. I lost control. I got rough with the girl."

Wilkinson nodded slowly, as if deliberating carefully what Tommy had just said. "You got rough," he echoed. "Is she dead, Tommy?"

"Yes."

Wilkinson, with care, poured himself another glass of wine. He raised it to his lips, holding the glass delicately by its stem with thumb and two fingers, tilted the glass, let the liquid flow into his mouth, swallowed. He placed the glass back onto the table. "Did I tell you I hate this stuff?"

Tommy didn't reply. He waited. He never quite knew how his boss would react to situations.

Wilkinson placed his knife and fork together on the dinner plate. He lifted a red cloth napkin to his mouth, dabbed the corners.

"There's a chainsaw in the garage," he said quietly. "I don't want any mess. Buy a couple of large suitcases. Put rocks in as well, and dump them in the water. Make sure it's deep. Clean the basement. If there's blood on the carpet, get rid of the carpet. No traces, you understand? You've done this often enough."

Tommy understood. He had no shortage of experience when it came to the removal of dead bodies.

"She doesn't matter," continued Wilkinson. "It was always going to be this way. Just a little sooner than I had planned. So long as Black doesn't find out. He's on a mission. We'll take care of him later, when he comes up with the goods."

"You mean, if he brings you the Blood Eagle? What if he doesn't?"

"Then it doesn't matter. At least I can say I tried. And what's the worst? A dead journalist, and a dead lawyer. Who gives a shit. Now fuck off."

58

Cromwell got the call from Lyle Taylor. He was alone, in his bedroom, half pissed. The Plaza was far superior to the Radisson, he decided. Not that it mattered. As soon as this bullshit was over, he would fly back to sunny California, and put it all down to a distant nightmare, to be washed away by poolside drinks, clear beaches, and new projects. The film to be shot in Scotland would be shelved. His appearance in Glasgow had sparked a series of events, which he could never have foreseen. Or perhaps he was being naïve. Perhaps he should have realised that you can never really outrun the past.

Dalrymple was in a connecting room. A competent, quiet man. Given to him by Lyle Taylor during his stay in Scotland, as a bodyguard-cum-fixer. A *procurer*, he thought grimly.

Cromwell was lying on the bed, dressed in a complimentary hotel bathrobe. In his hand, the handkerchief, still stained after all those years. A lifetime ago. A symbol of a debt he still owed, to someone he had tried to forget. But a debt – *this debt* – lasted forever.

His mobile buzzed.

The voice of Lyle Taylor, launching straight in, ignoring any pleasantries.

We have him.

"About fucking time. Have you got it?"

Not yet. But my Romanian friends will find it soon enough. They're gifted, when it comes to inflicting pain. He'll tell us where it is, no problem.

"This whole thing's a fucking mess."

Which we all started. Let's not forget. We're all in it. The four of us.

"How can I forget?"

He hung up.

He lay, drifting into a half sleep. A soft knock on his door brought him round. He sat up.

"Yes?"

The door opened. Dalrymple stood. He always looked the same, thought Cromwell. He never showed signs of fatigue. As if he were immune from all the shit swirling around.

"I got the call from Lyle," said Dalrymple. "This is good news. Hopefully, in a matter of hours, you'll have what you want. Black will talk. Make no mistake. I know these people. He'll talk, he'll die, and your problem goes away."

Cromwell lay back down, staring at the ceiling. It was high, the cornicing an intricate embroidery of gold and silver swirls. The Plaza Hotel was old, possibly the oldest hotel in Edinburgh, and as such, possessed all the trappings of a bygone vintage.

"Black's a hard nut to crack," Cromwell said. "I'm surprised they got him so easily."

"Not that hard. Have we still the same arrangement tomorrow?"

"Yes," he muttered.

"Good. Where?"

Cromwell's head began to ache. He didn't want conversation. He wanted to sleep, wake up, and go home.

He rolled on his side, reached over to a pad of paper on the bedside cabinet, tore off the top page, stretched his hand out.

"I've written the address down. You'll get a call when he's finished with her. Make sure you're on time."

Dalrymple entered the room, took the paper, glanced at it, tucked it in his inside jacket pocket.

"I'm coming with you," said Cromwell.

"What?"

"To the place you get the girls."

Dalrymple's flat features creased slightly in mild bemusement. "You're coming to the Farm?"

"Is that what you call it? Yes." He sat up. The act made his head spin. "The last girl you chose for me, she wasn't what I was looking for. It wasn't what *he* was looking for. I have to make sure she's right. We'll put her in my car. I'll drive her to her... destination. Just as long as you pick him up when he's finished."

Dalrymple shrugged. "It's up to you. It's your money."

He turned to leave.

"Dalrymple?"

"Yes, Mr Cromwell."

"The last girl – has anyone said anything? Anyone wondering about her?"

Dalrymple smiled. "Not a soul. You don't need to worry. These girls – they come, and they go. No one cares. They are... how shall I put it?"

"Disposable?"

"Exactly."

59

It was 10pm. Foster hadn't left his desk, other than to go for a snack, or fill up his coffee cup. When he latched on to something, time lost its meaning. He stuck at it with the tenacity of a Rottweiler.

DS Stephen Blair was winding down. Like Foster, he'd spent the day ploughing through files, retracing steps that were twenty years old. When he approached Foster, his face was grey – a combination of weariness and exasperation.

"It's late. I'm off. Sleep. Fresh start. You coming?"

Foster looked up. "Fancy a drink?"

"You're kidding?"

"I've had a thought. It might be nothing, but then, who knows? I'd like your slant. Over a pint?"

"What the fuck." Blair sighed. "What the hell else am I doing?"

The Mill. A pub on a corner of Shawlands, on the south side of the city. The exterior unappealing – lime-green paintwork chipped and fading, window boxes on rusted metal brackets overgrown with weeds and dead flowers, walls of dismal brown stone. Inside was marginally better. A cluster of wooden tables with wooden chairs, the floor a combination of black and red tiles, set in no discernible pattern. The wallpaper, like the outside, lime green, dotted with wooden framed pictures of strangers' faces and banal landscapes. The place, as ever, was not busy. Which was why Foster and Blair liked it.

A television was fixed onto a corner, showing the news, the sound muted. The bar was varnished wood, stretching the length of the room, behind which was a simple gantry of whisky and spirits. The barman nodded, and took their order. A minute later, he produced two pints of lager. They took them over to one of the vacant tables, and sat across from each other.

"I should be asleep," said Blair dolefully. He drank some lager. "I suppose this is the next best thing."

"Who needs sleep when Glasgow offers such salubrious nightlife." Foster made a show of looking around.

"You're right. We're truly blessed. I wonder why they never put the sound on the television."

"Why bother when the chat is so stimulating."

"Valid point. Right, old pal, tell me all about it."

"I need you to have an open mind. If you're going to laugh, then do it discreetly. Do it while pretending to cough. Disguise it, so as not to hurt my feelings."

"Understood. Your feelings will be spared."

"Excellent. Okay." Foster leaned forward slightly. "I've been looking through the files of the three girls. Nothing connecting them, correct?"

"Nothing was found twenty years ago," replied Blair. "The attacks were obviously planned, given the method of killing. He would have needed his implements, and a place to work in solitude. But other than the crime itself, no connection."

"And?"

"Our killer may have spotted them in the street, a coffee shop, the cinema. Anywhere. Does his homework, establish where they live, their background, their habits, and then strike. He's careful, he's meticulous, and clever." Blair shook his head, and took another gulp of lager. "But no connection."

"Fair enough. But what if we've been looking in the wrong direction?"

Blair grunted. "Wrong direction?"

"We're searching all we can about the dead girls. What if we searched against someone else?"

"Someone else?"

"Sure. Bob Wishart mentioned Ronnie Wilkinson. The father of Evelyn. A well-known criminal. I checked his record. He started as a teenager, worked his way up."

"What's known as a career criminal."

"Exactly. Twenty years ago, he was forty-six. When his daughter was killed. Coincidentally, six months previous to that, he'd been arrested. Money laundering. The charges didn't stick. That was the end of it."

Blair blew through his mouth. "So? He had a good lawyer. He could certainly afford it. There has to be a point to this."

"Bear with me. I went back to the first girl. Molly Deacon. Worlds apart from Evelyn Wilkinson. Nothing to connect them. But let's look beyond her. She had a brother. He owned a garage at the time. He was charged with assault. He got into a fight, put a guy in hospital. He was convicted and served six months."

"Shit happens."

"So it does. Now the second girl. Norma Stark. A lawyer. No connections whatsoever to the other two. But let's look beyond her. She was married. I checked against both her married name and maiden name, which was Devlin. I checked the name in the computer."

He took a slurp of the lager, resumed. "A lot of Devlins came up. One in particular. Gary Devlin. I did a little more digging. He'd been charged with fraud. Some sort of mortgage scam. He was found not guilty. But guess what, old chum. I bit more digging and ta dah! Guess what?"

"What. The suspense is numbing my mind."

"Our friendly, wrongly accused fraudster turns out to be Norma's uncle – her father's brother. We have three dead girls. At first glance, nothing in common. But, after a modicum of hard work and startling insight from yours truly, we discover that in fact there is a link. They each are related to people who've had a tussle with our wonderful criminal justice system."

"You asked me to disguise my laughter," said Blair, "but I'm finding this difficult to do. Half the families in Scotland have got relations who've had some trouble with the law, if you were to look far enough."

"This is true. But it's something. It shows there's a common feature. Which sparks a different line of enquiry. No?"

"I don't see it. I agree with the facts. But it's not enough. You could look in each of the girls' wardrobes and find they each owned a red pullover. These are facts. But on their own, that's all they are."

Foster placed his pint glass carefully on the glossy wooden tabletop. He said, in a theatrically sombre tone, "Did they really each have a red pullover?"

Blair grinned. "We should call Wishart, and ask him."

"No thanks. Am I wasting my time? Don't hold back."

"Four words."

"Yes?"

"It sounds like shit."

"Glad you held back."

"But I know you, Paul. You'll keep on it, and then after a

week of zero results, I'll let you explain the whole thing to Wishart. Just make sure I'm not in the room."

"I think there's something in it." He took another drink. "I really do. My antennae is twitching."

Blair sighed. "Christ help us all. I have three years until retirement. My game plan is to lay low, don't do anything stupid, and buy a new set of golf clubs. Have you told anyone else about this revelation?"

"Nobody, except you. Thought I would use you as my sounding board."

"Well," replied Blair, finishing his lager, "now that you've sounded me out, I can give you some advice, from an old cynical cop to a much younger, more interested cop."

"Which is?" Foster smiled.

"Keep this to yourself. Don't tell a soul. And move on quick."

60

What is an evil man? He who compels obedience to his private ends,
violates beauty, creates pain, ends life. The destruction of evil men
should be more than a knee-jerk reaction of conscience.
It should be a duty.

Anonymous

Black, sitting shackled to a chair, was hoisted up by four of
the men. Marco and his brother – *The Beast* – watched the
process like two hyenas. He was transported from the kitchen,
through a long drab corridor, and into another room. Bare walls,
the plaster cracking, the illumination from a light bulb hanging
from the ceiling by a single wire, rough floorboards. A mattress
was shoved over to one side. He was lowered to the centre of the
room. The men left, locking the door behind them, leaving
Black on his own. There was a single window, with filthy net
curtains, the outside of the glass coated in grease and green
slime and bird shit, offering little view.

It was mid-evening. Black struggled with the bonds, but they were tight, impossible to break free. His plan, so far, had gone a little awry. He had allowed himself to be caught, the idea being that he would be taken to the one called the Blood Eagle. It seemed he wasn't here. He'd made it clear that he would only give up the location of the Book of Dreams to that one individual. Which meant he would have to endure. If, however, he could get free, he might inflict a little damage himself, coerce from one of them the whereabouts and identity of their boss.

But it looked like he was going nowhere fast. He inhaled through his nose, exhaling through his mouth, calming his mind. Rachel was out there, somewhere. Her existence depended on his actions. If he failed, then he was in no doubt Wilkinson would follow through his threat. A thought lurked in the shadows – one which he tried to dispel. But it formed in his mind, took shape like a demon. They would kill her, whatever happened. Or indeed, she may already be dead.

He had to focus. He'd spent weeks in the vast dungeons of Saddam Hussein, had suffered torture beyond imagination. He had been trained by the best survivalists in the world. Soldiers of the Special Air Service. Trained to cope with physical and mental abuse. The mind. The mind was the key. The mind could get you through it. And if you were still breathing after all the shit, then you were winning.

Time drifted. The tawny light of evening melted away to a more solid darkness. Outside lighting illuminated the courtyard. The baying of the dogs had settled; now it started up again. He heard a voice outside. He swung round. His vision was obscured. He detected movement. One of the men – a blur only – walking towards a low structure. One of the sheds he'd seen earlier. He was carrying a bag. The dogs became frenzied. Feeding time, surmised Black.

Black waited. Minutes ticked by. In time, the dogs fell silent.

Now, voices in the hall outside, approaching. A key in the lock. The door opened. Black braced himself.

Four men entered. The brothers, and two of the men who had escorted Black from his flat. They positioned themselves in a line, regarding Black for several seconds. The skinny brother – Marco – did the talking.

"We hope you're comfortable."

"Unbelievably."

"That's nice."

Marco dragged a chair across, positioning it three feet opposite Black, and sat.

He gazed at Black, as if he were considering a painting on a wall.

"Tell us where you've put the book. Tell us now, and we'll be kind."

"You'll be kind? That's a relief. Let me talk to the Blood Eagle. I'll tell him. No problem."

Marco leaned back, raising a shoulder in an offhand manner.

"Who cares? I'm the Blood Eagle. Tell yourself that. Or if it suits, my brother there, he can be the Blood Eagle. What does it matter? Tell us where it is."

"It matters to me. What time is it?"

"The time? That's not something you need concern yourself with. I think my brother would like to chat. His way." He swung round, nodded at the fat man – The Beast. Marco stood, moved his chair to one side. The Beast stepped forward.

Black looked up. Dangling from one hand, he noted, was a scourge. His brother Marco described it in detail, for Black's benefit.

"My brother has always had a fascination for these things. Me, I've thought them a little crude. This particular one, however, he made himself. A calf hide grip wound tight round a wooden handle. Attached, six leather thongs. What makes it unique are the extras. My brother has always been imaginative in this way. It's a passion of his. Each of the thongs thread through a variety of... what would you say... supplements. Is that a good word? There's sheep bone, lead spikes, metal balls. Also, entwined throughout, wood nails. Imaginative, yes?"

Black gave a crooked grin. "Wonderful. Could he wash first? I might die of his stink. Then what happens. Your employer will be upset."

Marco continued, in soft lilting tones, unruffled.

"But the common view is of the victim strapped up, all shackled, against a wall, being whipped across the back. This is a misconception. There are far more sensitive places."

He stepped to one side, made a delicate gesture to his brother.

The Beast took a step forward, and lashed Black across the face. A nail caught in his cheek, rending the skin. Black gasped at the pain. The Beast struck again, and then a third time. Black felt blood trickle in his eyes. His vision swam; his head spun.

Another man stepped forward, carrying a knife. He cut away Black's shirt, tossed it in a corner, leaving him naked from the waist up.

The Beast looked down at Black, smiling, spoke in a rumbling voice. "Who the fuck's laughing now, tough guy."

He raised one great arm up, and down, working on Black's chest, each thong armed with its little cargo, designed to eviscerate. Black clenched his teeth. The agony was searing, struck him to the core. He groaned. Nine, ten times. Black wavered in and out of consciousness. Someone splashed cold water on him. The Beast stepped back, sweating with exertion.

"Not nice," said Marco. "And it's only going to get worse. Unless..."

Black rolled his tongue in his mouth, swallowed back the

pain. He took a deep breath. He gave a smile, trying to keep his voice steady. "I think you gentlemen have misjudged the situation."

Marco folded his arms, cocked his head curiously, inspected Black. "Tell us. What have we misjudged? Enlighten us. Please."

Black had to concentrate. The pain was all-consuming. His chest, ribs and stomach a frenzy of torn flesh, every breath like a knife in the lungs.

"Your bargaining power. You haven't any."

Marco laughed. The others followed his cue, laughed with him.

"You're a remarkable man, Adam Black. How can you say such a thing?"

"Time's running out."

"For us?" Marco laughed incredulously. "We have all the time in the world. You on the other hand..."

"Tell me the time," mumbled Black. He was fighting a battle with the pain. The pain at that moment, was winning.

Marco shrugged. "For what it's worth – it's just after midnight. I think a long night."

"You have eleven hours," said Black.

"Until what... brunch?" A ripple of laughter.

"The book you want, right now, is in a sealed envelope with a lawyer. If he doesn't get my phone-call by 11am tomorrow morning, then his instructions are simple. He opens the envelope, copies the contents of the book, and arranges a courier to transport them to three newspapers. Whether they publish is anyone's guess. But it's your gamble. And then you can have brunch. But I'll make the call, and get you the book, only if you bring your boss here. I want to meet him, face to face."

Marco didn't respond for several seconds, a fixed smile stuck on his face.

"You're lying," he said softly. "I can see it in your eyes." Another glance to his brother, who loomed forward, and lashed out, whipping Black across the face, neck, chest. Backwards, forwards. Ten seconds' worth. He stopped, taking deep breaths.

"You like that?" the Beast said. He raised his arm once more, swept it down, rendering a thunderous backhanded blow to the side of Black's face, the impact enough to knock the chair on its side.

Black groaned, drifted into an almost dreamlike state. The pain had gone. He teetered on the brink of unconsciousness.

"Get him up." The voice of Marco. To Black, it sounded like an echo of a voice, spoken from afar.

He sensed being lifted, the chair set back. More freezing water splashed on his face.

"Talk to us, Black. Where is it?"

This time, Black didn't bother looking up. "Tick-tock. Your funeral."

"Fair enough. Looks like a long night." He nodded to one of the other men. "Open the window. It's going to get hot in here." The man went to the window, and with some effort, pulled it up by two feet, where it stuck. The slightest breeze wafted in.

"That better?" said Marco. "Good."

Black sensed, rather than saw, a movement. The looming presence of the Beast, as he brought the scourge down again. For Black, the pain had gone. He closed his eyes, slipped into darkness.

61

Danika lay on her mattress, listening to the sounds of the night. In this place – The Farm – the sounds were nightmarish. The baying and barking of the dogs, the cries of a man in pain from a room in the big house. The laughter of men as the pain was inflicted. A symphony of terror. And when the man cried out, the howling of the dogs intensified. None of the girls were sleeping. Sleep wasn't possible, under such circumstances.

"What are they doing?" whispered the girl who had spoken to Danika earlier.

"Killing someone," responded Danika in a flat voice.

"Who?"

"I don't know."

The night wore on. In this unreal world, Danika found it difficult to keep track of time. An hour passed. Maybe two. Maybe more. The sound from the big house diminished to silence. The dogs, perhaps exhausted, also quietened. Suddenly, without Danika quite realising it, the place was silent. She got up, crept to the side of the barn, put her eye up to the space between the planks. Below, the courtyard, the house. The indoor lights were out. A stillness had settled. An aftermath of the brutality. The only illumination, the glow from a single sconce on an outside wall, by the door. It gave a weak, yellowy light, casting another shade to the nightmare. She took three deep breaths. If she didn't act now, she never would.

The wood was weak and rotten, attached by rusted nails. She grasped the plank, gave a short, sharp tug. It cracked, came away in her hand. Her heart rose to her mouth. She froze. No reaction. The dogs didn't clamour, the door to the house didn't open. The night, so it seemed, remained undisturbed.

"Are you crazy?" The same girl again, her voice low, a husky whisper.

Danika ignored her. She clenched her teeth, pulled the next plank. This time, no sound. It fell into her hands. Another deep breath. The third plank came away. There was space for her to squeeze through. She looked out. Below, a drop of about seven feet, to the flat roof of a smaller shed-like structure, wedged to the side of the barn. She turned, looked at the rows of mattresses, and the shadows who lay on top, aware they would all be watching her, terrified.

"I'm leaving," she said quietly. "Who's coming?"

No one moved.

"They'll catch you," said the girl. "What happens then? What happens to us?"

Danika had no reply to give. She turned away, studied the gap she had created, made a decision, wormed her way through, legs first. She lowered slowly, hung by her fingertips for a second, dropped the short distance onto the roof of the lower building. She crouched down, hugged the shadows, nerves stretched, expecting the worst. She crept along, hunkered down, until she reached the edge. Another seven-foot drop. She looked about. The place was quiet. She slid over, clinging to the edge, dropped quietly. She crouched again, remained still. No sound, except her quick breathing. She wavered. She could scurry to a perimeter wall, climb over, and run into the night. Run anywhere, so long as it was away from this place.

But the man. The man tied up and tortured. She knew the room where he'd been taken. From her view in the barn loft, she had seen moving shapes through a dirt smeared window, heard the sound of his pain. He had been taken to the same room where the fat man had killed Monica. The window was a short distance across the courtyard, in the big house opposite. She wondered if he were still alive. She wondered, even in that moment of extremity, if she could help him. Her eyes darted, left, right. The dogs were silent. The men were probably sleeping, secure in the knowledge their captives were too scared shitless to move an inch from the barn.

Another deep breath. She raced across the open space, a fleeting shadow, to the front wall of the big house, skin tingling, feeling exposed in the open space. She pressed herself against the stone, shut her eyes tight, expecting the dogs to start up. Silence still. With her back to the wall, she sidled to the window. It was a quarter open. Enough space for her to get through. She turned, peered in. Only darkness. A noise. A soft groan. A vague silhouette of a man, sitting. She held her breath. The man was alive. She could turn tail, and run, melt into the night. But Danika had listened to him being tortured, for hours. Her instinct, whether foolish or not, was to try to save him. Plus, if they escaped together, then perhaps two was better than one. The windowsill was at the height of her waist. She manoeuvred herself, slithered through the gap.

Her nostrils twitched at the smell of raw sweat. The room was a cluster of shadows. In the centre, the man, sitting on a chair, hands tied behind him, chin resting on his chest.

She crept up. His shirt had been removed, his skin ripped.

She touched him gently on his cheek. He started, turned. She jerked her hand back.

"Can you walk?" she whispered.

The man looked at her. He was trying to focus. "Who are you?"

"My name is Danika. I was taken by these men. Held in the big barn. But now we can escape."

"No," he said, voice a dry croak.

"If I can get this rope loose." She turned her attention to the rope tied round his wrists. She pulled and tugged.

"No, Danika. It won't work. Go back. They find you, they kill you. Go back."

"I can't loosen this rope," she said, starting to cry. "It's too tight."

"Go back, Danika. Please."

She faced him.

"There's water in that jug." He nodded to the door. Danika saw a shape on the floor. She went over – it was a large stoneware jug half full.

She brought it over, placed it carefully to his lips, tilted. He drank.

"Put it back," he said.

She did so, returned to him. "I can't untie the rope. If I had something sharp."

"Go back to the barn, please. You don't need to worry about me. How many are there of you?"

"Fourteen."

The man looked at Danika, his eyes two black orbs. "I can get you out of this. You have to believe me."

"How can you do anything? You're tied up. In the morning, they'll probably..." She couldn't finish the sentence.

"No one's going to kill me."

She touched his cheek. "I'm sorry. What's your name?"

"Adam Black."

"I'm sorry, Adam."

She made her way back to the window, turned. The man called Adam Black was looking at her. She climbed through the open window, and keeping to the deep shadows, scurried out and away.

62

Black watched the girl disappear into the darkness. He would have screamed at her, to stay put, don't run away, get back to the barn. The dogs weren't there for fun. They would find her, catch her, and then...

It occurred to him, he might do exactly the same, if he were her. And who could blame her? He took a deep breath, which hurt. But they hadn't killed him. And he'd had worse. They were under instruction. From the individual calling himself the Blood Eagle.

The Blood Eagle. The gangster – Ronald Wilkinson – wanted him so badly, he'd taken Rachel, in an effort to coerce Black into doing his bidding. A mad hair-brained scheme, but brutally simple – *The Blood Eagle for Rachel.* An easy equation, which in Wilkinson's world, made perfect sense.

Black closed his eyes, reined back a wave of pain, tried to think. He was here, to get up close. His plan, he thought ruefully, was perhaps as mad as Wilkinson's. But it was all he had. And provided he could endure, then as time ticked on, they would become more desperate. They would eventually concede – the Blood Eagle would come. Unless they killed Black first. The flaw was obvious. They could bring anyone to Black and tell him it was the Blood Eagle, and Black wouldn't know the difference. It was a chance he had to take. After that, it got complicated. Black had to bring the Blood Eagle to Wilkinson.

Time passed. He drifted into a sort of half sleep – a grey area on the periphery of wakefulness. A sudden noise startled him. He opened his eyes, blinked. The dogs were howling; men shouting. Activity in the courtyard. It was dawn, or shortly thereafter.

Black waited. He heard car doors, opening, slamming shut. The dogs were being transported. The cars drove off. Minutes dragged by. Black couldn't be sure. One hour? Two hours? Now, noise from another part of the house. Men arguing. Heavy footsteps. The rattle of keys, as the door was unlocked. The door opened. In came Marco, his fat brother behind him, followed by another man.

Marco's easy, languid manner was gone. He was smoking. He seemed strained.

"Where's the book?" he asked.

"Morning to you too," said Black.

The Beast launched forward, roaring, struck Black across the face. The blow made his head spin. Blood gushed from his nostrils.

"Where's the book?" repeated Marco.

Black took a second to find his voice.

"I think your fat ugly brother has broken my nose. Tell him, I'm going to break his fat fucking neck."

"Not the answer." Marco took a deep drag of his cigarette, leaned forward, pressed the tip on an open wound on Black's chest. He held it there for five seconds. Black emitted a choked gasp. The pain was excruciating.

"Now – where's the fucking book?"

Black took deep breaths, shook his head, as if the action would shrug away the pain.

He gazed at Marco, gave a ghastly smile.

"What was all the commotion? You got a runaway? Pressure, Marco. It gets worse, if I don't make that call."

"You're a stupid man, Black." He leaned forward again, waving the cigarette slowly in front of Black's face.

"In the eye, perhaps?" he whispered. He rested the burning tip on Black's cheek. The skin sizzled. Another five seconds. He lifted it away.

"Where's the book?"

"I'll tell the Blood Eagle," gasped Black. "Only him. Clock's ticking."

Marco straightened, stepped back. He gestured to the Beast. "Put his eye out."

The Beast unclipped a brown leather sheath attached to his belt, pulled out an eight-inch hunting knife. He smiled, took a step forward, raised the knife, hovering the point an inch from Black's right eye.

"Gonna stab you in the fucking eye."

A noise outside. Cars pulling into the courtyard. Horns beeping. The familiar sound of howling dogs. Men laughing. The Beast straightened, cast a glance out the window, turned to his brother.

"They're back," said Marco. "Let's go." He regarded Black with a sneer. "Don't get too comfortable."

63

Dalrymple's phone beeped early. He was awake, just out of the shower. He answered. He listened patiently to the voice on the other end.

"I'll call you back," he said. He hung up. He pondered the matter. This so-called *Book of Dreams* was becoming irksome. As was Adam Black. He had a call to make. Lyle Taylor. He pressed speed dial. It was early morning, but he knew Lyle, like himself, was an early riser. It was a call too important to delay.

Lyle – *What is it?*

Dalrymple – *Marco phoned.*

Lyle – *And?*

Dalrymple – *Black's not talking.*

Lyle – *Give him time. Our Romanian friends know what they're doing.*

Dalrymple – *We may not have time.*

Lyle – *What do you mean?*

Dalrymple – *Black claims to have given the book to a lawyer. The lawyer will send copies of it to the papers, unless Black makes a call by 11am. He's prepared to make the call if he meets the Blood Eagle. Then you get the book.*

Lyle – *What the hell's his game.*

Dalrymple – *I say kill him, and take what comes.*

Lyle – *You don't appreciate the sensitivity of the matter. I'm going to head up there. Now. I suggest you do the same.*

The call ended.

Dalrymple got quickly changed into track bottoms, training shoes, sweatshirt. He opened the connecting door between his room and Cromwell's. Cromwell was asleep. Dalrymple approached the side of the bed, gently shook the covers. Cromwell stirred.

"I got a call. I need to go to the Farm. You still want to come?"

Cromwell remained motionless for a few seconds, then propped himself up on one elbow.

"What time is it?"

"Six forty-five."

"Jesus fucking Christ. What call?"

"From Lyle Taylor. Looks like Adam Black is becoming a nuisance."

Cromwell dropped his head back on the pillow. "I knew that guy was trouble. Taylor should have handled it."

"You still want to come?"

Cromwell gave a long sigh. "Yes. I want to check that you choose the right girl. It's important."

Dalrymple shrugged. "If that's what you want."

"When do we go?"

"Now."

Lyle Taylor was at his house when he got the call from Dalrymple. He had already eaten breakfast – muesli, some fresh tomato juice. Also, he'd made fresh coffee from a percolator. He filled a cup for himself, and one for his brother. Lyle had picked him up from hospital the evening before, heavily sedated. He placed the cup on a saucer, and carried it and his own through to the conservatory. His brother was sitting on a bamboo-framed chair, dressed already, gazing at the garden. He'd refused to eat anything.

He placed the coffee on a glass-topped table, and sat opposite.

"Your garden was never as good as mine," said his brother.

"You had a talent for it, Martin," said Lyle. "You were a *horticulturist*. It was a talent."

Martin Lyle gave a sarcastic laugh. "You would say that."

"It's true."

"You'd say anything to get what you want. Manipulative. What am I doing here?"

"You know why," said Lyle gently. "You're not well."

Lyle reached over, picked up both the cup and saucer, took a sip, balancing the saucer on his lap.

Martin hesitated. "I did something."

"What did you do?"

"I killed a woman. I think. It comes in flashes. Maybe I'm dreaming."

"Tell me what you remember."

"I gave the man Adam Black my book. I think. Then, I realised it was wrong. That I shouldn't have done it. I wanted it back. I broke into his house. It wasn't there. I went to his girlfriend's. Something happened. A neighbour came. I killed her. Maybe. Sometimes everything's clear. Sometimes I'm swimming through a fog."

"How did you know where he lived?"

"Who?"

"Adam Black."

"I've been following him."

"Why?"

"Because..." Martin ran fingers through his hair. "Because I think he can help."

"Help what?"

"You wouldn't understand."

"Please, tell me."

Martin turned suddenly, to look at him, eyes glinting in the morning sunshine. "Was it you?"

"Was it me what?"

"Did you kill my wife?"

"Ah."

Another sip. Then, "Do you want to know who killed her?"

A tremor seemed to pass through Martin's face. "Yes."

"Then I need to take you somewhere. We need to leave now. First, we have to pay a visit to someone along the way."

"Where are you taking me?"

"To the beginning, Martin. Where it all began."

Lyle helped his brother into the passenger seat of the Jaguar 4x4 parked in the expansive driveway of his house. Before he got in, he pulled out his mobile phone. He had to speak to someone.

The Blood Eagle.

64

Black could hear men talking. Since Marco and the others had left the room, he reckoned maybe an hour had passed. Maybe more. Time was meaningless in this new world. And yet crucial. Black had his own deadline to meet – that set by Ronnie Wilkinson.

The talking grew louder. The familiar sound of the door unlocking. This time, four men. No sign of Marco, or the Beast. They each carried pistols – 9mm Berettas – except one, who held a sub-machine gun loosely in his hands.

One of them made his way behind Black, crouched, untied the rope.

"Stand up." The accent was thick, guttural.

Black swivelled his shoulders, jiggled his arms and hands, bringing life to them. The pain in his face and chest, where he'd been lashed, was a dull throb. He took deep breaths through his mouth – his nose was blocked, from congealed blood. He stood.

"I need to piss," he said.

"Sure. Against the wall."

Black regarded him with bemusement. "If you say so." He went to the far wall, relieved himself.

"Move." The man gestured with his pistol.

Black went out first, followed by the others. He walked back through the corridor, into the kitchen, where another two men were waiting, each brandishing a shotgun.

"Outside."

Black emerged into the courtyard. The sun was hidden behind a straggle of cloud, giving a grey cast to the morning. A breeze had picked up. In the centre, Marco and his brother were standing beside a chair. Sitting on it, thick insulating tape binding her wrists and ankles, was a girl. She was gagged. Black recognised her. The girl who had tried to free him. Danika.

She was naked, her face bone white and streaked with tears. It appeared, at first glance, she was unharmed. She looked up at him, eyes wide in stark terror. She tried to speak, the gag rendering the sound to a desperate moan.

"She ran away," explained Marco. He was smoking a Capstan, unfiltered. "Silly girl." He stepped behind her, placed his hands on her shoulders, massaged her neck, the top of her back. She gave a choked gasp, squirmed.

"Hush," said Marco. "No need to be frightened. Adam Black is here to save you." Marco took a deep drag of the cigarette, smoke coiling around him, the air rich with the smell of strong tobacco.

"We warn them," he said, his voice almost sympathetic. "When they arrive, my brother makes a point of... what shall I say... *illustrating* to the girls that we will not tolerate bad behaviour. Bad behaviour, yes? This includes running away. But despite the dogs, and all the men with guns, and the fact that we are in the middle of fucking nowhere, she decides to escape. Escape into the Scottish wildlands." He bent, put his mouth to her ear. "How far did you think you'd get? No one ever escapes. Not from here."

He straightened, and appraised Black. "What do you call this bad behaviour? Rebelliousness? Defiance? Stupidity?"

"Courage," said Black, in a controlled voice.

"Courage," Marco echoed. "Is that what you both share, Mr Black? Where will courage get her, I wonder. Any suggestions?"

Black said nothing. Behind him, four men, three armed with pistols, one with a sub-machine gun. On either side, a man bearing a shotgun. All aimed in his direction. He was helpless.

"You seem to care little about your own well-being. I have a feeling we could spend all year with you, and you wouldn't talk. I admire that, Mr Black. It shows real strength of character. But I wonder if you have the same resolve, if we add a new dimension. What about Danika's well-being? Will you show the same... what did you say... courage?"

He turned to his brother, stepped back.

The Beast ambled over. He was wearing a bright yellow T-shirt, tented over his huge stomach, silver jogging trousers sitting low, showing the top of his underwear, open-toed sandals. Under each arm, large dark sweat stains. He was carrying a 9mm Beretta, similar to the others. He stopped beside the girl, raised the pistol to an inch from her temple, watching Black with eyes like two small dots of obsidian. His face broke into a leering grin.

"You see where this is going, yes?" Marco paused, inhaled, flicked ash onto the grey flagstones. "I'm going to ask you once more. Where is the book?"

Black's mind raced. "I told you. I've given it to a lawyer."

Marco gave a deep sigh. "I think you're talking bullshit. Where is the book, Mr Black? I'll count to three. If you haven't given me a satisfactory answer, then poor little Danika. Her head gets blown all over the ground, and we'll give what's left to the dogs."

"I don't have it," said Black. "Killing her won't make any

difference. I told you – it's with a lawyer. Bring the Blood Eagle. I'll make the call."

"One."

Black's thoughts tumbled over themselves. He'd spent a night in fear and pain. He couldn't think straight.

"This achieves nothing." He wiped sweat from his eyes. "The girl dies, you still don't have the book. Where's the profit in killing her?"

"Two."

Black tensed. It didn't matter what he said. She was about to be executed. He looked into her eyes, bright and wide, her body trembling under the gun. He poised himself. He could leap out to the fat man, get his gun. Do the unexpected. These thoughts flashed through Black's mind in a fraction of a second. So be it. He braced himself, balancing on the balls of his feet. It was all too clear to him, that this was suicide. He would drop to the ground, in a hail of bullets, she would experience instant oblivion, shot at close range.

A car horn blared from the main gate. Everyone turned.

Two cars, both Range Rovers, were waiting to be let in. The Beast flicked a glance to his brother, who replied with an abrupt shake of his head. He lowered his pistol.

Marco regarded the girl. "God is smiling on you."

65

Two of the men scrambled over, opened the gates. The cars eased in slowly, parked up beside the group. One silver, the other sapphire black, the driver of each being the only occupant. The driver of the silver car got out. Black recognised him instantly. Dalrymple. He also recognised the man in the driver's seat of the black car, who chose to remain inside. Victor Cromwell. They locked eyes, briefly. Cromwell looked away.

Dalrymple stepped forward, an insolent half smile playing on his lips.

"Luck indeed!" he exclaimed. "How are you keeping, Mr Black?"

Black responded with a cold smile of his own. "Your friends have been entertaining me."

Dalrymple looked askance at the wounds on Black's chest. "They can be a little uncivilised, I admit. But you brought it upon yourself, I think."

He turned his attention to Danika, stroked the side of her face with his hand. She jerked her head away.

"What did you do, my beauty?" he said softly. He snapped his head round to Marco. "What the hell's happening here?"

Marco took a long last drag of his cigarette, tossed the stub on to the ground, crushed it with the sole of his boot. "She's a runaway. Escaped last night. We found her, and brought her back. We do what we do. We were going to kill her, and thought perhaps she might be of use to us. To force Black to talk."

"That's novel. And as a matter of interest, did Black talk?"

"We were about to find out."

"Really? Didn't I give explicit instructions." He pointed to the terrified form of Danika. "This one was special. She wasn't to be harmed. Yet here we are, me arriving at this shithole, to discover you're about to put a bullet in her head. Did I make myself unclear?"

Marco bowed his head. "Rules are rules. She ran away. The others have to learn."

"Sometimes I think you take the learning too far. Untie her, and get her clothes."

Marco immediately gestured to one of the men, speaking in his native dialect, his voice sharp. The man nodded, scurried to the barn.

Meanwhile Dalrymple focused back on Black. "Animals. Now you know what I have to put up with."

"Must be difficult."

"Indeed, yes. But the upside is the profit."

"Where there's muck, there's brass."

"Exactly right. You're getting the hang of this game."

The man returned from the barn, clutching some clothes. Marco barked another command. The man dropped the bundle on the ground, and with a knife, cut the tape binding the girl's wrists and ankles, and removed the gag from her mouth – a handkerchief crumpled into a ball, held in place by a piece of rag tied round her jaw.

She let out a sharp exhalation of breath, jumped to her feet.

She stooped, and pulled the clothes on – jeans, T-shirt, a pair of flip-flop shoes.

"Remember me?" said Dalrymple. She had her head down. She glanced at him, then Black, then kept her stare fixed on the ground.

"I asked you a question," said Dalrymple gently.

She responded with a miniscule shake of her head.

"Sure you do," continued Dalrymple, keeping up the same soft reassuring tone. "The motorway café. I remarked at the time how pretty you were. Give me your hand."

She didn't move, but glanced again at Black, her face a picture of sheer undiluted desperation. But there was little Black could do. He would be dead in the instant it took to squeeze a trigger.

"Don't look at him," continued Dalrymple, a metallic ring to his voice. "Give me your hand. If you don't, I'll give you back."

She looked up, and stared at him, glassy-eyed, stretched out her hand.

"There we are," said Dalrymple. "That was easy." He took it, and led her to the side of the black Range Rover. The window slid down.

"Will she do?"

Cromwell stared at the broken forlorn figure, standing limp before him, her head down. "She's perfect."

"I thought you would approve."

Cromwell leaned over to the passenger seat, picked up a hand-sized zipped pouch, passed it through the window to Dalrymple. Black watched the scene unfold in fascination. Dalrymple released her hand, turned away, unzipped the pouch, took out a small clear plastic needle and syringe. It was filled with a clear liquid. Danika stood, listless, staring into the middle-distance. She was in shock, Black realised.

Dalrymple turned, embraced her, and delicately injected the

liquid into the side of her neck. She winced slightly. Dalrymple stood back, gazing at her, as if studying an experiment. The change was dramatic. Her head lolled, her shoulders slumped, her eyes drooped. She staggered slightly on her feet. Probably Rohypnol, surmised Black. A tablet crushed in water, and injected. The effects quick and powerful.

Dalrymple, in an almost gentlemanly fashion, caught her from keeling on her side. She leaned heavily into him. He held her, guided to the rear passenger door of Cromwell's car, opened it, steered her in. She collapsed immediately on the seats. He closed the door behind her. Cromwell spoke to him.

"He'll be here in five minutes. He wants me to wait."

Dalrymple looked slightly surprised, turned to Black.

"It looks as if your wish is to be granted. The Blood Eagle is coming. He's looking forward to meeting you."

66

B lack's options were limited. Surrounded by Marco, his fat brother, and six men, bristling with fire power, he had no place to go. Except a shallow grave in the Scottish wilderness, he thought grimly. But Dalrymple's words rang true. It seemed as if his wish *was* about to be granted. What then? Black had no idea. Improvisation. Usually, a sure-fire recipe for disaster. But Black was in a corner.

He discreetly sized up the men around him. Marco appeared unarmed, though he might be concealing a weapon. The Beast had a Beretta and a long sheathed knife attached to a thick leather belt. The six others carried amongst them three Berettas, two shotguns and a sub-machine gun. Black scrutinised them – their movements were languid, easy. The weapons were held low, their postures casual. It was plain to see they were complacent. Too used to dealing with terrified young women. As such, they possessed an inflated opinion of their own skill. They hadn't bothered retying his hands. Bad move.

"Where are you taking her?" he asked.

Dalrymple shrugged. "It doesn't matter. No one's going to miss her."

"Her parents might."

"It's just bad luck. This is something you both have in common."

"Where do you fit in? You like to drug young woman for a bit of date rape? You pimp them out to your handsome Hollywood master, so you come to this shithole?"

"Shut it," growled one of the men.

"It's all right," said Dalrymple, his voice affable, almost amused. "He's asked a question, and I'm happy to humour. I work for the man you're about to meet. I help him with, shall we say... the administrative side of things. The packages are brought here, by these fine gentlemen, and I make sure they are more or less intact, and then distributed in an efficient and profitable manner."

"Packages?"

Dalrymple continued in a silken voice. "My employer and Victor know each other from way back. Victor went to America. They never lost touch. When Victor came back to visit Scotland, my employer asked me to look after him. There's a lot of crazy people out there, Mr Black. Movie stars are perfect targets for the deranged and maladjusted. Victor asked if he could sample some of the... packages. And voila! It fitted in perfectly. Here I am, supplying a need."

"I'm trying to think of the right description for you – pimp, ponce, scumbag. I can't think. There's too many."

Dalrymple sighed. "For a man in your position, you show remarkable bravado."

The sound of a car engine made him turn.

"Talk of the devil."

Another car pulled up. A Jaguar 4x4. Inside, two men. The driver, Black did not know. The passenger, he did. His thoughts flashed back to an early quiet Saturday morning in a Starbucks coffee shop, to when the whole sorry mess began. To an old man who handed him a book.

The same old man was sitting in the car, gazing ahead, eyes not fixed on anything in particular. The driver got out. He was in his seventies, luxuriant white hair swept back off his forehead and over his ears. Tanned. Long straight nose, clear blue eyes, somewhat narrow chin. Dressed with a suave elegance – powder-blue cotton summer suit, open-necked white silk shirt, soft blue shoes.

"Looks like a popular place," he said.

Dalrymple nodded. "All on account of Mr Black."

The man brought his attention to fully bear on Black.

"You, my friend, are a regular pain in the arse. My name is Lyle Taylor. I believe you wanted to meet me."

Black said nothing.

"The strong, silent type. We'll see how that pans out."

He made his way to the side of Cromwell's car, peered through the window at the girl sprawled on the rear seats, then spoke to Cromwell through his open window. "I see Dalrymple has come up with the goods. She's a beauty."

Cromwell said nothing.

"We've been summoned," said Lyle.

Cromwell frowned in puzzlement. "Why?"

Lyle inclined his head at the old man sitting in his car.

"Why do you think?"

"This has nothing to do with me," growled Cromwell.

"But it has everything to do with you, and you know it. Orders are orders. We do what we're told."

Cromwell didn't respond immediately. To Black, watching closely, he seemed decidedly upset.

"Fuck it," said Cromwell. "Don't you see I have things to do?"

Lyle was unmoved. "What you do with the girl is your

business. I don't want to know, and I don't care. But what I do care about, is that you follow orders. As I do."

Cromwell was silent for a space, then said, "Where? When?"

"Five this afternoon. A table on the pale horse."

"Jesus Christ," muttered Cromwell. "So fucking dramatic. A fucking trip down memory lane."

"Not all memories are good."

"Who gives a shit. Let's hope the place is still standing."

"It is. I can assure you."

The car window slid up. The conversation was over. Cromwell circled the car round the courtyard, drove back out the open gates, and into the sweeping plains of the Rannoch Moors.

Lyle swivelled and looked directly at Black. "Here we are then. I have arrived. As requested. The Blood Eagle."

67

Foster was in work early. He hadn't slept well, his mind turning over the file notes. Call it a sixth sense, a bloodhound instinct. He knew he was on to something. He just couldn't pinpoint it. It was like grasping at shadows. Yet there was substance behind the shadows. He could smell it.

He was surprised Blair wasn't in. They'd spoken over pints of lager the night before, and Blair had been intrigued by Foster's hypothesis. They'd left on the basis that they'd crack on together, early. Blair was due to retire in less than three years, but he was as fit as any young copper, and like Foster, when he had the scent, he didn't let go.

Foster buzzed him on his mobile. It was switched off. Unusual, he thought. Foster stood at the whiteboard on the wall of the incident room, gazing at the photographs of the victims. Four young woman. The fourth, an unknown quantity. The only clue, a rough tattoo on her wrist. A number. Which, probably, signified ownership.

A woman brought in from the continent, coerced as part of a trafficking gang. The trouble was, such gangs were well organised and clandestine. Difficult to crack, if not impossible.

Her identity would doubtless remain a mystery for all eternity, he thought ruefully. She would have parents, brothers, sisters. Somewhere a family, anxious for her return. He sighed, studied the pictures of the three other girls. Before and after. All of them bright-eyed, smiling, blissfully unaware of the monstrous violations to be inflicted on them, as illustrated by the subsequent photographs. All of them on show, mutilated beyond imagination.

"There's no getting used to it," came a voice behind him; a voice he knew well enough.

He turned. DCI Wishart was standing at the door of his office, tie loose and hanging low, rough-shaven, sad drooping eyes, blue shirt and grey flannels crumpled. It looked like he'd spent the night on the couch in his room, thought Foster, which wouldn't be the first time.

"It's like a door's been left open," said Foster.

"Uh huh?"

"And suddenly you can see into the mind of a psychopath. It's all there. In bright lights. All the detail. All the colours. We're glimpsing something, that no person should ever see..."

"Evil," finished Wishart. "Pure and simple. Which is why we have to catch this fuck. Where's your buddy?"

"Blair? No idea. Sleeping?"

Wishart grunted. "Then wake him up, and tell him to get his arse in here."

Wishart shut the door. The conversation was over. Foster went to his desk, leafed through files he'd already read. Not on the victims, but their families. In particular, the felons. The black sheep. It was a link, regardless of how tenuous. He studied, immersed himself, flicking his head from the written notes in the files, to downloads on the computer screen. Time drifted.

By 11am the place was full, the room full of noise. Constant telephones. Still no sign of Blair. Foster tried his mobile again.

Still switched off. Ill? Maybe. But in the time he'd known the man, he couldn't recall one day's sickness.

It was 11.30am. The phones were buzzing. The murder hadn't yet been disclosed to the media, but calls were being made, calls were being returned, reopening lines of enquiry twenty years old. Family, friends, acquaintances, work colleagues. It wouldn't be long before people twigged. The Blood Eagle was back.

Foster straightened in his chair, stretched, raised his eyes to stare at the ceiling. He'd found a link. It was crazy, it was mad, it was inconceivable. He turned to Blair's empty desk. He tried the mobile once again. Nothing. He took a deep breath. He shuffled some papers. It was there, in black and white. All a person had to do was look. And he consoled himself by the fact that his theory was probably bullshit. Still, it was a connection. He peered over at the photographs on the whiteboard. Four young women, kidnapped, mutilated, killed.

"Fuck," he whispered. He tried Blair's phone again. Switched off. He stood, made his way to Wishart's office at the end of the room. He was about to knock, when the door suddenly opened, Wishart's large frame before him.

"Sir, I–"

"We've had a call," said Wishart. Foster stared. "A man and a woman's been seen entering a derelict miners' club, just off the Glasgow Road."

"I think I know it."

"The girl looked drunk. He was half dragging her, so we're told. I've got uniform going over. Get Blair and get the fuck over there."

Foster swallowed. "Well, that's the thing. Blair isn't here."

"What? Where is the lazy bastard?"

"Sir, I've tried–"

"Fuck it," interrupted Wishart. "I'll go with you. Then I'll shove a rocket up Blair's arse."

Wishart grabbed a jacket off a peg on the wall, strode out towards the exit.

Foster followed, hoping to Christ he was wrong.

68

"Now that I'm here, we can get down to business, yes? And maybe cut away all the bullshit. Talking of which, I believe you have to make a call?"

Black gazed at the man before him. Suddenly, he was out of ideas. And when that happened, he fell back on old skills.

"Sure. A deal's a deal, after all. I believe one of these handsome gentlemen took my mobile phone."

"Give it to him," said Lyle.

Marco barked out a command. One of the men pulled out Black's phone from a pocket in his jeans, and handed it tentatively to Black.

"On loudspeaker, please," said Lyle.

Black keyed in his password. Colour materialised on the screen – a green field, an orange sky. He swiped it. Columns of apps appeared. He pressed one in particular, which opened into a time setting. He made a quick adjustment. It was a slender chance, but one which might conceivably save his life.

"Hurry the fuck up," said Marco.

"Please," said Black. "All these guns make me nervous."

"Easy on the man," said Dalrymple in a languid voice. "He's under pressure. Aren't you, Mr Black?"

Black opened "contacts", and scrolled down a list of names on the screen, tapped the relevant one, then tapped the loudspeaker symbol. Three seconds passed, then the noise of a phone ringing.

It was answered by a polite female. "Hepburn Frank."

"Hi. Can I speak to Kenny Hepburn?"

"I'll put you through. Who will I say is calling?"

"Adam Black."

"Thank you."

Nothing was said. Black waited. Another five seconds.

"Adam?"

"Kenny."

"What's up?"

"Nothing, in particular. How's the family?"

A pause. The voice responded, hesitant. "Everything good. And you?"

"Everything good this end. You take care."

Black hung up.

Lyle clapped his hands. "Bravo. Now, tell us where the fucking book is."

"It's in my flat. Your Romanian friends were careless. The built-in cupboard in the bedroom has a false back. Push it. You'll find the book."

Lyle nodded graciously, looked at Marco, who immediately spoke into his phone.

"We can have someone there in five minutes," said Lyle. "Then we'll see. While we're waiting, you can indulge me. Why so desperate to meet? Most people would rather spend their time in other places. Yet you came here willingly. All for an audience with the Blood Eagle. Why, Mr Black?"

Black regarded the men around him, focused on Lyle. "It's difficult to concentrate with guns pointing at my head."

"I'm afraid that's something you'll have to put up with. Tell me, please. I'm burning up with curiosity."

Black shrugged. Sometimes, the truth was the only way.

"A man called Ronnie Wilkinson has my girlfriend as his... guest. Like you, he's a fucking lowlife scumbag. He wants me to bring to him, either dead or alive, the Blood Eagle. If I don't, he'll kill her. And he's not the type of man to bullshit."

Lyle's lips curled at the edges into the semblance of a smile.

"Why would he want that?"

"His daughter was murdered twenty years ago. By the Blood Eagle. I think he wants a measure of revenge."

The smile stayed fixed on Lyle's face. "But what if there's no connection?"

"It doesn't matter. Ronnie Wilkinson is a bitter man with a psychotic nature. It is what it is. Now you know."

"Crazy world," said Lyle. "He's in for a disappointment."

Black said nothing.

"You know how this is going to end, don't you?" said Lyle.

"Not good."

"Indeed not."

The phone rang. Marco answered. He listened, looked at Lyle.

"He has it."

Lyle gestured, raising his hands. "How simple was that?"

He gave another courteous nod.

"I would like to say it was a pleasure, Mr Black. I'll leave you with my friends. I suspect you will not enjoy the experience." He turned to Dalrymple, who had been watching the scene unfold quietly from the side lines. "Kill him, and bury him deep. Or else feed him to those fucking dogs."

He got into his car, gave Black a final farewell smile, circled round the courtyard, and left.

Dalrymple appraised Black. "It's the end for you, my friend."

Black gave a sardonic smile. "Everything has to end."

69

Feel no fear before the multitude of men, do not run in panic, but let each man bear his shield straight toward the fore-fighters, regarding his own life as hateful, and holding the dark spirits of death as dear as the radiance of the sun.
War song of the ancient Spartans.

When there's nothing left, and you've nowhere to go, and there's fuck all petrol in the tank, then how it ends is the only thing that matters. For those last brief seconds, go out like blazing fucking gods.

Staff Sergeant's Instruction to men of the 22nd Regiment of the SAS.

Five minutes passed. Nobody had moved. Black remained standing, surrounded. Dalrymple had given an order to shoot Black, which had sparked off a heated argument between Marco and his brother, shouting at each other in their native language in sharp staccato bursts, incomprehensible to Black.

Black's nerves were set on a hair-trigger, every muscle tense and poised to spring – where to, he had no godly idea. Oblivion, probably. But his options were limited. Strike for the first man, then see what happened. But the argument between the brothers was unexpected. And Black needed the unexpected to stand a chance.

"What the fuck's going on?" Dalrymple asked.

Marco answered. "My brother wants to have satisfaction. Black has insulted him. A bullet in the head is too quick."

"Meaning?"

"He wants a bit of fun."

Dalrymple blew through his mouth, shaking his head. "What is it with you people. Nothing's simple. You hear that, Mr Black, the Beast wants a bit of fun? This is their home. I don't think I can really object."

Three important lessons Black had learned in Special Forces. If captured, the first thing was to make invisible. Don't look at the enemy in the eye. Say as little as possible. Shrink, both mentally and physically. If it looked bad, and you knew violence was imminent, then do the opposite. Become bold. Distract. Put them off balance. Search for a weakness, and in the process, exploit it. If that proved unsuccessful, then the third thing was easy. Die like a man, and take as many of the fuckers down as you can.

In the present scenario, Black was at lesson two, and hurtling towards lesson three.

Black looked at the massive bulk of the Beast, gave him a measured stare –

"You are one fat ugly fucker."

The Beast grunted, took a step forward, to be restrained by his brother.

Dalrymple stood to one side, clearly enjoying himself. He snapped his finger at one of the men. "Cold beer?"

Marco translated. The man hurried into the house, and a few seconds later, came out with a bottle of Budweiser, which he gave to Dalrymple. He screwed off the top, took a swig.

The Beast said something. Marco listened, nodded.

"He wants to execute Black. The old way."

"The old way!" repeated Dalrymple. "Fucking hell. Serious stuff. Sounds ominous, Mr Black."

Black didn't respond. The Beast lumbered off, to one of the ramshackle outbuildings surrounding the courtyard. He tugged open the door, its hinges creaking, the bottom scraping against the ground. He went inside. Black waited, heart thumping. A stillness had settled on the place. The breeze had died to nothing, the dogs were quiet. The sun was bright in a cloudless sky. There was no talking, no chat. This indeed was serious stuff.

The Beast reappeared. In both hands, he held a plain wooden bench, four feet long, about a foot and a half high. He placed it in the centre of the courtyard. He looked at the crowd of men, grinned, went back to the barn. Another few seconds elapsed. He emerged back into the daylight, holding a long-handled axe.

"Medieval," quipped Dalrymple. He made a sympathetic gesture. "It doesn't even look that sharp. Not looking good, Mr Black."

Black's nerves were stretched, tight as piano wire. A thought flashed through his mind. The scene setting before him was reminiscent of a similar situation, a million years ago, in the dungeons in Iraq. Where beheading was commonplace. He got out of that. Would he get out of this? Black didn't like his chances.

Now, the Beast stood by the bench, the axe gripped in both hands. He'd tucked his pistol in his belt. He raised one meaty arm, beckoned Black forward.

"Move it," said Marco. The group made their way forward, like a shoal of fish, Black in the middle.

Dalrymple fell in behind them. "Any last wishes?" he said, laughing.

Black ignored him. Including Dalrymple, there were seven men clustered about him, one man directly behind, his pistol pointed an inch from the back of his head. Two on one side, three on the other. Dalrymple at the rear. They were all armed, but the spectacle was a distraction. Other than the one behind Black, their focus was diverted, weapons pointing at nothing in particular.

In five heartbeats, they reached the bench. The men circled round. The one behind Black remained where he was, arm outstretched. Black could feel the muzzle of the weapon pressed against his scalp.

The Beast spoke. "Kneel!"

Black took deep breaths, trying to calm his pounding heart. Any second now.

"Kneel!"

The man behind him kicked Black in the back of the legs, above the knee. His legs folded forward. Black collapsed down. Now, the Beast loomed in, axe dangling in one hand, bustling away the gunman behind Black, his massive size preventing anyone else coming close.

He spoke again, accent thick, sluggish, pointing at the bench.

"Put your fucking head down."

Black looked up, gave a thin-lipped smile.

"Christ, you stink."

The Beast glared down at Black, eyes bulging in wrath. He straightened, adjusted the axe, grasping it in both hands, raised it high, as if poised to chop wood, ready to split Black's head in two.

Suddenly, a voice. Black's voice. *"Wake the fuck up, Captain Black!"*

Everything froze. The Beast stopped, eyes wide and startled. It was the sound of Black's alarm, blaring from his mobile phone.

It was all Black needed.

He lunged forward, into the Beast, who staggered back on one foot, the axe useless. The men around him couldn't shoot, their options restricted. One inaccurate shot, and they'd miss Black, and hit their friend. Black saw all this in a second. The Beast still held the axe handle, both hands occupied. Black grabbed the pistol from his belt, fired once, twice into the Beast's stomach, spun in a half crouch, a lifetime of training kicking in, rendering his movements almost instinctive.

He got three shots off before anyone knew what was happening. The man called Marco took a bullet in the face, imploding with the force, nose and jaw eviscerated. One took a bullet in the neck, the third crumpled, the top of his head shorn away. The Beast fell like a toppled tree, clutching his guts, his yellow T-shirt bright with blood.

Black leapt, rolled, fired again, all in the space of three seconds. His targets were easy. It was happening too fast for them to comprehend. Ill-prepared to deal with any real threat, they fired off rounds without focus. Black, on the other hand, was entirely focused. He pulled the trigger of the Beretta semi-automatic. One in the shoulder, spinning the man like a top. One direct in the chest, bouncing him off his feet, one in the groin, destroying genitals and upper legs.

Dalrymple was running to his car, turning every five strides, firing. Black sprinted after him. He passed the man with the shoulder wound, shot him again in the head, which burst open onto the flagstones in a sudden tapestry of blood and bone. He swept up his fallen pistol. Dalrymple was a yard from his car,

Black close behind. Black with two guns, started firing like a western gunslinger, hitting the tyres, the windows, the side of the bonnet. In an instant, the car was useless. Dalrymple ran past, towards the open gate. Black followed. Dalrymple was fast. Black, after a night in the company of the Beast, was seriously handicapped. He was in pain, he was exhausted. Dalrymple was fresh, and ex-military. He would outrun Black in the wilderness, hunker down, hide, and thus escape.

Black could not allow that to happen. He sank down on one knee, took a second to calm, aimed, fired. Dalrymple was whipped off his feet, a bullet in the back of the leg. He rose slowly, half dragged himself forward, trailing his shot leg, and in the process turning and firing. The shots were wild. Black ran another ten yards, crouched again, aimed, fired a second shot. Dalrymple fell on his side, the other leg shot at the knee. He shrieked, crawled forward, using his elbows, leaving a trail of blood.

Black had no need to run. He made his way to Dalrymple in long strides. Dalrymple swivelled round, face contorted, aimed. Black casually stepped on his arm, pressing his gun hand flat on the ground. Black stooped, kept his foot on his elbow, grabbed the wrist, jerked one way, snapping the bone. Dalrymple gave an inarticulate shout. He released the pistol from nerveless fingers. Black kicked it away. He pulled Dalrymple up by the shoulders of his jacket, turned him over on his back.

"Not quite what you were expecting, *old boy*," said Black.

Dalrymple stared up at him, hatred burning in his eyes. "Fuck you."

"For a man with two shot legs and a broken arm, you don't have a very kindly disposition."

Dalrymple gave a ghastly smile. "Just get it done."

"Where did he take the girl?"

"What do you care?"

"I understand."

Black stood on Dalrymple's shattered knee. Dalrymple gave forth a scream, arching his spine in pain.

"I repeat, where did Cromwell take the girl?"

"You're going to kill me," Dalrymple gasped. "So why should I tell you?"

"Sometimes death is better than pain. Ever been tortured? There's nothing quite like it. It feels like it lasts a life time. Death becomes almost... welcome."

Dalrymple said nothing.

"Fair enough."

Black crouched again, manoeuvred his hands, breaking Dalrymple's other arm, at the wrist.

Dalrymple groaned. He was losing blood at an alarming rate.

"Look at me," said Black. "I'm ex-military too. I was a captain in the Special Air Service. I served with the 22nd Regiment, in Afghanistan, Iraq, Bosnia. Everywhere. I have to call the police to this shithole, and tell them what went down. They'll bring ambulances. I give you my word, as one soldier to another, and as an ex-officer, that I will not kill you, that I will make sure you get that ambulance, that you get through this. What have you got to lose?" Black stared into his eyes. "I give you my word."

"Your word?" His eyes flickered. His right leg was pulsing blood. "Inside pocket. You'll find an address."

Black opened Dalrymple's jacket, reached inside, retrieved a piece of notepaper.

"What does he do with them?" Black asked.

"Unpleasant things. Better not to know. I'm supposed to pick him up when it's over. At the address."

"Pick him up? Who? Cromwell?"

"Enough questions." Dalrymple wheezed. "I'm dying."

"I know."

Black stood, looked down at him.

Dalrymple managed a rattling laugh. "It was worth a try. Fuck your word, Black."

"My sentiments exactly."

Black shot him once in the chest, then the head.

Black ran back into the courtyard. Dead men were scattered all about, except one. The Beast had somehow crawled back into the main house, a line of blood behind him, like slime from a snail. Black approached the front door. It was useless trying to listen for any sounds, the baying of the dogs drowning everything out. Black crouched, went inside. Blood on the kitchen tiles, trailing into the passage beyond. Warily, Black followed. On the wooden floorboards, moaning softly, was the Beast. Black loomed over him.

"Hope you're not trying to avoid me," he said. "That would just be plain rude."

The Beast was on his stomach. He mumbled something.

"I can't hear you," said Black.

"Please," he moaned. "I need help."

"Ah. That's what I thought you said." Black tucked the pistols in his pockets, grabbed handfuls of The Beast's hair, and dragged him round and back into the kitchen, the blood acting as a lubricant, so that his bulk slid across the floor. Black kept going, dragging him through and out into the courtyard, all to the sound of screaming and shrieking, as the open wounds on The Beast's stomach scraped and bumped on the ground.

Black stopped at the bench. He picked up the axe. The Beast started to sob, tried to lift himself up. He got on one knee, hands pressed on his stomach, blood pulsing through his fingers. He stared at the axe in Black's hand. His round face morphed between terror and pain.

"You wanted a bit of fun," said Black. "The old way. Let's keep on that theme, you fucking fat piece of shit."

Black raised the axe. The Beast tried to shout, but managed

only a dry croak. Black brought it down, splitting his head, the blade wedging six inches into the skull. The Beast remained still for a second, then toppled on his side. Black pulled out the pistols from his pocket, and shot him four times for good measure.

Black made his way to the barn, where the girls were being held. He opened the door, went in.

"You're free!" he shouted.

Movement from upstairs. A head peeked over the edge of the mezzanine level.

"Who are you?"

"Come down. It's over."

One by one, they climbed down the ladder. They made their way out, blinking in the sunlight. A group of young, dishevelled women, terrified, bewildered, disbelieving.

"We saw what you did," said one, her English broken, her voice hesitant.

Black nodded. "I'll call the police. Explain what happened. They'll come for you. You have nothing to fear now."

Some started crying, shedding days, weeks, of torment and dread.

"You're safe," said Black gently. "You're all going home. To your loved ones."

"What's your name?"

"My name? Adam Black."

Black turned to make his way back to the main house, but stopped when the woman spoke again.

"Where are you going, Adam Black? You're hurting."

Which was true. His chest and shoulders were on fire, courtesy of The Beast and his love of the scourge.

"I'm going to find out where the hell we are. Call the police. Then I'm going to find Danika."

Plus, he was still to meet the Blood Eagle. The man who

called himself Lyle Taylor was bullshitting, and Black knew it. He'd heard the conversation between him and Cromwell. They had spoken without concern that he was listening, assuming it didn't matter, that Black was a dead man. Someone was giving orders. The Blood Eagle. The Blood Eagle had arranged a meeting. And he had a good idea where that might be.

70

They took Wishart's car. Foster drove. The Miners' Club was eight miles from the station, sitting in a small patch of countryside between Rutherglen and Cambuslang. The reason Foster knew about it was because he'd been called out there two years earlier.

The place had been targeted by arsonists. He remembered it well. A squat pavilion, the walls burnt black, the glass melted, the interior reduced to ash. Amazingly, the roof hadn't collapsed. He also remembered the aftermath.

There had been no insurance. The open spaces where the windows and doors had been, were boarded up. The place was classified as dangerous, entry was forbidden, the local council deciding to demolish. But it never happened. The carcass of the building remained, blackened, rotten, derelict.

They spoke little during the drive, each consumed in their own thoughts. Foster decided not to air his theory. Judging on how the day went, it could prove to be bullshit.

He'd tried to contact Blair again, on the hands-free, without success.

"I'm going to kick that man's arse," grumbled Wishart. "Now

is not the time to become a fucking hermit. Mobiles should be switched on and ready at all times."

The building was a half mile from the main road, hidden by trees and bushes. The single access road was as derelict as the building, the car bouncing and lurching over potholes.

They arrived, parked twenty yards from the main entrance, in a tarmacadamed area once a car park, now rutted and cracked with weeds.

Foster surveyed the scene. It seemed uniform hadn't arrived. The place looked deserted. Some of the window boarding had been removed, ripped away, leaving dark gaps – probably addicts, seeking a little privacy to squeeze heroin into their veins.

They both got out. It was late morning. The scene was almost tranquil, thought Foster. The day was still, the sun bright, little sound save distant traffic a half mile away. The trees didn't rustle. The bushes didn't stir.

"Should we wait?"

Wishart responded without hesitation.

"If the bastard's in there, then I don't want a dead girl on my conscience just because the cavalry were late."

Foster couldn't disagree.

The windows were only three feet from the ground. Wishart went first, clutching a pocket flashlight. He pulled himself through a gap in the boarding, and entered. Foster followed. A smell of rot assailed his nostrils. Wishart flashed the torch beam. Objects sprang into vision – cluttered metal chairs, an upturned table, items unrecognisable. Lockers along one wall. They had entered what Foster could only describe as a storage room. A door opposite. They made their way delicately. The bare floorboards were springy. Foster was worried his foot might sink straight through. They entered a corridor, doors on either side. Wishart opened each door, as quietly as he could, Foster at his shoulder. Toilets, empty rooms, a cloakroom, all bare and ruined, daylight glinting through holes in the walls.

The corridor opened into a much larger room at the end. The function hall, reckoned Foster. Here, the remnants of a bar, along one side. A few metal tables lay scattered about, some chairs. The bare frames of some pool tables. An open space in the centre of the room. Discarded needles on the floor. Everywhere, the smell of decay.

"There's nothing here," said Foster. "A complete waste of time." He cleared his throat. "I meant to tell you, back at the station. I've found something. It might be nothing."

Wishart turned to face him. "What?"

"I think there might be something connecting the first three victims. But it's crazy. And yet... it's there."

"Tell me, Foster. Tell me all about this connection."

71

B lack got to work. He went into the kitchen, and washed the wounds on his chest. He rummaged through cupboards, until he found what he was looking for. A bottle of booze. Brandy. He took a gulp, then soaked the cuts and abrasions, causing instant mind-wrenching pain. He dabbed them dry with a towel. Without ceremony, he stripped off a shirt from one of the dead men, put it on. It was tight, but it would do. He found the driver of the SUV – the top of his head a tangled mess – and got the car keys. All the while, the girls watched, huddled together, hardly daring to believe they were free. Black made his way to the barn where the car had been parked, pulled open the main double door, bleeped the alarm, got in.

He drove out the main gates, leaving the Farm behind him. He made a frustratingly slow way through the wilderness of the Rannoch Moors, barely registering the scenery. One thing was certain – he would not be eager to return. He got to the main road. Opposite, he saw a sign for the Kingshouse Hotel. It was then he called the police – *men dead; trafficked women; take the single-track road at the sign for the Kingshouse Hotel; half hour drive through the moors until you get to a farm.*

Black drove south towards Glasgow. Fifteen minutes later, three police cars and an ambulance blazed by him, heading north. The girls would be safe now. Black took a deep breath, drove fast. The car had satnav. He'd be there in two hours, maybe a little over. Black couldn't fathom why the hell Cromwell had taken the girl to a disused social club, in the outskirts of Glasgow. But Danika had tried to help him. He would make it his business to return the favour.

It was approaching midday. The landscape flitted by. Black's thoughts were elsewhere. As ever, he was against the clock. Wilkinson had imposed a deadline. And if he failed? He chose not to consider the consequences. Rachel depended on him. He would not let her down. And if Wilkinson were foolish enough to harm her, then Black would burn his whole fucking world.

He got to Glasgow, took the bypass, headed past Rutherglen, then took a turn off, arrived at Glasgow Road. Then, to his left, the satnav guided him along a road virtually invisible, no better than the one through the Rannoch Moors. Black wondered what the hell was going through Cromwell's mind, coming to this place. Dalrymple could, of course, have been bullshitting. A last act of malevolence. Black arrived. There were two cars there. One he recognised instantly. Victor Cromwell's Range Rover. Black had come prepared, relieving his kidnappers of their Berettas, secure in the knowledge they no longer required them. He tucked one in the belt of his trousers, kept a hold of another.

He made his way to the building, entered through the same gap as Foster and Wishart had entered earlier that morning.

A soft sound echoed from deeper inside. A scrape of movement, a woman sobbing. Nerves stretched, Black crept through the gloom, along a passage, to the source. The building creaked at his passing. He got to a large room – more of a hall. He stopped, stared, trying to understand the scene before him.

The place was lit by candles, placed in a circle. In the centre, on the floor, was a metal trestle, the size and shape of a double bed. Like a rack. Ankles and wrists tied to each corner by cord, so that she lay spread eagled, was a young woman. Danika. Naked. Fussing round, checking the frame, the bonds, was a strange nightmarish figure. Black remained motionless, swallowing back a sudden chill of dread.

The creature was tall and stocky, wearing a white robe. The candlelight created a flickering shadowy orange cast to the room, accentuating the horror. The face was barely human. An eye was missing, leaving a bare socket, the lower half of the face lacking skin or any covering tissue, brought back to gleaming bone; the mouth was lipless; the nose split into two lumps of cartilage. The teeth were overlarge, unnaturally pointed. Long straggling hair hung to his shoulders. Beyond the circumference of the circle, two men lay sprawled on the ground, face down. a pool of dark viscous liquid forming around them.

Black stepped back into the shadows, watched.

The man stood behind the trestle, bent, grabbed a section, lifted, raising it up, so it stood on one end. The woman's moans got louder, taking substance. She was vertical, naked, bound. He concentrated on each bottom edge, pulling out metal platforms, locking in them in place. He shook the structure gently, to ensure it was stable. He took two steps back, regarding the girl. She had regained her senses. She looked at the creature before her. She screamed, fighting the cords. The trestle rattled, but held firm.

On the floor was a rolled out plastic sheet. On it were various items – knives, metal-cutting shears, scissors, hooks, other implements.

He bent down, picked up a metal rod, the end sharp to a point.

Danika stopped screaming, stared at him with wide eyes. "Please," she whispered. "Please let me go."

He spoke, voice low and husky. "You're beautiful. Too beautiful to let go." He raised the rod. "Where should I put this? In your eye?" He glanced down, between her legs. "Or somewhere else, maybe?"

Black emerged from the shadows, pointed the Beretta. "Touch her with that, and I swear I will rip your fucking heart out."

He had his back to Black. Slowly, he turned.

Black walked towards him, pistol aimed directly at his chest. "What the fuck are you?"

The figure said nothing, remained still.

"Drop it," said Black. The metal rod clanged to the floor.

Black stepped into the circle of candles. Now, close up, things took a different perspective. He realised the thing he confronted was just a man. A man wearing a mask.

"Take that fucking thing off."

Slowly, slowly he raised his hands, opened his jaws, removed a set of teeth from his mouth, grasped a fold at his neck, peeled back the face, to reveal another below.

Black knew the man. He'd been introduced by Rachel only two days earlier. He'd been in Black's flat. He had been worried for their safety.

Detective Chief Inspector Wishart.

"Hello, Adam. What an unpleasant surprise."

72

"Welcome to my world," said Wishart.

"What world is that?" replied Black. "The world of psychopaths?"

"It doesn't matter what you think. Here, I am God."

"Then you're a god looking down the barrel of a semi-automatic." Black nodded to the two men on the ground. "I assume one of them is Victor Cromwell. What happened? He was giving you a girl, and the deal went sour?"

Wishart gave a half-sardonic, half-wistful smile.

"You really don't know anything. Victor and I go way back. We struck a deal. An oath was made. Twenty years ago, long before anyone knew about Victor Cromwell, who at that time was just another struggling actor, waiting tables, delivering pizzas. But I knew him. I knew what he was, back then."

"What was that?"

"A perfectionist. An artist. I had arrested him for assault. He'd cut up a prostitute. But the way he'd done it. Such creativity. I recognised in him a rare talent. All it needed done was a little honing, moulding. You see, Adam, I've been doing this sort of thing for many, many years. But Victor took it to a whole new level. A level I wished to emulate."

"You struck a deal with Cromwell?"

"Of sorts. I found him three women. They were special. Hand-picked. Selected. I gave them to him, to work his magic." Wishart suddenly laughed – a harsh, metallic sound. "And what magic he worked. It was... magnificent. Or so I thought."

"The Blood Eagle," said Black.

"Three women, I handed to him, on a silver platter. And he was to reciprocate. We made a blood oath. He was to give me three women. Not random. Chosen carefully, with thought, as I did. Then, I would show him what I could do. I would surpass him. But he failed. He broke his end of the deal."

Black waited.

"He left, suddenly. Went to America. Became a movie star sensation. But I remembered. And when he returned, only last week, I reminded him of our pact. Our oath."

"You contacted Cromwell, and insisted he keep his side of the bargain. The Blood Eagle rises again."

"And he did keep his side. He brought girls to me." He turned, gazed at Danika. "Isn't she beautiful?" he said, in a hushed whisper.

"Why kill him?"

Wishart swivelled round, back to Black. His eyes glittered like white pearls in the candle flame.

"You're full of questions, Adam."

"Please. Humour me."

Wishart twitched his shoulders in a manner of rueful resignation. He spoke in a heavy voice.

"Because my hand was forced. The other man is Paul Foster. He was a clever, ambitious DS. Too clever, by far. He saw a connection. Twenty years ago. The three girls, at some point, had family members arrested and taken to the police station where I've always worked. That's how I chose them. I would take their statements, as a routine enquiry. Get to know them."

"Not quite routine."

"He saw a connection. He told his friend, Stephen Blair. Blair phoned me, last night, taking the credit. Blair's dismembered body is in the trunk of the car you saw outside."

"You've been busy."

"There's an irony to all this. Foster thought Blair was the link. He was the arresting officer, in each case, so I could hardly blame him. He wanted so desperately to tell me."

"And when he did, you killed him. Let me guess. You kill Cromwell, leave both bodies here, along with the displayed corpse of another young girl. The scene speaks for itself. Cromwell, the killer, Foster killed in the process. Everybody dead, and life goes on for DCI Wishart. Except I'm here."

"You're a complication."

"You can always set your Romanian hounds on me."

Wishart frowned. "What?"

Black moved on. Something was missing. He needed to be certain. "I'll tell the world the truth. That Victor Cromwell was the Blood Eagle, responsible for the deaths of three young women, all those years ago. And DCI Wishart. Who was he? A poor imitation. A man who tried to copycat. But an unworthy substitute. Not a god at all."

Wishart rose himself up, his voice shrill. "But Victor told me the truth, after all this time. Before I shoved a knife through his deceitful heart. He told me. He confessed."

"What did he tell you?"

"It wasn't him. He merely watched from the side lines. A spectator. A coward. None of it was him. He's a *voyeur*. He deceived me. Betrayed me. He didn't kill any of these girls. It was someone else. Someone close to him. Victor Cromwell was an imposter. A fraud."

Black seethed with impatience. "Who is the Blood Eagle?"

Wishart regarded Black, the bones on his face harsh in the candlelight.

"Victor Cromwell has a sister."

73

A noise. A groan. One of the men stirred. Black glanced down. Wishart gave a wild hoarse sound, flung himself forward, arms and legs wide, to be met by three bullets in rapid succession. Black would never miss from such close range. Two in the chest, one in the throat. Wishart staggered back, his neck an instant tangle of blood and vein, mouth gaping, trying to suck in air. Black stepped closer, shot him twice in the face. Suddenly he was not so dissimilar to the mask he'd removed.

Black grabbed a knife from the array of utensils on the ground, cut Danika free. She collapsed into his arms.

"You came for me," she said.

Her clothing was in a bundle beside the metal frame. "Put them on."

He went to the men on the floor. One was trying to prop himself up on an elbow, a ghastly wound in his stomach.

"Easy," said Black. "You're Foster?"

The man nodded. "Wishart did this..."

"Don't talk," said Black. Cromwell lay beside him, inert, dead. Black stretched over, stripped away Cromwell's shirt, pressed it against Foster's stomach.

"You're going to live," said Black.

Foster gave a ragged laugh. "Who could believe this."

Black a mirthless smile. "It's not about belief. It's about who lives and dies."

Foster took a deep painful breath. "Inside jacket pocket. Let me call this in."

Black nodded. He gently opened Foster's jacket, pulled out his mobile phone, gave it to him. Foster tapped the screen, fingers slick with his own blood.

"Who are you?"

"It doesn't matter. Get an ambulance. For her too. Her name's Danika. She needs to go home."

Black sensed a presence. Danika, dressed, was standing behind him. He got up. She hugged him, cried into his chest.

"Don't leave me," she whispered.

He stroked her hair. "You're safe now. You're going home. It's over." Gently, he released her.

Foster made the call. The cops would get there in ten minutes.

"Time I was leaving." Black smiled at Danika. "Where are you from?"

"Kosice. Slovakia."

"I'll not forget that."

Black left the building, got in the car once owned by a group of Romanians left dead on the Rannoch Moors. But he was no longer concerned with that. He had a meeting to attend, at 5pm.

At a table on the pale horse.

74

B lack drove without stopping. In a single day, he had killed eight men. Or was it nine? He'd lost count. And the day wasn't over. He clenched the steering wheel, keeping the tremble from his fingers. He was fuelled up on adrenalin. He prayed it would see him through to the end.

He parked the car in a layby a half mile from his destination, waited.

At 4pm, he armed himself, and made a move. He scrambled down a wooded incline, the ground grassy and strewn with moss-stained boulders, reaching a thin strip of shoreline. He kept to the trees, the grey-blue water lapping gently, almost at his feet.

He picked his way through the trees, a shadow amongst shadows, one eye ahead, one eye on the flat calm of the loch, aware the place could be watched from a stationary boat. A half hour later, he reached a stone wall, shoulder height. He peered over. It was as he recalled.

He had arrived at the place where it had all started. The Raven's Crown.

Black slipped over the wall, and in a crouching run, hugging the wall, he reached the rear entrance. To his left, the little wooden dock. He made his way round to the other side of the house, to the garden. Sitting there, on the patio area, the slabs decorated with a painted white horse, were four people, on metal high-backed garden chairs. Sitting round a circular table. On the table a bottle of white wine, and four glasses. And a book. Black recognised it. The so-called Book of Dreams.

They were talking quietly. Black took a deep breath, approached them, one hand round the Beretta.

"Good afternoon."

The four jerked their heads towards him. One of them, a man of Eastern extract, wearing a red tracksuit top, faded jeans, reached to a holster strapped over his shoulder.

"Please," said Black. "Try it. You've caught me in a killing mood."

Lyle Taylor gave a brassy laugh. "Jesus fucking Christ. We were just talking about you. Although we weren't considering resurrection. You should be dead, Black."

"Sorry to disappoint. I see you have the book."

"It was all about the book. I was expecting more. At least some lurid memoirs. But not even enough to fill a page." Lyle glanced at the man sitting next to him. "I don't really know what my brother was thinking of."

"Nor do I," replied Black. "Though it certainly created a distraction. Your brother met me in a coffee shop, and told me to find out who killed his wife. From small beginnings. He never gave me his name, by the way, which in some circles, would be deemed to be impolite."

"Now that's a start," said Lyle. He was smoking a cigarette, which he flicked onto the slabs underfoot. "Tell Mr Black your name."

"Fuck you."

"My brother has a brain tumour," continued Lyle in a silky

voice, apparently unperturbed at the dramatic turn of events. "There are things he cannot recall. Like his name, which is Martin, for the record. Plus, there are other events he cannot recall. Hence this little meeting, as a way of bringing back the past. How did you escape, by the way? I think I'll need to tighten up security. Maybe I should sack Dalrymple."

"I wouldn't worry about him. I made him redundant. Permanently. Like everyone else at the Farm. Which by now will have the police crawling over every inch."

Lyle gave a languid smile, took a deep drag of his cigarette.

"Now that really was rude of you."

"I try my best," said Black. "Aren't you going to introduce me?"

"Of course. This is Omor. He's very loyal. And particularly gifted with the knife. I'm sure he'll want to make your acquaintance at some later date."

"I'm sure he will," said Black.

Lyle gestured to the fourth person there. "And this is–"

"I know who this is," cut in Black. "We've met already."

75

"What was your name?" Black asked. "Elena? From Warsaw?"

The woman looked at Black with dark burning eyes.

"Where the Vistula River sparkles like spun silver. You should have been a poet, Mr Black. You were very gallant. At the hotel. A knight in shining armour. But it was part of the act. It was all *theatre*. To see how you would respond. It was me who took Luca and Andreas to the hotel. It was me waiting in the speedboat. We misjudged you. And look at you now. Holding us to ransom at the point of a gun. Who would ever have imagined such a thing."

"And here we all are," said Black. "Not theatre anymore, but real fucking life. What's this all about? Cleaning things up. Tidying things away. You have the book. You thought I was dead. Is it Martin's turn? It's down to you, isn't it, Elena? Or would you prefer me calling you by your other name?"

"What name is that?"

"The Blood Eagle."

"Call me what you want." She reached over, placed her fingers delicately round the stem of her wine glass, raised the glass to her lips, sipped, put the glass back on the table. "This is where it started. This building, by the side of the loch. Women were brought here. Before my time. Perhaps Lyle can tell you."

Lyle inhaled, flicked more ash away but said nothing.

Elena continued. "We brought the girls here. I suppose you would call this a brothel. We would call it a rather exclusive business. They came from all over. Some we bought, some came of their own free will, for a little extra money. Some we... took."

Black listened, sensitive for the slightest untoward movement. The man called Omor stared at him with an unnerving intensity. Waiting for the moment Black's concentration strayed. "Keep going."

"You're so like your father," said Martin Taylor, suddenly.

The statement took Black off guard. "What?"

"My brother is reminiscing," soothed his brother. "Sometimes his memories are clear, sometimes confused. Which is how this thing started."

"Tell me how it started."

"Twenty years ago. Maybe more. Margaret, my brother's wife, worked for the police with your father, Robin. Robin Black. Your father had headed a small task force, created to smash rings like ours. Anti-trafficking. Of course, Margaret knew nothing about her husband's involvement. Isn't it rich? Under her very nose, her husband was running the most sophisticated trafficking syndicate in the country. Which was useful to us as well. Margaret confided in Martin, unwittingly, so we were always one step ahead of the game. Your father died. Cancer, if I recall. Margaret stepped into his shoes. They were close to destroying us. We therefore had to destroy them. Do you know how to destroy an enemy, Adam?"

Black waited.

"You cut off its head. Twenty years ago, a young man visited our establishment here, the Raven's Crown. He had certain peccadillos, shall we say. He enjoyed the company of whores, but his preference was mutilation. One summer evening, he went too far, slit a girl's throat. He was in such a state. Wasn't he, Martin? You remember this, don't you?"

Martin Taylor stared stonily at the loch, refusing to speak.

"Sometimes I think my brother remembers more than he cares to tell, and is laughing at us all the time. I digress. This young man killed the girl. She was a nobody. Just another slut, you understand. But suddenly, she was more useful dead than alive. We saw an opportunity. We explained that there would be no police, that we would take care of the situation, that we would look after *him*. If he completed one simple task."

Black listened. The sun cast a tawny glimmer on the surface of the loch, so still, so tranquil. The loch deceived, thought Black, veiling the evil on its shores.

"It was all so perfect. Margaret had no idea about this place. Martin suggested they come here, for dinner. He was always so persuasive, my brother." He glanced at him. "Or is it manipulative?"

He turned back to Black. "We arranged matters, so that the place was empty. They sat here, at this very spot, on this patio, on the pale horse. Sipping what? A crisp Chardonnay? My brother would know. Then, the gardens were magnificent. Difficult to imagine, I know. Time and neglect take their toll. But she would have been happy, in that moment. My brother excused himself, to see to more drinks, leaving his wife here, alone. Cue our young friend, ready to redress the balance. To complete his task."

The corners of Lyle's mouth twitched into a thin-lipped smile.

"He used his knife. I often wonder how exactly he performed the action. Did he lean over, from behind, and stab her? Did he sit down beside her, initiate a conversation, distract her, then plunge the blade in?"

Lyle gave a long sigh.

"The next chapter, I remember well. As would my brother, if he were able. The young man came rushing back into the hotel, breathless, telling us he had 'done the deed'. We both came out, to this spot. There she was, where Elena is sitting at this moment, slumped over the table, and the blood! Everywhere, soaking onto the patio. Suddenly the horse was no longer white. But life is full of twists, is it not, Mr Black?"

"It can be," replied Black, all the while watching Martin Lyle's face for a reaction, a display of emotion. It remained set as steel.

"Poor, dear Margaret. She wasn't dead. She saw my brother, tried to get up, hold him. Pleading, she was. Her rescuer had arrived." Lyle stopped. He took a drink of the wine. He looked up at Black. "Families and their secrets."

"Finish the story."

Again, he looked at his brother. "Shall I? Or do you wish to have the honour?"

No response. Lyle shrugged.

"My dear gentle brother whipped out a Swiss army knife from his pocket, pushed the blade through her throat, and sliced one way, then the other, and in such a manner, cut off her head."

76

A silence fell. Lyle took a final drag, then dropped the cigarette end on the slabs, and crushed it with the sole of his shoe.

"And that young man...?" said Black.

"Then, he was called Vasile Sotropa." Lyle was staring at Elena. "Born in Poland. An unemployed actor. After what happened, we paid for him to leave. He went to America..."

"And thus, Victor Cromwell was born."

"Spot on, Mr Black," he said, his voice quiet, subdued. "And here we sit. On the pale horse. Six feet below us, wrapped up in tarpaulin, is the body of my brother's wife, rotting and betrayed."

He looked at the book on the table. "I suppose this book – this *Book of Dreams* – is Margaret's revenge. Our atonement. For sins passed. My brother told me about your meeting in the coffee shop. But he was confused. His dates were mixed up. He had never been in your office. But you struck a chord, somewhere in his mind. The connection between you and your father. And by doing so, he dragged you in to this little mess, by sheer accident."

Another drink of wine. "And it was our intention, dear brother, to put you down there alongside your wife, for all the fucking chaos you've caused. On the instruction of the Blood Eagle." He turned his attention back to Elena. "Correct? Until you came along, Mr Black."

Suddenly, Martin stood, the metal legs of the chair scraping against the stone.

He glowered at Black, daring him to shoot, his face deathly pale, mouth twisted in a sneer.

"Liar!" he roared. He wore a grey cotton summer jacket. From a pocket he produced a kitchen knife. He swivelled round, thrust it into his brother's eye, deep, to the hilt. Lyle shrieked, the impact knocking his chair back, onto the ground. Omor, thinking to benefit from the confusion, grabbed for his pistol. The sound of a bullet echoed across the still calm of Loch Lomond, as Black shot Omor in the head.

Lyle writhed and twitched on the ground, his movements lessening, until he stopped, the blade fixed six inches through his eye.

"He's a liar," croaked his brother.

"I don't think so," said Black. "I think, like him, you're one evil bastard. Your only redeeming feature is the tumour in your head, which hopefully will do its work soon enough. If you move, I'll kill you."

He turned to Elena, who had remained in her chair, apparently unfazed by the commotion.

Black regarded her. Fortyish. Slim. Undoubtedly beautiful. Dark hair curled to her shoulders, eyes glittering a startling blue. Tanned oval face.

"Your surname is Sotropa? Victor Cromwell, otherwise Vasile Sotropa, is your brother. You're the one in charge. You're the Blood Eagle. And you took the name from the past, when you and your brother mutilated those young women, all those years ago."

"My brother. The coward. The girls were brought to him, by a man whose identity he kept secret."

"His name was Wishart. He was a policeman, until this morning, when I killed him."

"Do you kill everyone, Black?"

"I have a strict diet of murderers and psychopaths."

"They were brought, and we worked on them." Her eyes seemed to lose focus. Was she reminiscing? wondered Black. "*I* worked on them. He watched. He liked to watch. He liked to hear their screams and see them beg. For me, it was creation. They were nothing. I changed them. Changed them into something new and precious. Did you see my work, Adam? I made them... glorious."

"Glorious," repeated Black. "Your victims, if they were alive, would perhaps have their own views on the matter. You kept the name. Blood Eagle. It has a definite ring to it. Brings a chill to the spine. Talking of which – how could such a sweet young thing become the head of an outfit such as this? It doesn't seem possible."

"You're going to kill me. What difference does it make?"

"Indulge me."

She paused. Martin Taylor had sat back down, his face slack, eyes distant.

"Shall we humour him, Martin?" she said gently. Her glass had toppled, leaving a pool of wine on the tabletop. She dipped a finger in, licked the tip with a darting pink tongue.

"We were lovers. Martin and I. His brother was only half right." She sat, staring into space, as if preoccupied with private thoughts. Eventually she spoke. "He killed his wife. But he did it for me."

Maybe Martin was listening, maybe not. Black couldn't be certain. His face registered no emotion.

"He would do anything I asked. I started controlling the finances. It soon occurred to the brothers that I was clever with money. Clever with business. They allowed me greater scope. I introduced our Romanian connections, set up the Farm, and other places. Business grew. The Blood Eagle was feared. And respected. So it went. Until Martin gave you the book. And now we're here." She glanced at a slim Rolex on her wrist.

"He's not coming," said Black. "Your brother is dead. Stabbed through the heart, and lying alone in a shithole. Dalrymple is dead, along with your handsome Romanian boys, and as we speak, those young girls are with the police, safe, and looking forward to going home. Your world is finished. It's over."

She stared at Black, expressionless. Suddenly, to Black, her beauty had evaporated, and all he saw was the hardened face of a stone-cold killer.

"What now?" she asked, tonelessly.

"With the help of your brother, you murdered three women. Those are the only the ones I know about."

"You know nothing."

"I know this," said Black. "Your time has come." He shot her between the eyes, the back of her head disappearing in a froth of blood, bone and black curls.

Martin stirred. "It was lies," he muttered. Black watched in dread fascination, as he stood once again, shuffled round to the other side of the table, to the body of Omor. Martin bent, picked up the semi-automatic on the ground beside him. He turned, straightened, appraised Black.

"Who do you believe?" he asked.

"I believe it's time you finished this."

Martin nodded. "I knew you were exactly the right man." He placed the barrel of the gun in his mouth, fired.

Black took a deep breath. He got out his mobile phone, pressed the number he was given. A voice answered instantly. The voice of Ronald Wilkinson.

77

"I know who killed your daughter. Those involved are all dead. I can tell you everything when we meet."

"Where are you?"

"I'm at an abandoned hotel called The Raven's Crown, on the shore of Loch Lomond. Two miles past Ardlui. You'll find it, if you look hard enough. Bring Rachel with you. Take her to the dock at the back. I'll be watching. If she's not with you, then the meeting won't happen, and I'll know she's dead. And if she's dead, then I come after you."

A pause. "I think we have to be reasonable about this," said Wilkinson. "Rachel is perfectly safe. But we would rather you come here. To my restaurant, where we can have a civilised chat. If all goes well, you and Rachel can leave, unharmed."

"Let me talk to her."

"She's not here."

"Then call me back in five minutes. I want to hear her voice."

Black hung up. He waited, on tenterhooks. He walked down to the wooden pier, at the rear of the hotel, watched the light glimmer on the surface of the water. Less than fifty yards away, strewn across a slabbed patio area of an overgrown garden, were four dead bodies.

The phone buzzed.

It wasn't Wilkinson's voice. It was the voice of Tommy. The man Black had encountered in the coffee shop.

"We'll come to you. We'll be there in two hours. We'll bring Rachel."

The saga was nearing its end. He would get Rachel, they would leave, run away from people like Wilkinson, The Blood Eagle, killers. Run far away, where no one could find them.

78

Ronnie Wilkinson was dining in his restaurant, on fresh spinach and ricotta lasagne, with a side of garlic bread, when he got the call. Tommy was downstairs in the main bar area, who was promptly summoned, and instructed to phone Black back, and relay Wilkinson's response.

"I don't mean to sound stupid, boss. But how can we meet Black without his girlfriend?"

"Anything's possible, if you exercise your mind. Don't you know? Anyhow, I don't pay you to think. I pay you to do." He outlined his plan, which Tommy realised was surprisingly simple.

Wilkinson tore off a wedge of garlic bread, downed it in a gulp of red wine.

"You bring him here," he said. "I'll be waiting. And I want him alive. And I swear to Jesus fucking Christ, if you can't carry out this simple command, then listen closely."

Wilkinson leaned forward, as did Tommy. "I will cut your fucking head off. No second chances. You understand this, Tommy?"

Tommy blinked, swallowed. "Understood."

~

Black waited. He had two Berettas – one was half full, the other a full clip, with fifteen rounds. The pistol used by Martin Taylor on himself was a Glock, which he prised from his lifeless fingers. He also retrieved the kitchen knife from the skull of his brother, wiping it clean on the long grass. They would come, full of weapons. Black had to return the compliment. He hoped none would be used. For Rachel's sake.

He dragged the four bodies into the deep shrubbery at the back of the garden. There was nothing he could do about the blood on the paving stones, but doubted anyone would notice. He entered the hotel, checking the rooms, for no other reason than to ensure they were empty. He once again entered the dining room, where he had killed two men, their bodies long gone, the only clue as to their presence a dull stain on the carpet.

There was only one road into the hotel – a single lane. There were cars parked at the front, belonging to Lyle and Elena. Black had retrieved their keys. Lately, he'd got used to rifling through pockets of the dead. He drove each car to the layby where he'd left his own, a half mile further up the road, jogged back. He positioned himself amongst the trees and bushes, invisible, and hunkered in.

The cars arrived. Black heard the sound of tyres crunching over the small stones of the lane, the soft purr of engines.

He sat still. Doors closing. Then, his name being shouted. He didn't move. He waited.

Now, a group of men filed round the side of the building. There, the man called Tommy, a pistol in one hand. Each appeared armed, ranging from pistols to shotguns. There was no sign of Wilkinson. Stumbling behind Tommy, a slighter figure, being led by a length of thin rope tied around her wrists. A cloth bag over her head. Black's heart leapt. The same build as Rachel. He recognised the pale blue running shoes, pale blue jeans, blue top with puff sleeves. They stopped at the wooden pier. Tommy was calling for him. Ten men, one woman.

Black hesitated. He was outnumbered and outgunned. There was zero chance of taking Rachel without a firefight. He had little leverage. They had a hostage. He had nothing, except information, and Wilkinson hadn't come to hear it. Which meant they intended taking him back. Black had no choice. Rachel was only a few feet from him, terrified. He would gladly die for her. The trick was to make sure *she* didn't die. He took several deep breaths, calming himself. He didn't really know how this would pan out, but there was only one way to find out. He edged forward, readied himself, to stand up, emerge from his hiding place.

He stopped. He squinted at the group, disturbed by a prickling beneath the surface of his mind. A sudden well of dread filled his chest. He remained still, hardly daring to breathe. Time seemed to stop. He withdrew back into the shadows.

Rachel was dead.

He would kill them all.

79

Cry 'Havoc!' and let slip the dogs of war

William Shakespeare: Julius Caesar

B lack was back in the SUV, and heading out, to anywhere, when his mobile phone buzzed. It was Wilkinson. Black picked up.

"What happened?"

Black answered in a measured voice. "Change of plan."

"There's no fucking change of plan!" barked Wilkinson. "You get to the restaurant now, or I swear your bitch dies."

"Where is she?"

"She's on her way back from that fucking hotel. I swear, Black, I'll kill her myself unless you get your fucking arse over here!"

"Different rules now. My rules."

"What the fuck does that mean?"

"It means you can kill her, if you wish. You're a dead man.

You, and everybody who works for you. You'll not know where or when, but you'll spend every second of every minute wondering. Welcome to your new world, Wilkinson, where I am your worst fucking nightmare. Where I watch you die."

He hung up. He drove, on autopilot, oblivious of the land on either side, uncaring of the direction.

He gripped the steering wheel until his fingers turned white.

He began to cry.

80

Three weeks later
The restaurant which Wilkinson owned – The Thirsty Fox – opened officially at 12.15 for lunch. The chef arrived at 11am to make preparations, along with an assistant. He kept a strict kitchen. Scrupulously clean, well-stocked, well-organised. The special he had planned was a steak and blue cheese pie, a recipe he'd picked up on the internet. He'd add his own twist; some English mustard, and perhaps a little Guinness.

He noticed immediately a cardboard box on the stainless-steel carving table, the size and shape of a cake box. A delivery? He couldn't think. A gift from Mr Wilkinson? Unlikely. It was tied with string. He opened a drawer, got a pair of scissors, cut, opened the top.

He staggered back, screamed. His assistant rushed over, recoiled in horror when he saw the contents.

A severed head. The chef knew who it was. Ronnie Wilkinson's enforcer. His right-hand man. The one called Tommy.

81

Ronnie Wilkinson was a gangster, had been all his adult life. Violence and death were common parlance in his world. The death of Tommy shook him, but did not scare him. He knew it was Black, and he knew he was next on his roster of death. He'd lived with threat all his life. He reacted in the best way he knew – he doubled his guard. Other than that, life remained the same. He refused to be intimidated. He went to his restaurant, he drank in his pub, he went home at night.

He owned several houses. His main home was the building Rachel had been taken to, in the north of the city, in a plush area called Bearsden. He lived alone, his daughter dead, then divorced from his wife soon after. Three floors, including the basement, set in an acre of garden. There was no garden to speak of, as he had removed the flowers and shrubs, and covered most of it in burnt-orange slabbing. At night, while he slept, two men were stationed at the main double-door entrance, two men at the rear entrance. Inside, three men in the kitchen, drinking coffee, every half hour one patrolling the rooms. Plus four men in the basement where Rachel had been murdered, as back-up.

During the day, always four cars. An entourage of muscle.

When he ate in his restaurant, always four men, sitting at tables next to his, plus one on each door outside, and two more in the bar downstairs, quietly watching.

To Wilkinson's mind, he was untouchable, his house and restaurant impregnable. He almost wished Black would try something, so he could watch him die like a dog.

Two days passed.

Midnight. Witching hour.

~

Two days earlier

Black had been watching Wilkinson for several days, studying his movements, which primarily involved travelling from his house to his restaurant, and then back again. Security was tight. He was surrounded by men, most of the time. Getting close was difficult, if not impossible. Black knew, once he'd delivered the package to his restaurant, Wilkinson would further ramp up his security. Black had anticipated this. He'd parked his car a hundred yards away, on the road adjacent to the front entrance, and when Wilkinson and his entourage had left the house that morning, presumably after being told by one slightly shocked chef there was a head on his kitchen unit, Black waited for his opportunity. There were no guards. They had all left with Wilkinson. There may have been an alarm, but this was irrelevant.

Thirty minutes later, bang on time, two women pulled up outside the gated entrance. They'd come by taxi. They got out, opened the gate, made their way to the house. One had a key. They let themselves in. Cleaners. Same time every day. Black could set his watch by them. He got out of his car, taking with him a small holdall containing some food, a litre bottle of water, a coil of rope. He strolled to the front entrance, rang the bell. The noise chimed through the interior. The door was frosted glass, set in a cathedral-style frame. An image approached. The door opened. A woman answered.

Black gave his best smile.

"Mr Wilkinson sent me back. Said he'd left something in his bedroom. A file. Do you mind...?"

The woman, in her mid-forties, face worn from a lifetime of cigarettes, shrugged. "Sure."

"Great. I'll be just a minute. I'll see myself out."

"Whatever you say."

She left the door open, and made her way through to the back of the house. Black entered into the main hall. Another woman appeared, holding a carpet hoover in one hand, a cloth in the other. She smiled. Black smiled back. She disappeared in the same direction as her colleague.

Ahead, a wide sweeping staircase. Black raced up, three steps at time. He got to the upper hall. He checked each of the rooms. The biggest was undoubtedly the one occupied by Wilkinson. His clothes were scattered on the bed, to be lifted for laundry. Another door off it, opening to an en suite the size of most people's living rooms, complete with jacuzzi and sauna. Black went back out into the main hall.

There, in the ceiling, a trap door, for access to the roof space. It was what he hoped for. Now, it was down to luck. The trap door had a small latch. Black looked in an airing cupboard, shelves stacked with baskets, towels, bed sheets, pillowcases, other oddments. There! Standing in a corner was a wooden pole, a metal hook at one end. Black got it, went back into the hall.

Suddenly a voice, coming from downstairs. "You found what you're looking for?"

"No problem!" Black placed the pole by the wall, went down

stairs, to the front door. There was no sign of anyone. "That's me away now!"

"Okay," came a voice from another part of the house. Black opened the door, shut it loudly, crept back up the stairs, and using the pole hook, caught the latch, pulled. The trap door swung open, attached by two long hinges, revealing a set of extendable metal loft ladders. Black used the pole, caught the lowest rung, pulled the ladders down. He climbed up, pulled the ladders in, closed the hatch.

Midnight – two days later

Black, nerves sharpened to a knife edge, eased the ladders down. Men padded about, on the ground floor. He heard the murmur of their voices. Slowly, with exquisite care, he took each rung at a time, one step, two, trying to balance the weight, to avoid any sound.

He reached the bottom, crept along the hallway. In his hand, he held a Ka-bar hunting knife, preferred by the American Marines. In his jacket pocket, the Beretta, a souvenir from his time at the Farm. Looped round his shoulder, the rope. He approached the top of the stairway. Wilkinson's room was past the stair entrance, at the other end of the hall. A noise. The soft creak of movement. Someone was coming up.

Black flattened against the wall, waited. A man appeared, turned, confronted Black, his face suddenly slack with surprise. Black thrust the knife up, under his jaw, sliced. The man went limp, collapsing into Black's arms. Black manoeuvred him onto the carpet. The dead man would be missed in ten minutes. Black still had time.

He got to Wilkinson's door, opened, slipped in. The room

was in darkness. At the far side, the sound of soft snoring. Black remembered the layout. To his left, there was a wide tapestried chair, on four short wooden legs. Quietly, he staggered it across to block the bedroom door. He turned, switched on the light.

Wilkinson groaned, voice sluggish.

Black strode over, Beretta in his hand.

"What the fuck..." Wilkinson propped himself up on one elbow, hair tousled, bleary-eyed, cheeks sagging.

"It's good to catch up," said Black.

Wilkinson stared, trying to focus, still somewhere in dreamland. "How the hell...?"

"Never mind that," said Black, crouching, pressing the muzzle of the gun against Wilkinson's forehead.

Wilkinson worked his lips, tried to talk, managing only a low incoherent mumble.

"Tommy explained everything," said Black. "His dying words were full of apology, how he was sorry he murdered Rachel in your basement. I think, at the end, he was truly remorseful."

Wilkinson found his speech. "It wasn't supposed to have happened. Tommy was a fucking loose cannon." He blinked away sweat. "You were there, weren't you?"

"At the hotel? Of course."

Wilkinson's breathing was heavy, lungs wheezing. "How did you know?"

"How did I know it wasn't Rachel?" Black's voice was a monotone, lacking emotion. "My hat goes off to you. Whoever she was, was wearing Rachel's clothes. You must have stripped her off while she lay in her own blood. You almost had me. But Rachel didn't have bright red nail varnish. Nor did she wear any rings." Black reached over, grabbed a handful of Wilkinson's hair, pulled him close, hissed in his ear.

"Here's the best bit. I know who the Blood Eagle is. I know who killed your daughter."

Wilkinson went rigid. Black heard him swallow. "Tell me," he gasped.

Black pulled away.

"Please!"

"Remember the game we played in your restaurant? One bullet, six chambers. I remember it well, as you might imagine."

"Who killed my daughter?"

"Here's a variation of the game. One bullet. One chamber. I pull the trigger. You die."

"Tell me, Black!"

Black looked at him, and felt nothing. "No."

He shot him once, between the eyes. His head bounced back onto the pillows, the wall behind a sudden sparkle of red stars.

Black stood, gazing at the dead body of Wilkinson. Noises now, from another section of the house. He fired another two shots, into Wilkinson's chest, then more rounds into the walls. He had chosen not to use a silencer. They would all come running, like bees round honey.

Black got to the window, opened it. He tied one end of the rope round the bottom of the bed frame, flung its length through the open window. There was commotion at the bedroom door, as those on the other side tried to batter it open. Black fired a shot straight at it, for good measure, the noise beyond suddenly stilled.

Black grasped the rope, climbed out, and lowered himself to the concrete paving below. As he had expected, the guards had flocked upstairs.

Black disappeared into the shadows of the night.

82

Donovan's was the only Irish pub in Kosice. It was a Saturday night, and the place was crammed with young students getting drunk. On a small wooden stage, a band played. A guitarist, a fiddler, a singer, beating out a lively jig. The place buzzed with noise.

The tables were rough wood, the seats nothing more than long benches. Black sat at one such table, in a corner nestled in the shadows, on his own, a pint of beer in front of him. He was watching the bar. One individual interested him in particular. A young man, laughing with a girl no older than twenty. He was lean, handsome, animated, flashing a perfect white smile. The girl was clearly attracted. Black got up, made his way to stand beside him.

He tapped the man's shoulder. The man turned, a bewildered look on his face.

"Can I help you?" he said with a strong English accent.

"I think you can," said Black. "You're Patrick Friel, yes?"

"Do I know you? Excuse me, I'm with company."

He turned his back. Black again tapped him on the shoulder.

The man turned round, a second time, the bewilderment changed to irritation. "Listen…"

"You don't know me. But you know Danika. She's the girl you sold to Romanian slavers."

Friel remained motionless. Black held his stare.

"She's alive, if you're interested."

Friel attempted bluster. "I have no idea what you're talking about. I think you have the wrong person, friend. What did you say your name was?"

"My name? Adam Black. And I'm not your friend."

THE END

A NOTE FROM THE PUBLISHER

Thank you for reading this book. If you enjoyed it please do consider leaving a review on Amazon to help others find it too.

We hate typos. All of our books have been rigorously edited and proofread, but sometimes mistakes do slip through. If you have spotted a typo, please do let us know and we can get it amended within hours.

info@bloodhoundbooks.com

Printed in Great Britain
by Amazon